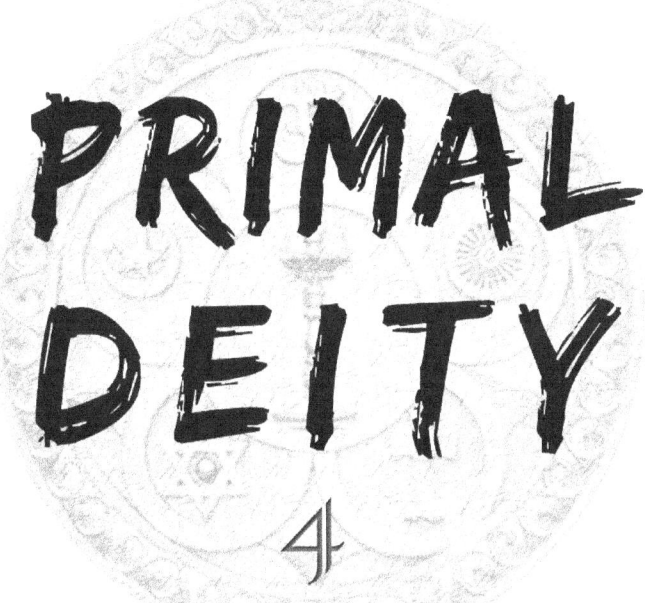

PRIMAL DEITY

4

Early Detection

ALLEN OZARK

Edited by Bella Fox

Published by Sumner House Publishing

ISBN: 978-1-7334656-6-3

Experience the Primal Deity Series…

www.primaldeity.com

In loving memory of my friend

Connie Lerner

1961 - 2020

Dedication

This book is dedicated to my little Emmie-Lou. Daddy loves you, now and forever, until the day I take my last breath, and till infinity and beyond.

PRIMAL DEITY

4

Early Detection

Chapter 1

This by far is the strangest thing I've ever experienced. As I canvass my wildly interesting life, certain things standout. I remember my mother telling me she really wasn't my mother, and my real mother was some dead hooker. I exaggerate, but that's about what it amounted to. Honestly, I remember not even caring who my real mother was. I still haven't tried to track that side of my family down, and for some strange reason, I don't feel bad about it. I recall being pistol-whipped by a psychotic school principal—who by the way wasn't even a principal, and instead was the criminal mastermind behind a mentally challenged, videogame-playing serial killer—and a pimp of underage girls, who just happened to be my high school BFF, rest his poor soul. *Talk about complicated.* I also remember walking into a drug lord's hacienda after being told by an entire team of special trained, battle-hardened Navy Seals I would be perfectly safe the entire time. After a violent firefight broke out, I had an epiphany. There I was, down on the floor, my nostrils engorged from a near overdose of cocaine, laughing at all the bullets whizzing back and forth right over my head. That's when I realized my team didn't like me very much. After the gunfire stopped, I cried. They literally sent me in as bait. Like a fresh side of beef, they hurled me right into a hungry lion's den. They didn't give a shit about me. Had it not been for Lieutenant Xavier Slade, rest his soul, I probably would've been a stain on the walls. I remember a thin, angry African running up to me in a little hallway with a really big gun, yelling and screaming at me, hoping to put me out of my misery. And, I remember having to kill the one man I trusted almost as much as Dad because, as it turns out, he was a traitor to his country. I see Dominic every night in my dreams. He just stares at me with a big hole in his stomach with his guts hanging out. It breaks my heart. I also remember falling in love with the only woman I think I'll ever love only to watch her brains get splattered all over the walls of a little holding cell somewhere out in the Arizona desert. I miss Vanessa so much.

I think it's safe to say all of that is strange. But this takes the cake....

So, here I am, in bed, wide awake, with my niece on top of me—bless her adorable little chunky butt—my sister wrapped up in my right arm, and my ex—a.k.a. my sister's goddamn husband—drooling on the other side. If I wasn't facing utter doom, I'd say this is about as low as I can get. However, there's an 800-pound gorilla, sitting over in the corner, reminding me today is the day I'm supposed to do something I vowed I'd never do in a million years—betray my country. I think what makes it worse is I fully intend to do it to save a handful of people trapped in this immaculate tomb, specifically my family.

Since the day I woke up inside this place, all I could wonder was how the Secret Service could build an identical White House off in some far away land, and then somehow forget about it. I always figured the CIA was chockfull of squirrely, unethical heathens, but even in my eyes, this is some kind of ridiculous.

I haven't slept a wink all night—probably because of the completely ridiculous story I told my family about why I have to leave today and why they have to stay in what they assumed was the White House until the urge struck them to ask a bunch of very reasonable questions any ordinary citizen would like, "Where's the President?" or "Why is there so little staff here?" All of us Southerlands may have issues of varying degree, but not one came onto this earth a dummy, and we don't roll with any dummies either. Even though Bill acts like he ain't got the sense God tried to give him, he still is not dumb enough to believe the government's lies.

Chris and his wife went back to their room around midnight, but I stayed with Bill, Theresa, and the little munchkin. We watched the most hilarious Disney movie ever, *Big Hero 6*. I swear that big, white Stay Puff marshmallow man was a total badass. He had the heart and spirit of a lion. I wish I felt that way right now, but I feel more like a little worm on a massive hook.

CIA Director Pearson got the better of me. I should've seen it coming. All the chaos and confusion didn't make an ounce of sense, and our good Doctor Hughes was a little too "good" to believe. If only I could get my hands on him, he'd never operate another helicopter for the rest of his short life. They should know to keep him away from me by now. No telling what I'd do up close and personal. Fortunately, they keep me and my family away from everyone. They told Bill it was a security concern and, because of my undercover mission, they're all at risk. I guess there is some truth to that because they really are, but Pearson is the only real threat.

Unfortunately, my hands are tied. I am not without some skills, so I know I could fight my way out of this place. Security is heavy, but not at night, and even during the day, there are exits that are barely monitored. However, if I leave now, I know they will kill my family—maybe everyone else in here too. Pearson exhibited precision a like a brain surgeon the way he contained everything surrounding this illegal, immoral, off-the-books mission. Nearly everyone I encountered up to this point who didn't die, has been rounded up, stuck in this replica White House, and kept far away from me. I doubt they are as heavily guarded as we are, but I'm almost certain they have been fed a complete line of bullshit about me under the auspices of "thwarting terror." Pearson should get an academy award for his performance.

I could continue torturing myself about what I should and should not have done, but I promised I wouldn't do that anymore. My new team and I were supposed to leave weeks ago for Riyadh, but the Economic Summit was pushed back as a result of credible threats against the President. I doubt these threats are credible at all. Chances are, it's all just part of Pearson's plan—that or maybe something's wrong with the bomb. *Who knows?* What I do know is, as soon as I'm done enjoying time with my family this morning, I'm going to get back on the clock. I need to find a way to get myself and Vice President Keller out of this mess. Yes, I need to keep my family safe, but no one family is greater than a whole nation, and I don't care what Pearson and his butt-buddy President Wood think. Their plan, despite their twisted belief they are patriots, will blow up in all our faces. I'm not worried about saving them from themselves. I need to save humanity from their treachery.

I have to do something. If not, millions will die. I've seen the specs on Doctor Taylor's doomsday device, and it makes Chernobyl look like a spill at the Coca Cola plant. I think that's exactly what Wood wants though—to rule with fear—fear of hate and violence. If that bomb goes off in Riyadh, he will no doubt have his way. I don't know what to do, but I can't let that happen.

"Bill," I whisper, shaking my arm under his head. "Bill .... Wake up."

He lifts himself up off me, wiping the drool from his mouth with the sleeve of his dark blue pajamas. Bill lets out a long yawn.

"My arm's asleep," I whisper.

Bill chuckles a little, looking around. "What time is it?" he asks, softly.

"I dunno," I reply.

Bill scratches his head and rolls over. He looks back over his shoulder. "It's seven already," he says. He scoots around on the bed and looks at all of us piled up together. He smiles the biggest smile I've ever seen.

"What?" I ask, quietly.

He's still smiling. "All my girls together at last," he says.

I mouth "Fuck you" slowly and shoot him a bird with my numb hand.

Bill shakes his head and laughs. He reaches over with both hands to pick Angie up off my chest.

I raise my hand. "No, wait." I put my arms around her and snuggle her tightly. "Just one more minute."

Bill smiles again and backs off. "We told her about you and showed her your picture every day. She always talks about you ... talks about when she's going to see you and says you're going to do her hair because she hates when Theresa does it."

"Hell, Bill I can barely do my own hair," I reply smiling. "Chile she'd be baldheaded messing 'round with me."

We both laugh a little. Angie moves around on me. Bill picks her up, carries her over, and puts her in the other bed.

"She loves you already, you know?" comes a soft voice.

I look to my other side down at Theresa, who's snuggling up to me. "T...."

"Yes," she replies.

I pause a moment for dramatic effect. "Your breath is horrible," I say softly.

We both laugh loudly.

"Bitch, you are burning my nose hair with your dragon breath!" says Theresa.

"Shhhh, the baby's still sleep", I reply, pointing to the other bed. I try to get up.

"No, stay here a moment," Theresa begs.

I run my fingers through her hair and kiss her forehead. "You miss Momma," don't you?" I ask.

Theresa nods. She shuts her eyes tight and squeezes her arms around me. "Yeah, but don't get any ideas. I overheard you talking to Chris about your girlfriend."

I frown. "Ass. You know what Theresa, you just-"

"I'm sorry," she interrupts. "I wasn't ... I didn't mean anything-"

I sigh. "Forget it. It's okay ... nosy bitch!"

"Stop it ... I don't ever want to fight with you again," she says softly. "I'm sorry if I-"

"Seriously, forget it," I say. "I gotta get up, T. After breakfast, I have to head out."

"What time is it?" she asks.

"It's after seven," says Bill softly. "I've got breakfast coming up. We should eat together since you're going to be gone for a while, Alex."

I pat Theresa's back a few times. "Here let me up, I'm gonna grab a shower."

"You really have to go?" she asks.

I gently push her off. "Afraid so, sis." I climb down out of the big bed and plant my feet firmly on the floor. I stand up and stretch as high as I can with both hands, yawning loudly. "I have to report for duty at nine, and wheels are up by noon." I wiggle my toes around on the carpet pile. I turn and stare at Theresa and I can't help but smile at her. "I'm gonna go down, take a shower. and get dressed. I'll be back for breakfast." I walk slowly to the door.

"Alex...?"

I turn around. "Yeah?"

Theresa waves me over.

I walk back over to the bed. "Yes, sweetie?"

Theresa blows right in my face and starts laughing.

I shove her back on the bed. "You filthy beast! Ewe!"

"Ahem!" Bill clears his throat and nods his head to the side in Angie's direction. "She's awake," he warns.

I cover my mouth. "I'm so sorry baby. Auntie Alex said a bad word."

Angie rubs her eyes and hops down off of the bed. She runs up and nearly tackles me. "Where are you going?" she asks.

I squeeze her tight. "I'm just going down to get cleaned up and ready for breakfast. I'll be back, I promise."

She smiles. "Okay. And you're going to eat with us?"

I nod. "Mmmm huh, I want blueberry pancakes too. Are you gonna make me some pancakes?" I tickle her tummy a little.

She laughs. "No, I am not old enough to cook."

"Well, pretty girl, I think somebody around here ought to be able to get us some pancakes, right?"

She nods. "Yes." She smiles a toothy grin.

I hug her tightly and she kisses my cheek. I stand up and caress her hair. "She's so beautiful." I touch her face and we share one last smile before she runs over and hops back in bed with her mom.

"I'll walk you out," Bill offers.

Bill and I walk to the door together.

"You are coming back?" he asks, opening the door for me.

I roll my eyes. "What did I just say, Bill?"

He smiles. "Just making sure."

"Well, make sure breakfast is here 'cause I'm starving, and-"

"Alex, I ordered blueberry pancakes, bacon and black coffee for you."

I frown and whisper, "Awe Bill, after all this time of you fucking my sister you actually remembered what I eat for breakfast. How sweet." I leave him standing in the doorway with his mouth wide open. I'm not mad at him at all—I just like busting his balls whenever circumstances permit. With everything that lies ahead, it might have been the last chance I got, so I couldn't pass it up.

Halfway down the hallway, my happy skip turns into a dreary shuffle. In less than two hours I will either help end the world as we know it or ... quite frankly I don't see any other options.

I enter my room and strip off my pajamas. I walk into the bathroom and grab my toothbrush. I squeeze out some toothpaste on the bristles and power it on. Then, I proceed to slowly brush each tooth, my gums, and my tongue. I stare at my reflection in the mirror, wondering what evil secrets the early morning is hiding from me.

I turn on the hot water and grab a towel. I step in the shower and close the doors. I just let the steaming hot water pound against my skin, and I breathe slowly. I need to clear my mind and be ready for whatever happens. I have to stay sharp and find any opportunity I can to exploit the enemy's weakness. I just pray they actually have one.

Chapter 2

I'm all showered and dressed up in my costume, which is what I call it because that's exactly what it is. I'm not an FBI Agent and I'm no DEA Agent and I'm not a Justice Agent either. I'm just a criminal. Technically, I'm not even a criminal. I'm just a puppet in a hat.

I leave my room and head back to Bill and Theresa's where the aroma of breakfast grabs me like a ghost and pulls me face first towards their door. I walk in and the room smells of hot delicious breakfast. It reminds me of waking up back in the day at home after Momma'd been working in the kitchen for hours. Inside, everyone's already seated. There's a plate stacked high with blueberry pancakes waiting on me. I casually walk over to my chair and sit down. I open up my napkin and lay it on my lap.

"Chris, why don't you say grace?" Bill suggests.

Chris looks at me and smiles. He reaches out on both sides and grabs his wife Teri's hand and Theresa's. I reach to my left and grab Theresa's hand and reach for Bill on my right. As we all lock hands, Chris prays.

"Lord Jesus, thank you for all the blessings you have given us. Thank you for bringing Alex back to us. Lord, you have been so good to all of us, and we feel your grace on this earth every day. Lord we know those who hold us hostage here that their spirit is not right...."

I open my eyes and look at Chris, who continues praying with his eyes closed.

"...But we ask that you weigh heavy on their hearts to keep their demons at bay," Chris prays. "We ask that you keep us safe and you grant Alex the strength she needs to come back to us once more. For it is by your love and your hand that all things are possible, so we ask you to lay hands on Alex and keep her safe from any and all harm until the day we hold her in our arms again. Thank you for this food and for the hands that prepared it. In your heavenly name we pray, Jesus, amen."

My eyes are still open. I don't realize that I'm crying until I feel Theresa pressing her napkin against my cheek.

"You knew?" I ask, weeping.

Bill stands up, walks over and touches my arm. "Doesn't matter what anybody says," he confesses, "if somebody tells me to come with them because you said so, that means you're in trouble. That was the first thing you taught me when you started undercover work, remember?"

I nod.

Bill looks around the table. "We can all see it on your face," he says. "We knew the moment they brought us here they were manipulating us to get to you."

I shake my head. "But, why-"

"If we're gonna die," Chris says softly, "We're gonna do it together. This family's been split up too long. Never again."

Everyone piles on me for a group hug, even little Angie, who I doubt understands what's really going on, but she doesn't care and neither do I. There's so much love in this room from the most unlikely of characters. All our years of hate and fighting seem to mean absolutely nothing to any of us right now. I do my best to stop crying, and everyone sits back down in front of their plates. We all look around at each other for a moment.

"Can I eat now, Mommy?" Angie whispers.

We all laugh.

"Yes baby," Theresa answers, "eat your breakfast."

I try and eat part of my pancakes, but my throat feels swollen and it's hard to swallow. I put my fork down and take a deep breath. "They want me to do something bad," I announce.

Bill shakes his head a little. "Alex, you don't have to tell us-"

"Bill, just listen. They want me to do something bad. If I don't do it, then ... I don't have a choice. I can't lose you guys not like this. Not again. I-"

"May I say something?" asks Teri.

I smile at her. "Please."

"My dad, before he died, he used to tell me this story." She clears her throat. "A story about Doctor J."

I instantly smile bigger.

Teri continues, "He failed to yield the right of way ... he was right, dead right as he sped along, but now-"

Chris, Bill, Theresa and I all in unison yell, "He's just as dead as if he was wrong!"

Teri bursts out in laughter, and Bill laughs loudly too.

"Pop used to say that all the time," Bill says.

I nod and smile. "He sure did."

"Sometimes doing the right thing isn't the right thing to do," Teri says. She looks like she is holding back a tear. "We know what we signed up for here. You have your duty and we have ours. We have to think about more than just us."

I smile and nod. In fact, we all nod. Teri was right. Chris puts his hand on the back of Teri's neck and pulls her in for a kiss. He thinks he's whispering, but that boy can't whisper to save his life. I can hear him tell her he loves her.

I don't feel like eating though I know I should. I just sit and stare at my family. When I lost Vanessa and Tony, I never thought my heart would beat that way again for anyone, but I had no clue my family would ever love me like this—the way I love them, with all my heart.

We finish eating and say our goodbyes. It's all hugs and kisses and tears on my way out the door. I look back a few times and watch them all huddled up together, standing out in the hallway watching me disappear into the distance. We all know it may be the last time we see each other. All things considered I think we made the best of it.

I make my way down the hall, past a few guards and down the stairs to the level below.

"Agent Southerland," greets a man in a black suit, waiting for me at the bottom of the staircase.

I roll my eyes. "I'm not an agent anymore," I reply.

"Well, whatever you are, you're coming with me," says the man. He turns and starts walking.

I follow him down the hall. We walk through a security checkpoint in which he has to swipe a card, scan his handprint, and do voice authorization. Finally, we get through. The man stops at a window, flashes his credentials and checks his weapon in with the attendant.

"No guns allowed in here?" I ask casually.

The man smiles as he signs in on a security log. "I'm Mr. White, and I'll be escorting you to your briefing this morning."

I tilt my head left a little. "Mr. White, huh?"

"Yes," he replies. "Now please, come with me." He turns and walks quickly down the hallway.

I follow him once again for what seems to be a mile of closed doors. Finally, we reach the double doors at the end of the hallway. Mr. White opens the door and gestures for me to enter, so I do.

Inside the big room, down near the front, I see a group of men, and to my left, a quarantine room wrapped in clear plastic with people in biohazard suits inside, moving around a rather sizeable object. I stare intently in through the clear plastic, hoping the people inside would move so I can get a closer look, but they don't.

"Don't worry Southerland," says Mr. White, "all your questions will be answered soon."

Down front, the men are in a huddle. They go silent once we get in earshot of them.

"Mr. Black," says Mr. White.

A man breaks out of the huddle. "I see you've brought me a gift Mr. White."

Mr. White nods. "Agent Southerland, Mr. Black."

Before my fist can make contact with Mr. Black's face, the men pounce on me from all directions. It literally takes all they have to keep me from attacking Mr. Black, who chuckles oddly.

"You won't be fucking laughing when I rip your goddamn eyes out through your asshole, motherfucka!" I yell.

"I'll leave her in your capable hands Mr. Black," said Mr. White as he excuses himself.

Mr. White walks away, and I continue cursing, spitting and trying to fight my way to bloody revenge. "Cut the shit Hughes you goddamn piece of gutter trash!" I scream at the top of my lungs. "I'll kill you motherfucka—I'll goddamn fucking kill you! Let me go, bitches! Fight me like a fuckin' man!"

He shoves a tablet right up to my face. "No, you won't," he replies. "See that, Southerland? That's checkmate. Be glad they don't kill them right now. They know you told them."

I spit in his face. "Fuck you, you murdering son of a bitch!"

"I haven't killed anyone!" he exclaims. "Now sit down before I sit you down!"

The men push me around and over to a chair. They plop me down and hover over me.

Dr. Hughes nods. "Leave her. She's going to be fine. She knows better. Give us some room."

The men all back up a little at first, and then a little further, and then all the way to the back of the room.

Hughes moves his chair in front of mine. He sits down and smiles. "Alex," he says slowly.

"Fuck you!"

He tilts his head and smiles again. "Just what are you thinking in that head of yours?"

I curl my lips and frown at him. "You set us up. The choppers, the equipment—everything—you son of a bitch you set us up. Slade, Vanessa, Tony Crane, they're all dead 'cause you a greedy ass bitch, and I swear, on my father's grave, I'm gonna fucking kill you one way or another."

Hughes scoffs. "Look at me Alex."

"Yeah, I'm looking at you, bitch!"

He sighs and whispers, "I'm going to ask you the single most important question ever."

"MAN, FUCK YO' QUESTIONS!" I exclaim.

Hughes shakes his head. Still whispering, he asks, "Alex, did you see all the security badges and ID's Mr. White had?"

"What about 'em?" I snap.

He raises both hands to his sides. "Look at me, Alex," he says softly. "Do I look like Mr. White? Or do I look like you? No badges. Nothing."

I got quiet.

"Look over there." He points to the other side of the room. "See those cots? This isn't exactly freedom. We've been locked in here with a thermonuclear device, hoping and praying we make it through the night."

I squint at him. "But, but ... I saw you land the-"

He looks around in both directions to make sure no one is listening. "They have my mother," he says calmly. "She's um...." A tear streams down his cheek. "She's all I have left in this world. When the storms hit the gulf, Mom didn't stay, she left before it got bad, but my dad ... he was proud. A veteran. He didn't want to go. When the waters rose ... I wasn't ... see I was out on deployment and I couldn't ... I couldn't get back home, Alex. My brother tried to get Dad out, but." He shook his head again. "They both ... we buried them both...." He sniffles and wipes his tears. "So, you see, I can't lose her. I'll do whatever it takes to keep her safe. They'll kill her."

I touch his shoulder. I want to say something, but everything that comes to mind is judgmental and hypocritical. I want to tell him never compromise, but that's exactly what I'm doing. I close my eyes and look up at the ceiling. I sigh heavily. "Did you know?" I ask. "Did you know when you flew us to Virginia?"

He nods.

"Did you know Tesh was going to kill my friends?"

He nods again. Then, he shakes his head, still crying. "I'm sorry Alex. I really am, but this is the hand we've all been dealt. I was hoping you wouldn't walk through those doors today. I was hoping you had the strength none of us did. The men in black—Tesh's so called terrorists—they're not taking the bomb in ... we are. Why would you come here? I don't understand."

I touch his hand. "I didn't ask to come here, and I don't want my family to die because of me. This strong person everybody thinks I am ... I don't know who that person is. I'm just a soldier like you. You still have your mom. I lost both my mom and my dad. My mother tried to make me be more than what I am, but I'm just a soldier. I take orders. That made it easy for them to manipulate me."

"Us," he reminds. "They manipulated us."

"I'm sorry Hughes. I don't know what to say."

Hughes leans in and whispers in my ear, "Fight." He squeezes my hand tightly. "We needed a leader. We needed you. That's why you're here now. So, we fight." He leans back and nods.

I nod as well. "That our team back there?"

"Yeah." Hughes pulls out a handkerchief. He wipes his tears and then blows his nose. "Come on. Let me introduce you." He stands up and waives at the men in the back. "Come back over guys," he says.

The men slowly return to us. I stand up and straighten my clothes.

"Gentleman," says Dr. Hughes, "This is Alex Southerland."

I'm so embarrassed. I'm not sure why but I am. "I'm sorry, I-"

"No ma'am," interrupts the man closest to me. "I'm Mr. Red." He grabs my right hand with both his hands and moves in close. "John," he whispers, "John Kenner, Hundred and First."

I smile. "Ranger?"

"Yes ma'am," he replies proudly.

An older man to my left puts his hands on my shoulder. "They threatened us," he says. "Said we can't tell each other our real names, but I say fuck that! Fuck Pearson—yeah I said it. Fuck him! I'm Jose Serrano, CIA Station Chief, Islamabad-"

"CIA?" I ask.

Jose smiles. "Confused?"

I nod. "A little."

"Pearson and I joined up at the same time. We were at Langley together, but there are things he's willing to do to advance up the ranks I simply am not prepared to. Some lines you cross you can never come back from. Doctor Taylor contacted me. I made the mistake of approaching Pearson, hoping to reason with him. And as a result, he is now sending me to my death. I guess I could just let them kill me here, but my gut says I can find a way to stop this and keep my granddaughter safe." Jose's eyes begin to water. "My wife died, but my daughter and her daughter are here among us, prisoners of the devil."

14

I lunge forward and hug his neck. "I'm sorry, I-"

"It is okay," he replies, wrapping his arms around me and squeezing me tight.

I let Jose go and step back, wiping a tear from my right eye. I shake my head. "Whew, okay, thank you I needed that."

"You're most welcome, Agent Southerland."

"Alex," I reply. "Call me Alex. I'm not an agent of anything anymore."

Jose smiles and replies, "Neither am I. None of us are. This is the end of the line for us."

The man standing next to Jose reaches in. "Brian Tolliver," he greets with a firm handshake. "Defense Intelligence."

"Let me guess, Colonel Hammond?" I ask.

Brian nods. "I was on his team, but he's gone, and Pearson is calling the shots now. I guess he always was … it's all very confusing."

"So, you didn't agree with the intel that was going out on the Peter Tesh case, huh?"

"No ma'am I did not," replies Brian. "I'm pretty sure at this point it was all fabricated. They brought me and my wife here. We've been here a while. They made me come down here soon as the bomb arrived." He nods towards the plastic room with the bomb. "Just us and that God forsaken thing now." Brian frowns.

I'm about to respond, but the doors in the back of the room swing open again. I turn around and Mr. White walks back in wearing one of the black fallout suits. He's surrounded by other men, carrying large metal cases. They're about halfway to us now, and I realize someone is walking in single file behind Mr. White. The woman sidesteps to her left and I can see her face. My head spins around to Dr. Hughes who's shaking his head and frowning. I feel like someone just doused my head with accelerant and lit me on fire.

The woman walks up to me face-to-face. She tilts her head to the side. "You're not as smart as you think you are, Bureau!"

I grit my teeth and reply, "Rodriguez, why don't you take that suit off, so I can show these fine men how to kick a hole in a traitorous bitch's chest?"

She twists her lips up at me. "I'm here to make sure you complete your mission, Bureau. Seems the tables have turned." Rodriguez steps back looks around in each of our faces and yells in her thick Latin accent, "You hear that maricón? You do what the fuck I say, or I will detonate your ass. Your suits are equipped with self-destruct devices."

The men carrying the cases walk up and put a case down at each of our feet while Rodriquez continues her tirade.

"You try and betray me, boom!" she exclaims. "You do not follow orders, boom! You try and escape, boom! I don't like what you fucking say to me, fucking boom! And don't think for a second that I will give a itty bitty fuck about your dead ass. These suits keep things from penetrating out or in. Fuck with me and you'll be soup in a suit, got it?"

No one says a word.

"You betta fucking get it you fucking daffodils!" Rodriguez yells. "Now, get your suits on and get ready to brief."

Rodriquez walks towards the bomb, and we all drop down to our cases. I crack open my case, and there it is—a fallout suit, helmet and all. I touch the material of the suit and it's flexible, which is weird. It doesn't look like Rodriquez's suit at all. I hear Mr. White yelling from the distance for us to suit up. I undress, stripping down to nothing. I feel a tap on my shoulder. I turn around and John is standing in front of me, his face white as snow.

I raise both eyebrows. "What's up, John?" I ask.

"Well, not that I'm complaining," he reveals, sheepishly, "but, why are you stark naked?"

I smile and point to the one line of instructions inside my helmet that reads, "no non-organic materials inside the suit."

John steps back a little. "You speak Japanese?"

I smile.

"Well, numb nuts," yells Rodriguez, "I guess Southerland is smarter than she looks. The rest of you dumb fucks strip down to your balls. It's the only way you can get the suit on. Stupid fucking ass hats."

John looks me in the eye. "She's not a very nice lady, is she?"

I shake my head. "That's no lady my friend. Now, excuse me, Space Invader, I know we're in the same room and about to be naked all at the same time, but I just met you."

John's head turns red. "I'm so sorry, I-"

"I'm just fuckin' with you, soldier." I chuckle a little and then get back to the business of trying to stretch the suit up onto me.

All while I'm pulling and tugging in an upward direction with my ass on full display, I'm thinking, *Fallout suits my ass. Rodriguez gave us some bullshit—we're all gonna die.* I get the suit up to my chest and start tucking my breasts inside. Finally, I'm able to squeeze my arms down into the sleeves and pull it up. Looking down, my suit is like a wet, soggy bag—nothing like what Rodriguez and Mr. White are sporting. *Evidently, these guys lack the capacity to play fair.*

I pick up my helmet and look up. Rodriguez is staring.

"WHAT THE FUCK!" I exclaim.

"Put the helmet on, bitch!" she replies.

I point my helmet at her. "One more bitch and I'm gonna bust your goddamn mouth open, cunt!"

She laughs.

I hold my helmet up over my head and slowly lower it. It's completely dark except for a small line of light around the base of the helmet. Then, I see a cursor blinking at the top right of my helmet. It starts to blink faster and then the light at the bottom of my helmet disappears. The word 初期化し ます appears across the display, and suddenly it feels like my bones are about to break.

The display goes transparent and I drop to my knees. I yell in agony and drop down on all fours. The guys, still half-dressed, all crowd around me. I can hear myself scream, but they can't seem to hear me. The suit is sucking in and pushing out, hardening on every corner of my flesh, pinching and pressing against me from the tips of my fingers, up my arms, around my neck and down to my toes. Something keeps popping up on the screen but I'm in too much pain to translate it in my head. Finally, it stops. The display flashes for a moment and icons popup along both sides. I feel a pinch in my spine, which hurts about as much as whatever else was going on. I let out one last scream, and finally, it's over.

There's an exit icon near the bottom right, so I reach up for it, but nothing I do seems to activate it. I stare at it for a moment and think about getting out of that helmet. Instantly, my suit depressurizes around my neck, and I see light at the bottom of my helmet again. The display goes dark. I lift my helmet off with both hands, breathing erratically. I drop my helmet down on the ground beside me and sit back on my heels, shaking my head.

"Fucking crazy man!" I exclaim.

"What?" asks Jose.

Dr. Hughes touches my arm. "Are you alright, Alex?"

Rodriguez breaks through our huddle and looks at me with both disgust and delight. "That dumb bitch is fine!" she exclaims.

She leans down and knocks on my chest with her knuckles. I look down at my chest and it is hardened into a mold that looks like a tactical vest, only it runs along the lines of my shape. When Rodriguez taps the outside, it sounds like she's hitting a piece of steel with a rubber mallet.

"See, she's fine," Rodriguez announces. "Now, the rest of you fucks hurry up! And say one more goddamn name around here and...." she makes an exploding gesture with both hands, "fuckin' boom!"

"It's painful," I say softly. "The suit pumps up around you but it's painful and you get stuck with something towards the end. I don't know what it was. Felt like a needle or something. I can steel feel it deep in my back."

Hughes replies, "These suits are designed to keep us alive. Gotta be some kind of medicine delivery system."

"Yeah or the easiest way to kill us," John speculates.

Dr. Hughes looks up at him. "Could be."

"Everything's in Japanese," I tell them. "Be careful what you do, whoa what the shit?" I fall back onto my butt. "Y'all see that?" There's an entire display in front of my eyes. The same system as before. It's like a hologram. I wave my hands over the front of my suit and it distorts the hologram. "Holy shit!" I exclaim. "You can control the suit even without the helmet on."

The men get back over to their cases and finish suiting up. I can tell when their suits come online because they are squirming all over the place, taking a knee and gripping the edges of chairs and tables to get through. Each time one finishes, I see a teammate popup on my display. It would seem we are automatically synchronized.

I watch Rodriguez carefully. Our suits look just like hers after all, but she has some kind of device strapped to her left arm. I see her tap on it a few times and suddenly, she and Mr. White pop up on my team display. I get up to my feet. The suit is stiff, but it makes me feel stronger than ever before in my life. I stumble on my way over to Rodriguez, but after a few more steps find my balance. Rodriguez stops what she's doing and turns to me. She squints and sighs.

"I thought you were one of the good ones, Rodriguez," I say.

"What would make you think that, bitch?" she snaps. "Why? Cause I stormed the VP's residence with you? Dumb bitches are easily manipulated into doing-"

My punch nearly knocks her back to the rear doors. She falls to the floor, flat on her back, and her feet go up. I sprint over, following the trail of blood from her mouth with both arms extended. I kneel down and grab her throat. I clinch my right fist and rare back. "Say dumb bitch one more goddamn time and I'll fucking kill you!" But then, I hear a click and I look down. Rodriguez has her pistol pointed up at the bottom of my chin.

"Get off!" Rodriguez demands. She hops to her feet, steps forward, and pushes her pistol right in my face.

Mr. White casually walks up and touches the top of her arm, slowly lowering her gun from my face. "Ladies," he says softly, "We have a job to do. This will not get the job done sooner or easier." He offers Rodriguez a handkerchief.

Rodriguez takes the hanky and presses it up against her mouth, which is bleeding profusely now. She doesn't say a word. She just stares into my eyes and I in turn stare her down.

Mr. White tugs at her arm. "Let's get that looked at," he suggests.

It takes a few more pulls from Mr. White, but finally Rodriguez drops her gun down to the side of her leg and walks away with him.

I turn around and the guys are in their suits with their helmets off giggling like a bunch of schoolgirls.

Dr. Hughes shakes his head. "You're gonna get us all killed."

I shrug my shoulders. "What?"

"Hell, I been wanting to do that all day," Jose reveals.

We all let out a hearty laugh.

"Hughes, what's that thing on her arm?" I ask.

He leans in and whispers, "I'm not sure, but I believe it's a master control for all the suits. We have to find a way to get it off her. Then, we might have a fighting chance."

I tilt my head and frown. "Really?"

"I never said it would be easy, Alex," Hughes replies.

I turn around and to my surprise Mr. White is standing right behind me. Brian steps up to my right and Jose to my left.

"Whatever you're plotting, forget about it," warns Mr. White.

Brian gives Mr. White the *finger*. "Why don't you just back up off us, Whitey?" he says, holding both fists up. "You can get your lip busted too!"

"Come now Mr. Tolliver," White responds, "Are you forgetting about who's upstairs?"

Brian lowers his arm and sighs.

Mr. White smiles. "Play ball and you will be back with your families in a week—tops—everyone safe and sound. Now, you can all see your displays, yes?"

We all nod.

"Good then," says Mr. White. "The suits are quite automated. Think it and you will activate it. If you don't speak the language, that's not my problem, figure out how to change it. We are all linked now with communications. There is no range limitation as it bounces off satellite and is backed up short range by the equipment on our helicopters in case we do not have a line of sight. In the bottom of your cases, you will find a number of weapons. Equip yourselves. Wheels are up in 10...." He looks back at Rodriguez who is getting her mouth stitched up. "Let's say, 15 minutes. Questions....? No, then let's get moving, I will brief you in the air."

We turn and head back towards our cases.

"Agent Southerland," comes Mr. White's voice from behind.

I turn around.

Mr. White moves in close to me and speaks softly. "I don't have a dog in this fight. I am loyal to my superiors only, but she will kill you and your family when we are done. I don't know what you did to her, aside from just now, but I know she has been talking about killing you since you first arrived. She is CIA like me, but I have no allegiance to her. Just the country. Everything is compartmentalized, and I don't know what we are doing here, but-"

"The fuck are you talking to her for!" exclaims Rodriguez from a distance.

Mr. White smiles. "Watch your back. She can kill you with a push of a button on her wrist commander. Now, shake your head as if you are upset and push me away."

I do just as he suggests. He grips his gun as if he's going to draw down on me, but then after a moment he backs up and heads back over to Rodriguez.

I return to my case and kneel down. I open it and load up several weapons, two 9mm handguns and a M4 carbine machine gun. I look up and see Dr. Hughes experimenting with his suit and notice the coolest thing. He holds his gun down to his leg and lets it go and it snaps to his leg. It's hard to imagine but the suit all but reached out and grabbed it. I stand up and try the same thing, and sure enough my handgun snaps to my thigh. I hold the other up to the small of my back and it snaps to it as well. Then, I try and remove the one on my leg. As soon as I touch it, it releases.

"This is wild!" I exclaim. I pick up my M4, load it, and angle it across my back and it snaps to me as well. "Fuck!"

Dr. Hughes walks up to me. "Look," he says, showing me his gun. "There's technology in the grips and along the slides of these weapons. I suspect...."

"What?"

He reaches for my gun and he can't pull it off. "Yes, the weapons correspond with the suits. There's no way...."

"What...?" I ask.

He just shakes his head.

Tell me," I reply.

Hughes shakes his head again and speculates, "Who could've made something like this? All of it is way beyond anything in our arsenal."

I shake my head and touch his shoulder. "I don't know. All I know is we have to get that thing off Rodriguez's arm. It really does have a kill switch according to White. We'd never even see it coming."

Hughes nods, and returns to his case to finish arming himself.

I pick up my helmet and hop back and forth, foot to foot, trying to adjust to the constraints of the suit. It feels weird being naked inside a walking bomb, but I guess I have to get used to it. After all, it's not the first ridiculous thing I've done in the nude.

Rodriguez walks up to me, steaming. She gets in my face and lifts her left arm. She taps a few buttons on her wrist commander and tells me to place my fingertips on the display.

"Fuck you!" I exclaim.

"Do it or I'll shoot you in the face," she threatens.

I turn my nose up at her. "I'd still look prettier than you, cunt."

Rodriguez draws her handgun, so I reluctantly comply with her demand. Then, she tells me to repeat after her. I repeat a series of totally unrelated words and when finished, she presses the flashing icon on her fancy wristwatch. A noise comes from the right of us and catches my attention. I turn and look at the bomb. It lights up all over the front, and I see the display and it starts counting down from 48 hours— plenty of time for the Economic Summit to start and fill its halls with the unsuspecting elite.

"Wheels up in 15, you goddamn putas!" exclaims Rodriguez, storming out of the staging room.

I turn back to the guys. They're ready to go. I'm about to say something prophetic and inspiring when it all hits me like a ton of bricks—what I'm about to do, what I am powerless to stop, and my actions which are sure to usher in a new era of hate and war. I don't know if I have taken innocent lives before—I hope not. But this time, there's no question about it—if I do this thing they want me to do, the oceans will run red with the blood of the innocent. Instead of shooting my mouth off to the team, I kneel and do something that others might consider out of character for me during times like this—I pray.

Dear Jesus, our Lord and savior, give us a single glimmer of hope. I pray this one time I really need the stories to be true—that God really exists—that You are real, and Your love conquers all. Please, somehow, I ask You to deliver us from evil. I need that so badly, because right now, all I see is death in my future.

Chapter 3

The five of us—all suited up, fully equipped with gear and enough weapons to start a war—follow Rodriguez the traitor and Mr. White out to the front lawn where the two mysterious Black Hawk helicopters await us. I see a crew of men in military fatigues huddled near one of the choppers. *This is really happening,* I think.

Rodriguez turns and points to Dr. Hughes. "Follow the flight plan or I will turn you into clam chowder!" she threatens. She puts her left arm in the air to show off the unit strapped to her forearm. She means business.

Hughes nods, and we continue walking towards the second of the two helicopters. Rodriguez holds a radio up to her lips. I notice a man standing near the lead helicopter wave at her. The doors of the helicopter are open, so we climb in on both sides. Hughes takes his place in the cockpit and John joins him. Everyone is holding their helmets, but I put mine back on just in case something pops off unexpectedly because with me it usually does.

Rodriguez takes a seat. "We're going to rendezvous with Bravo at Dobbins Air Force Base. We'll meet our sponsor and head to the target location. Vice President Keller will meet us on the ground. No matter what, you keep him safe. Do your job and you just might live!" She taps her forearm a few times. "I can't threaten you enough," she says, "you fuck with me, I blow you up inside your suit, we Clorox it out, I stick some other worthless piece of shit in, and we keep moving. You mean nothing to me, comprender!" She looks directly at me.

I flip Rodriguez a bird which is hard to do since my suit is still a little stiff at the joints, but I manage to pull it off. She scoffs, and then tells Hughes to get moving.

The first helicopter takes off and breaks east across the open field. Hughes puts us in the air and follows. As soon as the first helicopter crosses above the tree line I notice a crooked line of white smoke coming from the trees, and it's growing longer by the second. It keeps coming straight towards us, and I have every intention of saying something, but I don't—I just grip the seat and the door with all my might to brace for impact.

Rodriguez sees me and looks out the door. "R! P! G!" she yells, but it's too late.

The cabin lights up. The explosion blasts Rodriguez and Brian out the other side of the chopper. I get thrown clear across to the other side of the chopper, but Jose breaks my fall. We are spinning around and going down fast.

"BRACE FOR IMPACT!" Dr. Hughes yells.

It all happens so fast. We land on our side. Dirt and grass explode up through the cabin, and Jose and I get banged all around inside. When we settle atop the earth, my head is ringing, but Jose isn't moving. I drag myself over to him and realize his neck is broken. He wasn't wearing his helmet. His eyes are open but, he's not moving—Jose's dead. The heads-up display in my helmet confirms it. His vitals are gone. I shut his eyes. Visibility is low, but my display automatically goes thermal and I can see two heat signatures up front.

"HUGHES!" I yell. "JOHN!"

"WE'RE OKAY!" comes a voice from the thick, black smoke in the cockpit. "Help me out of here."

I climb over the mess that used to be the cabin and see Hughes trapped in his seatbelt. "Jose didn't make it," I say.

"SHIT!" exclaims Hughes.

I cut Hughes down. John, who was seated beside Hughes in the cockpit is finally coming to as well. He has a big gash on his forehead, which is bleeding badly. He unsnaps his seatbelt harness and drops down.

"Where are our helmets?" asks John, clearly shaken up.

Hughes shakes his head.

"Who hit us?" John asks.

They both turn and look at me.

I shake my head. "I don't fucking know!"

"Rodriguez still alive?" asks John.

I look right at him. "I don't know man she flew out the door when we got hit."

John pulls his pistol and checks it. "Well let's find out before she turns us into meatloaf." He jumps up and grabs the edge of the bottom of the helicopter where the door used to be. He pulls himself up and reaches for me.

I jump up, grab his hand and he pulls me up. Dr. Hughes climbs out and hops down beside us. Then, he sprints towards the two bodies in the distance. John and I take off right behind him. I see one of the bodies moving and realize it's Rodriguez.

This bitch is still alive!

Hughes opens fire and so does Rodriguez. They hit each other and he goes down, falling backwards onto the lawn. Rodriguez goes down but she sits back up almost immediately. She tosses her weapon to her right and lifts her left arm up. I stop dead in my tracks and look at John.

"Get it off!" I yell. "Get out of that fuckin suit right-"

The sight of blood and guts erupting out of John's suit as his head flies off sends me over the edge.

"You goddamn fucking bitch!" I yell, charging at Rodriguez, gun first, firing at her head.

A round hits Rodriguez and knocks her back on the ground. Both her hands fly out to her sides. I hear gunshots behind me. Bullets are zipping past, but I don't care. I have to make sure she is dead or I'm a goner.

I run full speed up to Rodriguez's body and drop to my knees. There's blood all over the right side of her face and in her hair. Her face is swollen, and blood is pouring out of a gunshot wound. I think she's dead, but then she opens her eyes and swats my helmet with her right fist. Her blow has little effect on me. She's yelling at me but even if she's speaking Spanish, I can't understand her. All I know is she is fighting to get her hands on her wrist commander to end my life the way she did John's, and I can't let her do that, so I punch her face. And I punch her again, and again, and again until I can see her skull. Rodriguez's hands drop back down. Finally, she's dead.

I lift her wrist up for a closer look at the device in hopes of disabling it, but it gets shot out of my hand from behind.

Then, I get hit with rapid-fire burst from an automatic rifle. At least 10 rounds hit my back and flip me over Rodriguez's body. It feels like I've just been hit by a speeding train. Lying on my back and looking up, I see a shadowy figure standing over me blocking out the sun, his rifle aimed right at my head.

"Where is Alex Southerland?" comes a familiar voice.

"Tony...?"

He smacks my helmet with the end of his rifle. "I will fucking end you and everyone in this goddamn place if you don't tell me where she is."

"TONY!" I realize my external audio got muted somehow, so I focus on that icon and unmute it." "TONY, IT'S ME! DON'T SHOOT, IT'S ME!"

He pulls back with a confused expression on his face. "Alex?"

"Tony! You're alive!"

"What? Of course, I'm fucking alive, what the...."

"TONY!"

He grips his weapon and points it at my head again. "Take it off!" he orders, in disbelief. "RIGHT NOW!"

"JESUS, TONY!" I take my helmet off and look at him with my own eyes.

Here stands Tony, alive and well—in the flesh, wearing camouflage with black smears all over his face. *I can't believe my own eyes. He's alive!*

Tony takes one look at my face and drops his weapon down on the grass. He puts his hands up to his head and paces around for a moment. Then, he puts his hands on his hips. Then, he buries his face in his hands. "Alex!" he exclaims. "WHAT THE FUCK ARE YOU DOING!"

"Ghost one, ghost two is down. Proceed to Dobbins, I repeat deliver the package to Dobbins, over." comes a voice over the radio.

I shake my head and just look at Tony. I cover my mouth and try to stop the tears from streaming down my cheeks, but I can't.

Tony stops pacing and stares into my eyes. He smiles and just looks at me. Then, he snaps out of it. "Come on, we gotta go!" he exclaims, reaching for me. He yanks me up off the ground and starts pulling me, but I struggle and break free of his hold.

"No wait!" I move back over to Rodriguez's body and kneel down. "Fuck!" I yell.

"Alex, we gotta fucking go, right now!" Tony yells.

"You shot it!" I exclaim.

"What?" he asks, still shouting.

"You fucked it up man, we needed to-"

"ALEX!" he yells at the top of his lungs.

I see dirt kick straight up to my right from the impact of a bullet striking the ground. The bullet hit before I could even hear the gunshot. Someone is firing at us from long range. I look up and see men running towards us across the fake White House lawn. They are too far away to be accurate, but they're close enough to get lucky.

Tony grabs me again, firing a few wild shots into the distance with his pistol. "We gotta go goddammit!" he yells.

"No, wait!" I break free from him again and lunge forward towards my helmet. I grab my helmet and wrestle it back on. Then, I pull my rifle and fire at the men running full speed towards us. My helmet extends my sight with a built-in zoom feature, which helps me easily hit one of them. I knock him back on his ass and the others drop and scatter. "Go!" I yell. I look over my shoulder and see Tony recover his rifle and sprint towards the trees.

"Go!" Tony yells from behind.

I spin and run towards his position. He continues laying down cover fire. When I get to him, I yell "Go" and he takes off again. We take turns firing at the crowd and zig-zagging our way back towards the helicopter crash. Each time I fire, I take down a bad guy from a distance, but it's still not enough. It looks like they called every henchman in the rolodex.

Back near the chopper, I see a hand waving. Dr. Hughes is still alive. "Tony!" I yell, pointing at Hughes, "get him to the other side of the wreck, I'll cover you."

Tony pulls his rifle back up on his shoulder and slides over to Hughes. I switch my weapon to fully automatic and start spraying aimlessly at the bad guys. As soon as I see Tony and Dr. Hughes corner the heap of a mess that used to be the helicopter, I throw three hand grenades at the enemy and run for cover.

I circle around to Tony and Hughes. "Fire in the hole!" I yell.

Tony covers Hughes' head, and all three grenades go off. Despite the blasts, we still hear gunshots banging against the hull of the crippled helicopter. *These guys don't quit.*

"How is he?" I ask, my back pressed up against the only blade left on the propeller.

Tony shakes his head. "I'm sorry, Alex."

I crawl over to them, and Tony moves aside. He'd been putting pressure against Hughes' neck to try and stop the bleeding. Rodriguez hit him right in the artery, so unfortunately no amount of pressure would've kept him from bleeding out. Hughes is gone. From the corner of my eye, I see Tony praying. I touch Hughes' forehead and say goodbye. Then, the other side of the helicopter explodes and there's fire everywhere. The blast knocks Tony back a little, but he's right back on his feet.

"THAT WAS AN RPG!" he yells. "Alex, I'm sorry about your friend, but we gotta go!"

I shake my head. We start running together full speed towards the tree line.

"He's not my friend!" I exclaim, though I'm not sure why I'm compelled to tell him that. "Tony what the fuck are you doing here? And, how the hell are you still alive?" I ask as we hustle to the trees, bullets zipping past us. "I saw you-"

"I know about the bomb and everything," Tony yells. "I had to get you out of there before they made you arm it, now come on!"

Tony takes the lead and sprints past the first big pine tree. We run deeper into the woods. Pearson's men draw in close behind us and open fire. Tree bark flies all around us as we navigate the dark, dense forest. I run as fast as I can to keep up with Tony. Without warning, he stops dead in his tracks and turns back towards me. I stop too and look at him for a moment. Pearson's men are still firing on us, so I duck down behind a large tree stump. Tony holds up a detonator and presses down the button on top with his thumb. The blast is startling. I look over the top of my tree stump and the entire tree line in the distance is lit up, engulfed in flames. The screams and shrieks of men burning and running for their lives is music to my ears.

I stand beside Tony and watch the extraordinary blaze attack those traitors all at once. God knows how much explosives Tony used, but it looks like he'd booby trapped the place with everything he could find. There's no way they are getting through all that.

"Tony," I say calmly.

"Yeah, Alex?"

I snap my rifle to my back again, remove my helmet and hold it down by my side. "You're alive."

"Yup," he replies, emotionlessly.

"You've been busy," I say.

"Yup," he replies again.

"You just killed a lot of men," I say calmly.

"Had to stop that bomb," he responds. "You can't arm it if they can't follow us."

"Yeah, well, about that...."

"Alex...? About what?"

I clear my throat and continue staring at Tony's forest fire. "I already armed it." I turn and look at him.

Tony's hands spring straight up and cover his face. "GODDAMMIT, ALEX, WHAT THE GODDAMN, FUCKING FUCK! SHIT!"

"Tony," I say calmly, "I was trying to disable it and you shot me from behind and damaged the only device that could shut it down."

Tony turns to me. "Wait, so you're blaming me for this?"

I shrug my shoulders. "Well...?"

He looks up at the sky for a moment. Then he stares me down and points at me as if he wants to yell at me like I'm a little child. His body language tells me how angry he is, but he doesn't say a word. Eventually he just hangs his head down and sighs heavily. He shuts his eyes and shakes his head. "Come on." Tony turns away from the fire and waves me to him. "Follow me," he commands.

I follow him, using my helmet to swat bugs and spider webs from my path. "I'm sorry, Tony, I-"

"No, you're not," he says, leading the way.

"How do you know I'm not sorry?" I ask.

Tony replies, "It's all bullshit. It always is. You never mean you're sorry, you just say sorry because you think it's what other people want to hear, but you're a narcissistic sociopath, so I know you're not sorry."

"Eh, that's really fucked up, Tony."

He pushes his way through a thick line of bushes. "Well it's true," he says.

I frown. "I don't like the way that sounds, and you're being pretty fucking insensitive yourself, farm boy. My whole team died back there, and Pearson is going to kill my family, and we have to get to Dobbins Air Force Base."

Tony keeps moving, leading us deeper into the forest. "Dobbins?" he asks.

"Yeah," I respond, "the bomb is headed to Dobbins. We have to stop it."

"Uh huh," he replies, seemingly uninterested.

"Tony, I saw you shoot yourself!" I exclaim. "I thought you were dead all this time."

"Alex, don't be silly, I saw them drag you out of that bunker in Arizona."

"Then why the fuck didn't you say something you fucking asshole?"

"Can we talk about this later?" he asks.

I stop walking. "NO! I WANNA TALK ABOUT THIS FUCKING SHIT RIGHT NOW, FUCKING BASTARD YOU MADE ME BELIEVE YOU WERE DEAD, AND I'VE BEEN HURTING AND THEY KILLED VANESSA AND-"

"ALEX!" yells Tony, spinning around to face me. "They tased me when they busted into the cell. I had the gun, and I accidently squeezed the trigger. When I fired that shot, they hit me again with the taser and I fell to the ground. They drug you out. They secured me, and when I finally got out of there, I started looking for you. If you hadn't given me the tail numbers on those two helicopters, I never would've found you."

I stand there with my mouth open.

"Now can we go?" he asks, his tone now more frustrated than before.

I nod my head slowly. Tony turns back and starts walking again, pointing his rifle ahead and pushing his way out into the clearing. I follow and move in behind him. Tony walks towards some kind of dune buggy looking all-terrain vehicle.

"Well, how 'bout that," I whisper.

He goes around to the driver side, puts his rifle in the back and leans in with his arms hung over the top bars. He just stands there. I walk closer and realize he's tearing up.

"Tony, are you crying?" I ask.

He ignores me and sits down on the driver seat. I detach my rifle from the back of my suit and lay it down in the rear of the vehicle along with my helmet. I move around to the driver side. Tony is crying like a baby now, and I don't know why, nor do I care, I just want to be close to him. I climb in on top of him and immediately start kissing his lips, slowly at first, but then deeper, longer, and harder. I can taste his tears with every kiss and all I want to do is get out of this suit and fuck him right there in the middle of the woods, on the handlebars of this odd-looking dune buggy.

"What the hell are you doing?" he asks between his sniffles and my kisses.

"That's at least the third time you asked me that today." I kiss him again and again.

"Don't fuck with me, kid!" Tony exclaims, pushing me back by both arms.

I stare down into his eyes for a moment, thinking about what to say, but all I can think of is one thing, and so I say it. "I love you."

Tony scoffs. "What?" He pushes me up off him.

I force myself back down and kiss him more. "I love you," I say, rubbing my hands all over his head and squeezing his shoulders. "I love you." I kiss. "I fucking love you." I kiss again. By the fourth "I love you", he's pulling me in and wrapping his arms around me.

I stay on top of Tony, making out with him, trying to get him swallow my tongue, but then we hear helicopters approaching overhead, and it snaps us back to reality. We look up and see the choppers flying high and fast above the trees. They blast over the clearing in no time and continue behind us in the direction of the replica White House. I try to kiss Tony again because frankly I don't give a shit anymore about being killed, but he slams me back against the steering wheel.

"Alex," he says calmly, "we have to go, now sit on that seat over there, put your seatbelt on and don't say another word, or I'll leave your ass here."

I smile and comply with his demand. I climb off him and cross over to the passenger seat. I pull my seatbelt over across my chest and snap it into place down at the bottom of the seat. Then, I put my knees together and place my hands down on my knees. I turn and look at Tony. "I love you."

Tony frowns up big time. If I didn't know better, I think he wants to punch my lights out. Less than 30 minutes back together and I guess I'm already getting on his nerves.

Tony starts the motor and grips the steering wheel. "I love you too," he mumbles. Then, he slams down on the gas.

The front and rear wheels from Tony's 4x4 kick dirt and grass all over the place as he spins us into the shadows of the dense forest. The moment I saw Rodriguez that morning, I knew I had to find a way to take her down. I had to create an opportunity, but Tony beat me to the punch when he blasted us out of the sky. So, Rodriguez is dead now, but the bomb is still in play, so we're all still in danger—me, Tony, my family. I truly thought I'd never see Tony again, but thank God he showed up, back from the living dead. More than anything, he stopped me from facing the hardest decision of my life—killing innocent people in order to save the few I love. He effectively stopped me from making some classic, ridiculous, authority defying, morally bankrupt Alex Southerland move. However, in doing so, we just doomed a big white house full of people—including my family—to their death in order to try and save the rest of the world. My heart weeps, but in my mind—I'm okay with it.

Chapter 4

Tony and I drive through the forest on his little camouflage-painted dune buggy he probably painted himself for what feels like hours. The sun beats down on us from above and the threat of Pearson's men, hot on our trail, still looms. I have no clue whether my family or anyone else back at that compound is still alive, but I can't think about that right now. A hot nuclear weapon is in the wind—it's on its way to Marietta, Georgia, and there's no greater mission than stopping that thing from leaving U.S. soil. As I understand it, if that bomb goes off, it will tell a story all on its own—one that's far from the truth.

Between Tony jerking the steering wheel back and forth to miss giant trees by mere centimeters and all the sweat pouring down my back into my butt crack, I'm ready to get out and pitch a tent. I just grip the bars of the vehicle's roll cage and say a little prayer. The heat is getting to be more than I can stand in this ridiculous suit. I can't take it anymore. I reach to the back seat with both hands and grab my helmet.

Tony looks over at me. "That thing's probably bugged," he warns.

"I DON'T CARE!" I exclaim. "MY ASS IS MELTING!" I snap the helmet in place and once again I'm in complete darkness until the display boots up. Before all the commotion earlier, I was able to switch the interface from Japanese to English, which makes things a whole lot easier. As soon as I'm online, I see a row of new icons, other suits and they are in tracking mode. I quickly disable my location services and start moving through all the menu items. I switch my external communicator back on and turn to Tony.

"You look like a damn Martian in that thing!" he announces, laughing while making a serious left turn to avoid a boulder that came out of nowhere.

"Holy shit, man, you see that?" I turn and look at the supersized rock.

"You sound like a Martian too!" Tony shouts.

I laugh slowly like an evil alien from a horror film. "A sexy, black Martian?"

Tony looks right at my helmet and rolls his eyes. "You know, if I didn't love you, and I didn't need you, and I didn't just damn near lose my life trying to rescue you, I'd knock your ass out of that seat and keep driving!"

With my right hand, I make a jerk off gesture. "OH SHIT! MY ASS!"

"What?" Tony asks.

"HOLY FUCK!"

"What, Alex?"

"This thing is like totally drying and cooling the crack of my ass! Like fuck me, man!"

"Ass!" exclaims Tony.

I giggle. "What'd I say?"

Tony frowns. "You're a real fucking ass, Alex, you know that? Ungrateful fucking asshole!"

I roll my neck. "You kiss your mother with that mouth, farm boy?"

Tony slams on the brakes, and I nearly go flying out through the front. Thankfully, I'm wearing my seatbelt.

"The fuck was that for?" I ask.

"Shhhh!" Tony holds his fingers up to his lips. "We're here."

Tony points to a black SUV parked down near the road, which is currently being kept company by two men with AR15's. They are pacing around it, trying to look in through the windows, which are tinted jet black—even the windshield. Tony holds up his hand and points to his right, motioning for me to take that side, but I shake my head.

I take my helmet off. "Here, hold this," I whisper.

Tony squints, frowns, and violently shakes his head, motioning for me to stand down, but as always, I ignore him. Before he can get his hands on me, I'm already out of the dune buggy and moving towards the men. I look back and can see Tony is mad as hell with me. *What's new?*

I undock my pistol from my thigh and slowly make my way down to the vehicle, being careful not to make a sound. Once in arms reach, I look back and see Tony crouched beside the dune buggy, pointing his rifle in our direction. I raise my hand and motion for him to wait. I watch both men light up a cigarette, first the one on the left and then the other. I grip my pistol and position it behind my right thigh. Then, I casually walk around Tony's truck to greet them.

"Well, here I am, camping in the woods and the Universe sends me two sexy men to keep me company," I say, in a tone sultry enough to tempt a priest into fornicating.

They line up, one almost behind the other and grip their weapons. The lead man points his finger at me. "What are you doing? You shouldn't be here right now," he warns. His accent was thick, but I couldn't place it. "Go back to your camp!" he commands.

This man is downright salty, but his friend seems curious, so I rub my tummy with my left hand and advance a little more with my gun still down by my right side. I tilt my head to the side a little. "My girls and I are having trouble back at the camp, can one of you big, strong men, help us?" My mouth is open and I'm nearly licking my lips. *Men are so easy.*

"Yes," says the man in back. He pushes his way towards me, but the other guy grabs his arm and they begin to argue.

I can't make out what they are saying, but whatever it is, it damn sure ain't English. They both drop their weapons and let them hang by the shoulder straps as they wave their hands in each other's faces and get into a heated discussion. I'm not sure if I want to laugh or not, but I figure interrupting them would not be advantageous, so I draw my weapon and shoot them both right in the head. Their bodies drop before the two gunshots finish echoing down the road. All I can hear behind me is Tony yelling.

"ALEX!" he exclaims, loudly. "What the GODDAMN, MOTHERFUCK, GODDAMMIT JUST FUCKING WAIT, DON'T YOU FUCKING MOVE DAMMIT!" Tony is slurring just about every other word, all but tumbling down the hill, running as fast as he can with both our rifles in hand and my helmet under one arm. He is desperately trying to get to me. Maybe it's just my imagination, but I'm pretty sure I can see steam rising up off the top of his head.

Tony finally gets to me. He drops our rifles and lunges at me. He grabs me by both arms and slams me against the back of the truck. "YOU FUCKING MURDERED THEM!" he exclaims.

"Tony, I-"

"NO!" he yells, angrily, looking all around. "This is not how we do things, just what in the holy fuck are you thinking. Jesus, Alex, I'm sorry about your family, I am, but we can't kill cops, or we'll be just like those assholes back there. What the hell is wrong with you?"

I tilt my head and squint at Tony. "Are you finished?"

"What?" He looks confused.

"Tony, look at their vests."

He doesn't look. "What about their vests? You know what, you have no right to-"

"Look at the fucking vests, choir boy!" I exclaim. "They're not cops!"

Tony reluctantly steps back and looks down at the men. "Fuck, they're wired!" He looks back at me.

I tap my chest a few times. "Even with the helmet off, I still have access to my system. I can scan just about anything in sight and I could see the C4 on their chests and the wiring down their sleeves. I knew they were not law enforcement, and I couldn't take a chance on losing you to some mad roadside bombers."

Tony looks at me for a second. Then, he bends down and wrestles a detonator out of one of the dead men's hand. "Shit!"

"They would've killed us and anybody in the vicinity if they had the chance, Tony. I'm not a fucking murderer. I'm one of the good guys, remember...? And now, I'm fucking offended." I storm off around to the passenger side of the truck.

"Alex, I ... Alex, I couldn't see it ... I'm sorry."

"FUCK YOU, BOSS!" I exclaim. "Now get the ordinance. And let me in the goddamn truck! I'm fuckin' tired."

The doors unlock and I climb in. Tony remote starts the engine and I crank the air conditioning up on high. With my helmet off, my ass is sweating a river again. Honestly, I probably should be thinking about Bill and my family, but all I can think about is checking in to some sleazy motel and stripping this ridiculous suit off so I can get fucked.

I look up, and Tony damn near scares the life out of me. He's just standing looking in at me from the driver side window like a stalker. I throw both hands up and shake my head, mouthing, *dude, what?* Finally, he opens the door.

"Alex, I-"

I shake my head again. "Don't say it!" I warn.

Tony carefully lays the explosives he removed from the dead men's chest on the floorboard between our seats. Then, he reaches down and gets my helmet, which he hands to me. I stuff it down on the seat between my legs and rest my elbows on top of it. I watch Tony as he continues loading up.

"Here's your rifle," he says, carefully guiding it to me, butt first.

"Thank you." I take it and carefully lay it down beside the C4.

"Here's my rifle," he says, handing me his as well.

I take his rifle and place it down beside mine. Tony climbs into the driver seat and puts on his seat belt. Then, he nods at me, and I reluctantly put mine on too. With my suit on, it feels like the seatbelt is squeezing my spleen, but I suck it up and put up with it. If Tony drives this truck the way he drove that dune buggy, life I save may be my own.

Tony puts the truck in gear and looks up and down the road to make sure it's clear.

"Wait!" I exclaim. "Are these things hot?" I look down at the explosives.

Tony shakes his head. "No, I took care of it."

"Okay, what about the bodies?" I ask.

We both look back towards the rear of the truck simultaneously.

"Fuck 'em," Tony says, calmly. He steps on the gas and we speed off down the road, leaving the dune buggy for anyone to find right along with those two dead bodies.

I'm beginning to think we're either getting more reckless by the moment, or we collectively just don't give a fuck anymore. The things this farm boy is doing at this point is downright shocking. Whatever the reason for our overt acts, I hope we get to our destination before Pearson's men pick up our trail. As close as they were, they couldn't be that far behind, which means they may have heard those gunshots. We have to put some serious distance between us and them. Tony must be thinking the same thing because he's driving faster than I ever knew he could, and I'm pretty sure he just ran a stop sign. *Choir boy, my ass!*

"Where are we?" I ask as Tony barrels down an unknown back road.

He sighs heavily. "I don't feel like I should tell you."

I instantly cock an attitude. "And, why not?"

Tony looks at me for a moment and frowns. Then, he refocuses on the road. "I don't think I should tell you because you are fool enough to sneak off and try to storm the castle. It's what you always do."

I shake my head. "Not this time. My family's dead to me."

Tony gets angry. "DON'T SAY THAT, ALEX!"

"You killed them the moment you hit that chopper," I say softly.

"What did you just say?" asks Tony in a calm tone that does not match the situation. I don't respond, so Tony mumbles to himself, "Ungrateful bitch, I can't believe I'm risking life and limb and fucking career on this-"

I break out in an uncontrollable high-pitched laugh.

"What?"

"Fuck me, Tony," I yell, laughing louder and louder.

"The fuck, Alex...? Something is wrong with you!" he exclaims.

I continue laughing my ass off. "Tony...?"

"WHAT!" he yells, angrier than before.

"Did you just call me a bitch?"

He smiles the biggest smile ever. "I'm sorry, I-"

"No, don't fucking ruin it!" I interrupt. "You really did? You called me a fucking ungrateful bitch. O. M. G. This is like a special moment, like our first time." I look over at him and smile a very big smile.

Tony looks confused. "So ... you ... you like being called a bitch?"

"Hell no!" I exclaim. "Well, not really ... maybe, but ... shit, I don't know, Tony, just stop it you're ruining the moment." I reach over and touch the back of his neck and rub his hair. "You are really sweating," I say as I ogle his handsome face.

"Alex...?"

I bat my eyes. "Yes, Tony?"

"You're fucked up!" he exclaims.

I chuckle a bit. "Thank you."

"It's not a compliment," he replies, seriously.

I sigh. "Ass." I continue rubbing the back of his head. "Just drive the fucking car, and are you gonna fucking tell me or not? Look we're not in the office anymore. You saw me take those bastards out? Right?"

Tony nods. "Yeah, uh huh, I can just see where this is going."

"I'm not a bitch! I'm a lethal bitch! I'm the horniest goddamn bitch on the road! I'm-" I start crying. "I'm ... yeah, I'm fucked up and I ... I don't deserve to go on liv-"

"Alex...?"

I sniffle and wipe my nose with the back of my glove. "Yes, Tony?"

"I need you to relax."

I get defensive. "I am relaxed, I-"

"Stop!" he exclaims. "For once, stop and listen to me, cut the bullshit. You were in a helicopter crash. You just lost some men. You may have just lost your family too, and you just shot two men in the head. I think you're in shock."

I cry louder. "You crashed my helicopter! I hate you! And, I'm sorry. And I...." I realize he might be right, so I shut up and just sob loudly for the next few miles down the road. I try to speak again now, but I still can't. It feels like every bad thing I ever did is dancing atop my head, wearing clogs. All I feel is sadness. I almost get the words out, but I still can't, so I hold a finger up and cover my mouth with the other hand.

Tony reaches over with his right hand and runs his fingers through my hair while I cry. "You've been through a lot, kid" he says. "More than ... you just been through too much, and I understand if-"

"I love you, Tony." I stop crying.

Tony doesn't reply right away. We drive a few more miles down the road before he breaks the silence. "I love you too, Alex."

I wipe my tears and squeeze Tony's hand. At this moment, when everything in my world is a shit storm inside a cluster fuck, I'm right where I know I need to be—safe with my Tony at the steering wheel. I let go of his hand and push back into the far-right corner of my seat. I close my eyes and fall asleep peacefully.

Chapter 5

I awake in the car by myself. I can hear Tony's voice, but I can't see him. I yawn and stretch. It's cold as hell in here—Tony left the air conditioning on full blast for me. That was sweet. As embarrassing as it sounds, it seems these fallout suits are drool proof—I sure put that to the test. The ton of bricks that were banging on my head seemed to have fallen off. I can't remember the last time I intentionally killed anyone. *Wait, I tell a lie, I actually meant to kill that Rodriguez bitch ten times over.* For some reason, taking those two guys down back on the road pushed me over the edge, or maybe I was already over it. Either way, I think I took it really bad. Maybe it was the callous way I handled it. If I didn't know about the explosives, I would've tried to talk them down or knock them out, but I just rushed in, scoped them out and basically executed them. This suit is evil. It makes the average person powerful—invincible. It makes them a god. It makes me feel flip about human life. Even the scum sucking criminals have rights but having this much insight into everything around me makes me something I know I'm not—something I never wanted to be. I have to get out of this thing.

I push the engine stop button on the truck, open my door, and hop out. I turn around and see Tony a few paces away from the back of the truck. We are in the woods somewhere, parked in front of an old log cabin.

"What's up?" I ask, softly.

Tony waves me off and continues talking on his satellite phone. I stretch and roll my head around on my neck, trying to get used to standing up after sitting on my ass for so long. My suit seems to have stiffened up around my joints again, so I move around and bounce from foot-to-foot to loosen it up.

Tony hangs up the phone and turns to me. "Come on," he says, "we'll be safe in there. I have supplies and food—well something like food—and we've got clean water too. You hungry?"

I nod.

"Come on." He beckons for me to follow him. "Let's get you cleaned up and fed."

Tony turns and starts walking. I follow him to the door. He unlocks it and holds it open for me. I look all around before entering. The cabin is nestled deep inside the woods. There's no one in sight in any direction—no neighbors or anybody. It'd be a great place to off somebody. No one would ever find the remains.

Once inside, I stand and look around. The cabin is the epitome of simple living—basically just four walls—but there's a fireplace, a table, and a few beds over on the other side. All in all, for two people on the run, it's all we need.

Tony shuts the door. It'd been hot the entire day, but the sun is going down and it's cool inside the cabin.

"I put all your stuff back there near the bed on the right," Tony says. "I know it's a little chilly, and I don't mean to be a creep, but the way you're all contoured up in that thing, I'm guessing you aren't wearing anything it."

I smile.

"Well, I don't have any clothes that will fit you, and I'm pretty sure I left my go bag home, so when you come out of that thing, you're going to be cold. I'll start a fire and see if I can get some grub going, okay?"

I nod and pace around a bit. Tony starts throwing wood over into the fireplace, and I move back to the bed he pointed to. I sit down and lie back. I stare up at the ceiling, which looks like a den for cobweb-dwelling creatures. The power of this suit has my mind going a thousand miles per hour. It feels like I'm in the Shire with the ring of power in my little tattered jacket pocket, burning and calling me to slip it on my finger. But I'd rather be naked than run around in a suit of death, so I power it down.

As soon as I log off and exit the menu, my suit starts huffing and puffing and spitting out moisture, rapidly expanding off of my skin. It expands so much in the front that it pops opens like a deflated hot air balloon down my chest and returns to the baggy, stretchy state it was when I first removed it from its container. I smell like a dead rat crawled up my ass and died twice. It's like someone took a six-week-old fish, coated it with skunk juice, and then left it in a hot trash can all night. *I'm a sweaty, stankin ass mess.*

I pull my suit down and try my best to flip it as far inside out as it will go to let it air out. "Please tell me there's running water here, Tony," I say, wrapping myself up in a blanket I took from the bed.

He laughs. "Well, city girl, I drew a tub of water from the well before I went looking for you in case I found you stuck in the mud." Tony points to a big rusty tub across the one room cabin. "It's not hot, so you can either deal with a cold bath or you can wait till I get the fire going and boil some water to put in it. That'll warm it up some."

I roll my eyes. "It just keeps getting better and better," I mumble.

Tony laughs a hearty laugh and gets back to his fire-making duties.

I plop down on the only couch in the place and a cloud of dust flies up all around me. I cough a few times before proceeding to complain again. "You didn't think you'd rescue me did you?"

Tony smiles. "What makes you say that?"

"Cause your squeaky-clean ass forgot to dust." I run my hands over the plaid covered sofa cushion and draw back dusty palms.

"Well, it was either I dust or go save your ungrateful ass," Tony replies, sarcastically. "I chose the latter."

I frown. "I dunno, that fake ass White House is starting to look up."

Tony stops and drops his head. "Alex...!"

"I kid, Tony, seriously, I'm thankful, and I'm sorry about all the crying and shit because-"

"I thought you stopped swearing," he interrupts.

I gasp. "Uh, well when the fuck did you start cursing like a goddamn sailor, choir boy?"

Tony gives me the wickedest of stares. "I hate when you call me that."

"You know, Tony, I never knew you were such a bastard, I mean exactly what time did Gia crawl outta your ass and replace herself with a big hairy bitch bug?"

Tony angrily points at me. "Hey, don't fucking do that!"

"Your sleeve's on fire."

"What?"

"Your fucking sleeve!" I yell, rushing over to him.

Tony looks down and finally realizes he'd actually started the fire while arguing with me and got friendlier with it than he should've. I grab his arm and shove it in the cauldron of water on the floor. A little steam rises from the surface of the water as the flame on his sleeve dies out.

"You didn't feel that man?" I ask in disbelief.

Tony shakes his head. "My mind is ... it's been a long day. Look, give the fire a few minutes to get hot. I'll have some water for you ready soon and then I'll get some dinner going."

I drop my head and look him in the eyes. I touch both his shoulders and smile. "Thank you for saving me ... and for my bath. I'm sorry for being such a bitch as you say."

Tony frowns and stands up. "This is gonna take a bit, just make sure you move the wood around. I'm going to get some air."

Tony walks out the front door, and I sit on the floor with the iron poker jabbing chunks of wood around and playing with the fire. I don't know what's wrong with me, but I am being a bitch—a bratty one—and that's not like me. Then again, I do know what's wrong with me. All I can think about is my family being tortured by that black-hearted mongrel, Pearson, and all I want to do is go right back there and put his wrinkly balls in a vice grip. I want to water board him to his last goddamn breath. Tony's smart for not telling me where we are, but I'm not going to just sit by and let them kill my family. They are all I have left, and they just started liking me. Fuck that bomb. To hell with Dobbins. I'm not going there, and nobody can fucking make me. When Tony comes back in here, I'm going to make him tell me where he found me, and then I'm going to put an end to all Pearson's bullshit.

My internal rant is finished, and the fire is finally roaring. I lift up the heavy iron pot and hook it up at the top above the fire. I may be skinny and hungry, but I am still strong, and the stronger I feel in my mind, the harder I know I can hit Pearson and his bitch boy crew. *Hmm, Tony's right, I am cursing again. Jesus, not Blondie, I don't have time for her shit.* I can feel her climbing out of her demonic hole trying to take charge, and as strong as I want to be right now, I don't know if I am strong enough to stop her. Even though I smell like a horse's ass, my pussy's wet, which means she is up to something.

I drop the poker and put my face in my hands, trying to think of anything other than what I'm thinking right now, which involves Tony's cock in my mouth. Now, I'm wondering if it's big or short or fat or hairy, and I'm starting to tumble down Blondie's rabbit hole without a parachute or even a rope to climb back up. "This is fucking stupid!" I exclaim, leaping up off the floor and throwing my blanket down.

I run full speed across the room to the tub and jump in feet first. I scream louder than I think I ever have in my entire life. The water isn't just cold—it's freezing cold. I hit my head trying to climb back out. After bopping myself real good, I can't seem to get out. I flip and flop around with both hands and feet, trying to grab hold of the edge of the tub to get out. "GODDAMN! GODDAMN! GODDAMN!"

The door flings open and Tony comes through guns blazing. "The fuck's going on in here?"

"T... T... Tony!" I stutter, shivering and shaking, trying to cover my breasts and not drown. "G... get ... get me the fuck outta here!"

Tony puts his guns up and rushes over to me. He grabs me up and pulls me out of the tub. So, here I stand, freezing cold like a wet dog, naked and for the first time in a long time completely embarrassed.

Tony turns his head and looks up to the ceiling. "Are you okay?" he asks.

"Don... don't look, I-"

Tony shakes his head. "What on earth are you doing?"

"I ... cold... so cold, I j just wanted to take a bath and-"

He turns his attention to the boiling water over the fire. "And, you couldn't wait for the hot water?"

"IT'S COMPLICATED!" I exclaim, still shivering and dripping water all over the floor, which seems to be turning all the dust into mud. "Jesus, Black Jesus, help me please!"

Tony shakes his head again, and heads to the fire.

"You just gonna leave me like this?" I ask still panicking.

Tony sighs. He reaches down and picks up my blanket. Then he walks backwards slowly up to me, holding the blanket behind his back. "Here," he says, wiggling it at me.

I snatch the blanket and wrap it all around me—even over my head. I don't care that it's been on the nasty floor, I want to cover up, and not just because I feel frozen solid all the way to my bones. That was not sexy at all. Whatever chance Blondie thought she had with Tony, I'm pretty sure I just killed it with my "cat in water" performance.

Tony makes his way back over to the fire, takes another towel and grabs the handle of the pot over the fire. He lifts the pot up and carefully walks back over to the tub. The room fills with steam as he pours the boiling hot water into my freezing cold bathtub.

"You know not to jump in this without testing the water first, right?" asks Tony.

I cock an attitude. "You know what, fuck...." I pause for a moment. Then I nod and reply, "Yes, sir. Sorry, sir. I didn't think it was that cold."

Tony looks just as surprised as I feel.

Again, he shakes his head. "Alex, you are-"

"I'm fucked up, I know," I interrupt, hanging my head low and pushing the dust-mud around with my foot.

Tony touches my face with both hands and lifts my chin. He looks into my eyes and says, "No, you are going to be okay, I promise. Just try and relax. Everything's going to be fine."

I fall into his arms. "But I stink, Tony."

He patronizes me. "I know, and yes, you stink, but there's soap here."

I hit his chest with my fist. "You're a good man," I whisper. "Gia doesn't deserve you."

"Yeah, well you're right about one thing," he snaps.

"What? What's wrong with you and the Italian bird?" I ask.

"Nothing." Tony pushes me off. "Look, get cleaned up. Dinner isn't going to cook itself, okay?"

"Fine." I frown and stick my finger into the tub. The water is hot, but not too hot for me.

Tony heads back towards the fire. I watch every angry little step as he walks away. "She left me!" he exclaims.

"What...?" I'm totally shocked.

"I DON'T WANNA TALK ABOUT IT!" he shouts back over his shoulder.

Tony is salty as shit all of a sudden, so I just leave him be. I drop my blanket and slowly climb back down into the tub. I grab one of the bars of soap on the side of the tub and exhale slowly as I ease myself into the hot bath. I rub the soap around on my chest and my shoulders and under both arms while I watch Tony fiddle around in the kitchen area, which can only really be called a kitchen if you squint one eye after downing an entire bottle of whiskey.

My underarms smell like roses now, so I just lie back against the tub and sink down as far as I can into the water to let my bones soak. I enjoy the heat for as long as I can, and then I stand up and start washing my body with the little bar of soap. Tony thinks I'm not watching, but I see him out the corner of my eye, peeking back over his shoulder and looking at my body. *Goddammit Blondie!*

I soap up all over, hair included, and then sink back down in the water to rinse myself. Satisfied I'm nice and clean I step out of the tub and look around for a towel. I don't see one near the tub, but there are several over near the fire, so I boldly do exactly where Blondie wants me to. I walk right up to Tony, who's currently stirring something in the pot over the fire.

"Tony," I say softly.

"Yeah?" He doesn't look up.

"I need a towel," I tell him.

"Yeah, they're right over-" Tony's mouth drops as he turns and zooms in on my big wet breasts. He completely loses his shit, turning his eyes away and stumbling backwards towards the towels. He grabs one and holds it up while keeping his eyes pointed in the opposite direction.

"Tony, look at me."

"Uh, no! Alex, just take the damn towel!"

I cock my head and cross my arms. "No, bring it to me like a gentleman. The Tony I know would've had towels over near the tub, and I don't want to risk slipping up and falling over into the fire, so bring...! Me...! My...! Towel!"

Tony sighs. Then, he sighs. Then, he sighs again, but finally, he complies. He turns and looks at me with a blank stare, trying his best to not focus in on my lady parts. He takes a few steps towards me and opens the towel up. I spin around into it and wrap it around my body.

"See, now was that so hard?" I ask, looking down at the front of his pants.

Tony holds up a finger at me and looks like he wants to say something, but he doesn't. He just shakes his head and gets back to his stew, which is beginning to smell pretty damn good to me.

I walk over to the other side of the room and dry my hair as best I can with my towel. I dry the rest of my body and re-wrap myself in my towel.

"Is it ready yet?" I ask.

"Not yet," Tony replies.

"I need a broom," I say.

Tony looks back over his shoulder. "You fucking serious?"

I roll my neck at him and frown. "Yeah, do you have a fucking broom?"

"Jesus Christ," Tony mumbles, along with a few other choice words I can't quite make out. He stands up and walks out the back door. After a few minutes, he returns with a broom that looks like the Wright brothers used to sweep out their airplane hangar, but I don't say anything. I recognize I've been complaining about something damn near all day, so I just take the damn thing to try and de-dust the place.

I sweep a big pile of dust, dirt, and grime to the front door, open it and push it all out. Then, I do the same for the other side, relieving every corner, nook, and cranny of the cabin of its cobwebs, bugs, and a few other things I simply cannot identify. I push everything out the back. All while I'm sweeping, I'm thinking about Vanessa cleaning naked for me, rest her soul. In my mind I see me spanking her with a crop or whip or something and yelling at the top of my lungs for her to clean for mommy and bend over like the slut she is. She was into that sort of thing, and I swear I hated it, but I loved it too. Boy did I love it. *I wish she were here because I would so have a threesome with-*

"Alex...?"

I snap out of my twisted fantasy. "Yes, sir?" I respond.

"Come on," he says, "let's eat."

I rest the broom against the wall and shut the back door. Then I walk over to Tony and sit down near the fire. Tony hands me a bowl and something that barely resembles a spoon. I look down in the bowl and can't seem to identify the ingredients but it's hot and I'm hungry so, I start working up the nerve to dig in.

Tony laughs, and I look up at him. He's chowing down like a lumberjack and snickering at me.

I frown. "What?"

Tony can't seem to help himself. "It's seafood gumbo with chicken and sausage and a hint of garlic." He laughs a hearty laugh and continues eating.

I cock my head to the side, look back down in my bowl and stir it around a bit. "No, seriously, Tony, what is this?"

"Trust me, you don't want to know," he replies.

"Rabbit?"

He laughs again.

"Squirrel?"

Tony smiles really big. I shoot him a bird. "What, you think I don't eat squirrel stew?" I ask, scooping up a spoonful of meet and juice. I chew slowly and swallow. "Your squirrel's a little bland but other than that it's good."

He rolls his eyes. "I forgot you're the daughter of Zeus himself. I'm pretty sure your dad killed squirrels with lightning bolts."

My jaw uncontrollably drops. I frown up. "You know what, Tony, if I wasn't holding this goddamn bowl, I'd-"

"Shoot me a bird?" he interrupts.

I take another spoonful of stew. "Uh, fucking yes," I respond, talking with my mouth full. "Wait how did you cook them so fast, and how the hell are they so tender? Dad's were always as dry as his humor."

"Well, Alex, if you must know, I skin them, clean 'em and then cook them for about 20 minutes."

"With the head on?" I ask.

He nods. "Teeth and all. The brain acts like tenderizer," he explains. "Meat falls off the bone every time."

I eat a little more. "And you say I'm fucked up, but you up in this bitch cooking squirrel skulls in a big witch pot."

"Ass!" he exclaims.

We laugh and continue eating quietly. It's getting late and I'm tired. I finish my stew and drink some water. Then, I kiss Tony's forehead and make my way back over to my bed. I drop my blanket and climb under the dusty covers. I flip the pillow over and fall back down on it. I hear Tony rustling around, but I don't look to see what he's doing. I just stare up at the ceiling and think about my family. I hope they are still okay, but I doubt it. I close my eyes, take a few deep breaths, and then play possum for a while. I lie still in bed while Tony bathes. All while I hear him splashing around in the tub, I plot my next actions. Tony has information I need, and I'm not going to let the morning come without sweating it out of him, literally.

I hear Tony's feet hit the floor. He is out of the tub, and not before long, he's near. I crack my right eye open and see him standing between our beds. He's fully naked, still drying his chest and shoulders off. It's dark in the cabin, but the dim glow from the fire is just enough for me to see how big his back is, how slim his waist is, and how fine his ass is. For a white boy, Tony is built like a tank. He looks so thin in his suits and even tinier in his little toy soldier tactical gear today, but maybe that's what I wanted to see—like it's my Blondie defense mechanism to prevent me doing something stupid. I guess if, in my mind, I see him as undesirable, Blondie will ignore him, and I won't have to try and explain to Dad—rest his soul—that I spent my waking hours trying to "throat goat" his friends after his untimely death. See, when I say it like that, Blondie runs and hides. She is not completely without scruples. But, I'm in control right now, and this ain't for pleasure. I have a mission to complete.

I watch Tony move around and get ready to crawl into bed. I am a little conflicted. Yes, I want to manipulate him, but I actually have developed feelings. I really want to touch him, caress his skin, pull him into my body and kiss his ears from behind. I'd planned on fucking his brains out and making him tell me where my family is, but I guess I'm not as devious when Blondie is an absentee deity. She is never around when I need her, and I need her right now, because I can't stop feeling what I'm feeling, and I can tell what I'm feeling is about to get in the way of me getting what I need.

"Tony," I whisper.

He jumps back a little. "Oh shit, I didn't know you were awake. I'm sorry." He pulls his blanket up to try and cover his body.

I reach over, grab the blanket, and pull the end of it. Tony moves with the blanket, trying to keep it up above his waist, but he apparently is unaware of just how strong I am.

I shake my head, slowly and seductively, still pulling the blanket and Tony to my bed. "No, don't cover up, come here."

"Stop!" he commands, sternly.

I ignore him. Now, I'm pulling his blanket with both hands, and I can see him getting hard. His cock is eagerly poking out near the top of the blanket.

"Alex!" he shouts, "I'm fucking serious, now let go!"

I pull myself up off the bed with his blanket and wrap my arms around his neck. I kiss his lips, but he doesn't kiss me back. He tries to turn his head, so I tighten my grip around his neck, and lift my legs up around him. I wrap my thighs around his petite waist and lock my ankles behind his back, kissing him all over his face. The blanket hits the floor and I feel his stiff cock rise up against my pussy.

Tony grabs my shoulders and tries to pry me off, but I'm not going anywhere.

"I love you," I whisper between kisses.

Tony stops struggling. He kisses me back once. "I love you too, but we can't do this, and I know what you're doing anyway."

I continue kissing him. "What am I doing?" I ask, pushing my tongue into his mouth before each of my kisses.

"You want to know where your folks are," he mumbles, his words muffled by my wet tongue.

"Tony, I swear I will do whatever you tell me to," I tell him. I kiss him deeper and harder. "I swear I fucking will." I start pushing with my hips, thrusting my body up in the air and back down on his cock. "I swear to fucking God I will do what you tell me to, I just need to feel you inside me."

He shakes his head, but I grab a fistful of his hair.

"Stop it!" I exclaim, shaking my head. "Don't tell me no. Put it in, put it deep inside me right now! I need you and I know you need me too."

Tony's hands move down slowly in unison right to the small of my back, and then down to my ass. Finally, his hands find his cock, and then his cock finds my wet, hairy pussy. It's been so long since I could shave down there, but I don't care and apparently neither does he.

I nod slowly and continue kissing him. He's breathing so hard and fast it feels like his heart's going to pump its way right up out of his chest. I push my ass down and work my pussy onto the swollen head of his stiff cock. I wiggle my ass and move down along his shaft. His cock is long, and I want it all inside me. I squeeze his neck and bite his right earlobe.

"You feel so good inside me," I whisper. "Give it all to me, I need to feel you deep, please give it to me, please, Tony, I need it." I'm not sure why but I start crying, like uncontrollably crying, loudly, right there in his arms.

Tony wraps his arms around me and pushes his cock all the way up inside. I gasp and pull his hair hard. My eyes roll into the back of my head. Tony stands there with all my limbs wrapped around his body, and he pumps inside me slow and deep, pulling me onto his body so tight it feels like he can just crush me into him. He moves over and lowers me down onto the bed nice and easy. I spread my legs wide and give him full access. He gets on top and forces his cock in me, balls deep. He has his arms wrapped around my back and he is thrusting his hips and working his cock in my dripping wet pussy. I can't stop telling him how much I love him, and he can't stop telling me he's always loved me—how he will never let anybody hurt me ever again, and how he needs me. That right there is all I need to hear.

"Give me a baby!" I tell him.

"What?" Tony nearly launches up to the ceiling.

I wrap my legs around him and pull him deep in me. He struggles to break free, but I won't let him go. I pull him down on me. I can tell when a man is about to cum and it feels like he's about to bust uncontrollably inside me. I can see it in his eyes he wants to pull out, but he's still pumping my pussy like his life depends on it.

"Cum in my pussy, Tony," I beg, "cum deep in my pussy and get me pregnant!"

"No!"

"Yes, give me your baby!" I dig my nails into his back.

"ALEX! OH FUCK, ALEX, GOD, NO!"

"YES, YES, YES! FUCK I'M CUMMING BABY, CUM WITH ME! FILL THIS GODDAMN PUSSY UP!"

Tony yells and his body tenses up all over. I feel his load explode inside me all at once and I squirt all over him and me. He keeps trying to get up and out, but I keep squeezing my thighs to keep him in.

"Stop fighting me!" I say.

"You're on the pill, right?"

I chuckle a little. "Are you fucking kidding me, Tony? You just rescued me out of a hole in the forest. How the fuck would I be on the pill?"

"Jesus!" he exclaims. "We shouldn't have done this, what the hell are we doing here?"

"Tony....?"

"What?" He pushes up with both arms. "What in the world could you possibly say right now after this, Alex?"

I close my eyes for a moment and think. Then, I open my eyes and stare into his. "...Marry me."

"What did you just say?"

I sit up a little. "Marry me," I repeat.

"Your dad would fucking kill me if—I mean, I'm like a goddamn pedophile and-"

I put my finger over his mouth. "Daddy is gone, I am a grown woman, and I don't give a shit about Gia anymore. I need you. I don't want to play games, and I swear I am not trying to trick you. If you tell me to go to Dobbins I will go there. Divorce her ungrateful ass and marry me because my baby needs a father."

Tony shakes his head. "Gia already divorced me."

"Huh?" This news is totally shocking to me—fortunate, but still shocking. "What happened?" I ask.

Tony lowers himself back down. He moves to the side a little and rolls me over on top as he lies down on his back. I rest down on his chest. I can feel his cock pulsing inside me. He's still very hard and very deep in my pussy. His long, slender cock feels so good inside me. Like, he really just made love to me. Maybe it started out like fucking, but it didn't feel that way at all towards the end. I feel like I've just made love for only the third time in my life.

"Gia was upset with me for a long time," Tony explains.

"I don't understand," I reply, softly. "You're amazing. Why would she be-"

"I never gave up on you," he interrupts. "Not once. I ... she felt I was obsessed with you ... said you were dead and gone. That I needed to just let you go, but I couldn't. I think she could see how I really felt about you even before I could. Gia felt like number two to you, and she couldn't stand it. I came home after going back to Arizona for the third time trying to pick up your trail and I walked into an empty house. No Gia—just papers. At first, I thought I would be heart broken—I mean you know how it was with her, but-"

"You're not?"

He shakes his head. "Nah, I guess I'm not."

I smile, but I don't think he can see it with my face buried in his chest hair.

"She called me a sick cradle robber," he confesses.

I laugh a little.

"That's not funny, Alex, look at us!" he exclaims. "She's right, this is sick."

"Whatever."

"I'm 15 years older than you, and your dad-"

"Don't mention my dad again or I'm gonna fucking lose it!" I warn. "Look I love Dad. I do. And ... like you can pretend you knew him better than me, but you don't, Tony. You don't know him the way I did. He trusted you with my life. Now, I need to be your wife, and I need him and you to be okay with that."

"This is crazy," Tony says.

"What was crazy was Vanessa Sullivan's sex life. She wasn't a pistol—No, she was a goddamn bazooka."

"Seriously, Alex?"

"What?"

"You're seriously going to talk about your ex-girlfriend with my dick still in you? Geez!"

I lift my head up. "No, uh uh, you are not going to be jealous Mr. F B I. because I still love her, and I need for you to be okay with that too and not be jealous of a dead woman. And, I need to be able to talk about her and her strapons without you freaking out on me."

"You're really fucked up," he says.

I smile and kiss his lips. "Whatever. Now, are you going to do it or not? Why the fuck do I have to beg you to be my-"

"Alex, if we make it out of this shit alive, and you really are pregnant-"

"I'm pregnant dammit! I can feel it!"

Tony scoffs and rolls his eyes. "If you are and we're still both alive and not in a fucking wheelchair, we'll discuss it, okay? That's all I can give you at this point."

I frown like never before. "Fine!" I exclaim, plopping back down face first on his chest. "If that's all you can do right now, then fine, I'll take it, but we are going to talk about this later." I sigh, heavily and mumble, "Bet your ass was quick to say yes to Gia with your head all up her little bony white ass and-"

"ALEX...!"

I sigh again. "Fine ... I love you."

I squeeze Tony's shoulders and he rubs his hands through my hair and down to my back.

"I love you too," he says. "Now, get some rest. We have a long day ahead of us."

I snuggle into him, and we fall asleep together with me on top and Tony's penis still throbbing inside me. If I have my way, I'll never let him take it out again.

Chapter 6

Tony and I wake up in the same position we'd gone to sleep in only his cock finally slipped out of me at some point during the night. We're nearly glued together by our love juices. We are a sticky, sweaty mess. In hindsight, we probably should've put the fire out. It burned all through the night. Between the fire and the early morning sun, the cabin was hot like an oven.

"Morning," I greet, kissing him softly on his lips.

Tony opens his eyes quickly and then shuts them right back for a long moment. Then, he opens his eyes again, looks into mine, and kisses me the way I imagine he kissed Gia the morning after their wedding.

"How'd you find me?" I ask.

Tony curls his lips up. "See, I knew all you wanted was for me to tell-"

"No, I don't care about that anymore," I interrupt. "Whatever happens to my family ... you're my family now, you know, and we're here together. I promised I would do what you want me to do for a change, and I'm not going back on my word. Just tell me how you found me is all."

"Billings," Tony replies.

"Agent Billings?"

Tony nods.

"Secret Service Agent Billings?"

"Yes, Vice President Keller's detail," Tony confirms. "He had a hunch. Said he was around when Keller was giving everyone hell about building a replica White House. Told me he remembered the site they proposed to build it on. It was a long shot, but we'd exhausted every resource, and it's not like I'm some lowly field agent. Unless they had you in Gitmo, I should've been able to find you, and even if they did have you in Gitmo, I should've still been able to find you, but I couldn't. So, I followed up on his hunch. The first time, I drove up, parked, and hiked through the woods to the coordinates Billings gave me. When I saw it, I couldn't believe what I was seeing. It was really there, and if it was there, I knew you had to be there too. I went back, found this cabin, got ready, geared up and went in hard."

"It was DEA Director Pearson," I say.

"What?"

"Yeah, he's running the show," I explain. "You may know about the bomb, but you don't know what they are trying to do with it, do you?"

"I think they are going to set that bomb off in Georgia, and-"

"No." I shake my head. "Tony, that thing is set so that it looks like it came from Iraq. And I've already armed it. They are going to blow half the Summit up in Riyadh and kill as many people as they can. That's what those suits are for. They can withstand a nuclear blast, nuclear winter, they are damn near indestructible. My little voice says the President has one, and he's going to make sure Keller's in it when they set the bomb off. They need a patsy. He'll be the sole survivor and then it'll be just like Vanessa said, he will pin it all on me and Keller, and then the U.S. will take over the efforts to solve the financial crisis and dominate world security. Wood isn't going to the Summit. He's sending Keller. He's gonna pin all this on Keller."

"How do you know that?" Tony asks.

"Rodriquez, the woman I killed back there, she was in charge, and she told us Keller would meet us on the ground and we had to protect him at all costs. He's Wood's escape goat."

Tony rubs his chin. Then, he pushes me off. "Come on, get cleaned up," he says. "We don't have a lot of time here."

I sit up. "Okay, what's the plan, boss?"

Tony turns and looks at me. "Alex, we're not far from Keystone."

"South Dakota? Seriously?"

"I'm afraid so," he replies.

"Like fucking Mount Rushmore?" I ask.

Tony nods. "The very one. Listen, I can give you the coordinates and you can go back there, but even if your folks are still alive, it's you against all those men. You'll never make it in, and you'll never make it out of there alive even if you find your family. If you want, I-"

"Save it!" I exclaim. "We've got a bomb to stop."

Tony shakes his head. "Not we, you."

"Huh?" I rub my hands all over my face to try and fully wake myself up. "I'm confused."

"I need your help," Tony says. "I need to find Agent Billings. He and I fell out of communication, and I need him in order to do what I have to."

I raise an eyebrow. "Which is?"

"Arrest President Wood," Tony replies with a serious expression on his face.

I smile and shake my head. "No ... fucking ... way."

"I didn't know about Pearson, but I know about the others," Tony says. "I know about the Secretary of State, and-"

"Please tell me you kept it to yourself."

"I'm not an idiot, Alex! I am the Deputy Director of the FBI, remember?"

"Oh, thank God."

Tony sighs. "I told the Attorney General."

"GODDAMMIT, TONY!" I throw my hands up.

"It's not like that," he says, unconvincingly. "He's on our side. He's got our back."

I stand up off the bed and stretch. "So, how the hell are you out here all this time looking for me if you're still Bureau?"

"I'm on leave," Tony replies. "But, I'm still Bureau and so are you. The Director knows what we are up to and he's behind us all the way."

"Jesus, Tony, did you fucking tell everybody? Why don't you put it on YouTube or do a goddamn podcast?"

"Relax, Alex, I got this."

"This isn't going to work," I speculate. "You know Keller is back at that fake White House, right?"

"What?" Tony looks surprised.

"Yeah, Person is holding him along with my people and everybody from that fake ass trial they put me through."

Tony shakes his head in disbelief. "The fuck are you talking about?"

I pace around a little. "Oh no, you're the Deputy Director, you know everything ... asshole!"

"Just cut the shit and tell me what you know," Tony says in a frustrated tone.

I walk to the back door and open it. Tony follows and leans against the doorway. I lean my back against the door. The sunshine feels good on my naked body. I run my fingers though my hair and lay everything out for him.

"They detained me in Virginia," I explain, "after I shot the Vice President."

"That I know," says Tony. "Billings told me, but we saw Keller on television, and-"

"But did you ever see him in person?" I ask.

Tony thinks for a moment. Then, he shakes his head. "No, not once."

I nod. "Yeah, that's because they had him held up in the same bullshit place I was, exactly where you rescued me from. They brought me in and tricked me into thinking I'd killed Keller, you, those DEA agents, the asshole who tried to kill Vanessa back in California, I mean they had charges on my ass from decades ago and said I was still a Naval Officer so I was being charged in a military tribunal. They really had me too. I was starting to believe it towards the end like I'd really lost my marbles. I mean it was so real, but it wasn't. Pearson manipulated that situation too. That son of a bitch is everywhere. So not only did I get shipped off to a black site for them to beat the shit out of me for six months, after that, Pearson brings me to that fake ass White House and tells me it was all a ruse. Everybody except the people Tesh killed...." My eyes water up.

Tony touches my shoulder and pulls me in for a hug. "I saw the bodies back in Arizona, and I'm sorry for your loss, I really am."

"Thank you," I reply softly.

We stand there for a moment bathed in warm sun rays, totally naked and just embracing each other. Tony makes me feel like such a fucking lady. I really do love him. I hold back my tears and continue to share my story.

"Tony, they wanted me to think I'd done something terrible—the CIA—and wanted to force me into taking revenge on Keller, but Pearson said he told them it wouldn't work—he knew I wouldn't betray my country for revenge, so he kidnapped my family instead. I didn't want to think I could do it, but when I spent time with them, I ... I was going to do it. If you hadn't showed up, I swear I would've done it to save them."

Tony grabs my head with both hands. "No one is judging you."

I nod, slowly. "It's all a big game. I thought Keller was behind it and he was trying to make Wood look bad and pull a coup, but it wasn't that at all. They caused all this mayhem and all these attacks to create a ripple in the market and cause unrest around the world. They tweaked the market, they used fear as a weapon, and they are building up doubt in global security. With this financial crisis, they knew the world leaders would come together, and when they set that bomb off at the Summit, that will be all she wrote. The story will be complete. The world will be convinced that only President Wood and the grand United States of America can save everyone. They will privatize world security and dissolve any government or agency that challenges or opposes the supreme authority of The United States of Wood. But, think about it, man, what if this plan goes south? Hell, it already has. What if it gets out that Wood and Pearson were behind all this?"

"We'd be at war," Tony replies.

"It could seriously happen," I say.

Tony steps back a little with his hands on my shoulders. "Here's what we are going to do ... you're going to help me find Billings. When we find him, he's going to give me what I need to get to Wood, and then you and Billings are going to go to Riyadh and stop that bomb from going off."

I shake my head again. "Tony, I don't know how. You destroyed the only thing controlling it when you shot at Rodriguez."

"I don't know either," Tony says, "but I know you'll find a way—you always do. If anybody can do it, I know you can. You've got the suit, use it. Keep Billings safe, and you guys get that bomb the hell out of there. I'll arrest President Wood, and you and Billings meet me back here so we can get the Vice President out of that CIA White House and back to Washington. We cannot allow the Secretary of State to take the oval or he will pardon Wood and they will be back in business."

I scoff. "You make it all sound so easy."

Tony grabs my head again with both hands. "Look at me ... look at me, Alex."

I lift my eyes up to him.

"You and me together, we can do this, and yes...."

"Yes, what?" I ask.

Tony smiles. "Yes, I will marry you."

I light up and smile big. "Oh my God, Tony! Yes!" I kiss his lips. "Yes!" I kiss his cheek. "Yes!" I kiss his lips again.

Tony squeezes me tight and plants the biggest, most loving kiss ever right on my forehead. I melt in his arms.

"But there are going to be some changes," he warns.

I hug him tightly. "I don't care. I just want you."

"Okay, okay." Tony hugs me tightly. "Come on, Alex, let's get a quick bath and get moving."

I push him off me. "Fuck that! I'm not taking a bath for three days! I need to make sure your little soldiers fire up and make twins."

I'm not sure if Tony's eyes could roll back any further into his skull but they certainly came close.

"You are ... something ... something is really wrong with you," says Tony. He stomps away and goes straight for the tub. He climbs in and just sits in there for a moment, shivering.

I'm probably driving him crazy, but I don't give a tinker's damn. I want a baby—Tony's baby. Actually, I wanted Vanessa's baby, but that sounds too weird and fucked up to make any sense. This is the next best thing, and I need to believe I'm pregnant before I die, which very well could be today.

I start working my suit back into the right configuration so I can put it on again. Between that and watching Tony take his cold, angry bath, I'm in heaven. I'm sure he feels some kind of way about all this, and I don't blame him. Hell, I'd feel like a real asshole for fucking my friend's daughter, getting her pregnant, and everything else in between, but since I'm not that guy, I don't really give a fuck. If we live through this, Tony is putting a ring on it and walking my blackass down the aisle if it's the last fucking thing he does on this God forsaken earth.

It doesn't take long for Tony to get clean and suited back up. It takes me even less time as I just stick my sweaty, smelly cum-filled cunt right back in my suit and press the on button. It shrinks back down on me, bulks up the armor and I'm ready to rock again. As soon as my display comes on, I go right back into stealth mode to try and hide from anyone tracking me. I'm certain they are doing everything they can to track this suit down. I push my hair down in the back and walk over to Tony, who is lacing up his boots. He looks so cute with his little combat gear on.

"Eh, toothbrush?"

Tony smiles that amazing smile of his. "I only have one," he replies. "It's right over there." He points to the chair near the tub.

I put both hands on my hips. "So, I'm supposed to brush my teeth with your bathwater?"

"You can be a real jackass sometimes, Alex. Why the hell would you-"

I giggle.

"I'm beginning to hate you spent any time at all with David," Tony confesses, "It's like walking around with a less wrinkly version of him."

"Less wrinkly and way sexier!" I exclaim as I walk over to his toothbrush.

"Yeah, that too," Tony responds.

I brush my teeth and tongue and I do actually wash my face in Tony's bathwater, which if I wasn't standing in the shittiest cabin in Sherwood Forest would be the grossest thing in the world. In my mind it's like being splashed by some dirty old bum's ass-water in my face. I just try not to think about it.

I dry my face off with a blanket and start stretching and bouncing all around, getting my suit flexible again. My pistol and extra magazines are still stuck to my suit, but I need my rifle, so I walk over to it. Tony had it resting up against the wall near the front door along with the disarmed explosives from the men I killed. I pick my rifle up and check it. Then, I swing it up and over and attach it to the back of my suit at an angle for quick access.

Tony holsters his weapons and joins me at the front door. He picks up his rifle too. "So, any ideas on finding Billings?" he asks.

"As a matter of fact, I do have an idea," I reply. "So, this thing here, wait, where's my helmet?"

"Hang on, I'll get it." Tony walks over and grabs my helmet.

"Okay, so, I see that this suit is connected to multiple resources, geo stuff, criminal databases, everything, but there is this one satellite feed that seems to be able to track anyone from their biometrics, right?"

"Uh huh," Tony says.

"So, I'm thinking, we find him using this app thingy. We plug in his DNA or his fingerprint maybe ... hell his phone number, I don't know. Maybe it will track him down for us."

Tony scoffs. "That's pretty fucking thin."

"You got a better idea?"

Tony replies, "You nor I have his fingerprints or his DNA, so we gotta do this the old fashion way. Last time I saw him we were in Virginia, but then he said he was going to lay low somewhere for a while. Secret Service agents busted up our meeting and we got split up, but ... let me think for a second here...."

"We can't just go flying out here, looking under rocks, Tony, we need-"

"Chattanooga!" he exclaims. "I swear he told me Chattanooga, and I mean like the actual choo choo. The station."

I roll my eyes. "Now that sounds fucking thin—the Chattanooga Choo Choo? Are you serious?"

Tony points at me. "Hey, I found you, didn't I?"

"Yeah, but this is some kind of weak ass, hunchy bullshit, boss."

"Sometimes a hunch is enough," he responds. "Trust me, Alex, he's there."

I look up at the ceiling and sigh. "It's like 18 hours away, right? How do you even know he's still there if he was ever even there?"

Tony thought for a moment. "Either way, we've got to intercept that bomb. Tennessee is on the way. You think that fancy suit can access the DOD network?"

I nod. "I think I see where you're going with this. Find the plan or manifest for outbound transports to Riyadh and that'll tell us when the bomb is going and where."

"Exactly!" says Tony. "We get to Tennessee and can't find Billings, then it's you and me all the way. We stop the bomb, we come back for Wood and Pearson."

"One problem."

"What?" asks Tony.

"You know they are looking for this suit," I speculate. "I start poking around the DOD network, they're going to find me fast. I don't think I can do it and stay in stealth mode. Options to find me are limited in stealth 'cause it removes public access, but when I go out of stealth, all bets are off."

"Let's do it outside," Tony says. "We get our gear in the truck, you do your thing, go back into stealth, and then we get the fuck outta Dodge."

"They're going to find us," I warn. "They will use satellite imagery to track any vehicles coming from this cabin and guess what, there's only one."

"At least we'll have a head start," Tony says, optimistically. "It'll be enough."

I kiss him on the lips again, and softly say, "You know when I said I'd do anything you told me, I didn't realize it would be some stupid shit like this that would get me killed less than 24-hours of you rescuing me—if that's what you wanna call that particular cluster fuck."

"First, you're welcome," he retorts, "and second, this isn't stupid ... it's all we got."

I nod and take my helmet from Tony. I push the front door open, take a few steps out into the open and look up. I put my helmet on and boot up the display. I see Tony run past me and he starts loading up the truck. He closes the tailgate and runs around to the driver side. As soon as he gets in and cranks up, I turn off stealth mode and work my way through the menus. I see the DOD network and dive in. A few searches later and I see a flight plan for a C135 to Riyadh. I drill down and check the manifest. I see troops and equipment, but one particular item is unmarked. There's no description, but the dimensions and weight are right on. It's got to be the bomb.

"Tony, I found it!"

He stuck his hand out the window and gave me a thumbs up.

More than a dozen icons pop up on my screen. "Oh shit!"

Tony sticks his head out the window. The reverse lights on the truck come on and he speeds back up to me. I go back into stealth mode and take a mental note of all the operators I see. I recognized some of them from back at Pearson's. The first chopper must've dropped the bomb off and doubled back. There's a small army of men in pursuit of us. I run around and hop into the passenger seat.

"WE GOTTA GO NOW!" I yell.

Tony slams his foot down on the accelerator and we dart off to the bottom of the hill and out onto the main road.

"What happened?" he asks.

"THEY'RE CLOSE!" I yell.

"Who?"

"GUYS FROM THE FIRST CHOPPER, TONY, WE GOTTA GO MAN!"

Tony jams the pedal to the floor, and we blast down the road. As soon as we pull out into the clearing, I see a Blackhawk fly overhead in the direction of the cabin.

"Whoa, you see that?" I ask.

"What?" Tony looks up out of the top of the windshield. "I don't see anything."

"They just flew over," I say.

"Okay, what guys from what chopper?" he asks.

"The ones you neglected to shoot down in order to shoot me down out of the sky." I take my helmet off and put it down on the floorboard. "They must've dropped that bomb off in Georgia and hauled ass back up here."

"Well I only had one RPG—I just hit what I could." Tony bangs his fist on the steering wheel. "Our window just got smaller. We gotta ditch this car."

Chapter 7

Tony and I cover a lot of road in a short period of time. We take turns driving since we're both still tired from the previous day's events. When I'm not driving, I try my best to sleep or at least close my eyes and rest. I'm starting to regret my decision to not wash because even with the A/C on, I'm still sweating between my thighs and down the back of my suit. I dare not put my helmet on because that probably would be a dead giveaway. Uh, hello, 9-1-1, there's a lady driving an SUV wearing a motorcycle helmet. I can just imagine how that would go, so I tough it out and point my half of the vents directly at my face.

We head east and take I-29 South. Tony drives for hours, keeping one eye on the road and the other in the rearview mirror. I can't help but turn around periodically just to see who's sticking behind us, but we're not being followed—at least not yet.

We cross the Nebraska border around three in the afternoon. Another hour on the road and Tony seems to be growing more jittery by the moment.

"Reach back there in that bag—the blue one," Tony orders. "Grab one of those burner phones."

I turn around and grab the blue bag on the middle of the back seat. I unzip it and pull out a small black smart phone. "Got it."

"Find a used dealership," he says.

"We stealing a ride?" I ask.

"Alex!" Tony swerves into the right lane and speeds up.

"Joking—hang on." I power on the phone and wait for it to boot up. I open the web browser and do a search for *used cars near me*. "Hey, there's a Ford dealership, and a-"

"Buy here, pay here!" he exclaims.

"Okay, I got a Payless Auto Sales on 90th Street, but you gotta get off on this exit."

"Where, here?" he asks.

"Yeah, Tony right here go take 680 right now, exit 61!"

"Shit!" He swerves to take the exit and heads straight for the fast lane.

We continue west on 680 for about 15 minutes and then take exit four to get to Maple Street. We follow Maple Street and turn onto 90th. I spot a yellow building that looks like it used to be a gas station. It has a big red "buy here pay here" sign on the front.

"Right there!" I exclaim, pointing at the sign.

Tony wheels us onto the lot and parks right up front. We both get out and I follow Tony over to a black Ford Taurus. He walks around it a few times, squats down and looks at the tires, and then he runs his hand across the hood.

"One of the best cars Ford ever made," comes a voice from behind.

Tony and I turn around.

"Brent, Brent Thomas," says a man, offering Tony a handshake.

"Joseph Banks," Tony replies.

I turn and cover my mouth to prevent myself from laughing out loud.

"This a 98?" asks Tony.

"Ninety-nine," Brent replies, "top of the line. Used to be a government car. Took real good care of it. Only got 75,000 miles on her."

Tony looks over the car again. "How much?"

"$4000." Brent smiles.

Tony shakes his head. "You're kidding, right?"

"You paying cash?" asks Brent.

Tony nods.

Brent taps Tony on the shoulder. "I could knock it down a little for you."

Tony gives me the nod and puts his arm around Brent. "Let me run something past you...."

"I'm listening brother Joseph," says Brent.

I run back to the truck and start unloading it. I'm not sure what Tony is up to, but I know what that nod means—get the fucking car. I drag everything over to the Taurus while Tony and Brent head into the office. They return and Brent has a big smile on his face—even bigger than before. Tony unlocks the Taurus and I proceed to load it up. Whatever Tony said or did to the man, he was in a very good mood, because he didn't even seem to notice all the guns I was sticking into that car.

"Pleasure doing business with you, Joe!" Brent exclaims. He turns around and heads back inside.

"The fuck did you do, blow him?" I whisper.

Tony rolls his eyes. He leans in and whispers, "Get in the truck and take off down the road. Ditch it and start walking back this way. I'll head in the opposite direction and double back to pick you up."

I take the keys to the truck and run back to it. I climb into the driver seat, start the motor, and speed off down the street. I drive a few clicks down the road. I pull into a shopping center, park the truck, roll the windows down and leave the key in it. I casually walk off and start making my way back to the dealership. After a few minutes of walking, Tony pulls up and stops right by me. He pushes the passenger door open and I climb in and shut the door.

"You okay?" he asks.

I nod. "Yeah, let's go."

We make our way back to the freeway and take 680 back to 29 South. Hopefully, we threw the bad guys off our scent switching vehicles, but there's no guarantee.

"So, how'd you get the car?" I ask again as we speed down 29.

Tony looks over at me for a second. "Well I didn't blow the man if that's what you're asking."

I bust out laughing.

"Ass!" Tony exclaims. "I gave him ten grand for the keys, pink slip, and no paperwork or questions asked."

"Fuck me man, I would've blown him, and you could've gave me that money!"

"Alex, you're not that good," he replies.

I shift myself around in my seat and smack his arm.

Tony pulls away. "Ouch, that armor hurts! I'm driving here."

"You don't think I could get a car off some ole greasy ass used car salesman that spends his whole day sniffing beaners' ass and taking their paychecks so he can repossess and repeat?"

Tony's right eyebrow shot up. "Beaners?"

"Uh, yeah, Mexicans, they-"

"Alex, what the hell, just stop it with the racist-"

"I'M NOT FUCKIN' RACIST!" I exclaim. "They eat beans and rice and shit every day. Don't get mad at me, I'm just the messenger."

Tony rubs his forehead violently. "Jesus, just give me a break, will you?"

"Fine ... you want me to be quiet, I'll be quiet. You wanna run around giving Mexican's tens of thousands of dollars for raggedy ass cars then-"

"The man wasn't even Mexi-" Tony grips the steering wheel really tightly. "Just—you know what, Alex, shut up, I'm trying to think and fucking drive this raggedy ass shit!"

I turn back towards the window and try my best to muffle my snickering with the palms of my hands.

"AND PUT YOUR SEATBELT ON!" he yells.

I quietly sit back in my seat and snap my seatbelt in place. I lean back against the headrest. "Want me to drive for a bit?"

"No," Tony replies sharply.

I wait about another minute. "You mad at me?"

"NO!" Tony exclaims.

I wait another minute. "Love you."

"Alex, you're freaking me out with all this love foolishness. You don't love people! You fuck them and use them! You're a damn sociopath!"

"Wow, you really know how to sweet talk a girl," I say, sarcastically.

"This is ridiculous," Tony says. "I'm in love with the female Ted Bundy. I bet if you weren't law, you'd probably be boiling people in acid right now. And, don't think for a second I forgot about how you executed those two men back there. Jesus Christ what am I doing, I'm a lunatic! I can't believe it. I follow the evillest nice man on planet earth around like a puppy, and then fall in love with his evil daughter."

I start crying a little. "You really love me...?"

"Yeah," he says softly. "I'm not just saying it. Look, I know you're into women now, and-"

"What...? Tony, I-"

"Just let me finish!" he exclaims. "All of this is crazy, okay?"

"Okay, but-"

"Alex! It's crazy, but yes, I do, I really do ... I'm in love with you, and I don't want you just toying with my emotions. I've seen you manipulate people and I can't do it, okay? Not with all that's going on. If you want to be with me for real, just tell me but don't mess me around."

"Tony, look at me."

"No."

"Look at me!"

"I'm fucking driving, Alex!"

"I don't care, now fucking look at me!"

He takes his eyes off the road and looks into my eyes.

"I love you." I reach over and put my hand palm up on the center console. "I love you, and I want to be your wife. Maybe I don't know what love is like you do, but you can teach me. You can show me. I'm not a lesbian. I don't know where you keep getting that from."

Tony takes his right hand off the wheel and squeezes mine. "I saw her," he says. "I can't compete with any one like that, and if that's who you want, I can't-"

"It happened," I reply. "I don't know why, and it took me a long time to be okay with it, but it happened, and I ... I just know I love her. She showed me I could be who I am. And, okay I'm a sociopath, and maybe I don't just naturally do all that lovey, dovey shit, I'm like my dad, but I can work on it and I can do it. I loved her until she died, and I will love you until my last breath. Please, I swear, you don't have to protect yourself from me. I won't hurt you. And, you don't have to be jealous either ... Vanessa's gone, and she ain't never coming back." I stare at him for a few moments. "I've never seen you like this, you know this side of you before."

"What do you mean?" he asks.

"You're like ... vulnerable...."

Tony sighs, heavily. "Alex, this isn't work, this is ... it's us, I mean it's odd to even say it, but this is you and me starting a relationship, and I'm already outgunned by the competition. I'm old and-"

"You're not old, Tony."

He breathes out really hard. "Like I say, I'm old and I don't even know if I want kids or anything, it's just ... and, what if someone else like Vanessa Sullivan comes along?" he asks. "I'm not exactly an exciting person, you know?"

I lick my lips and lower my head a little, giving him the "fuck me" eyes. "You look pretty exciting to me." I unbuckle my seat belt.

"What are you doing?" asks Tony.

I climb up onto my seat with my knees and move the center console up and out of my way. I crawl over to Tony and start kissing him and rubbing between his thighs.

Tony swerves a little out of our lane, but quickly corrects the car. "I...." He kisses me and closes his eyes. "Alex, I-" He opens his eyes again and yells, "Oh shit!"

Tony flings the steering wheel and jumps one lane over to prevent from running smack dab into the back of a tractor trailer. I plop back down on my seat and we share a brief "Oh shit" gaze. Then, we both start laughing.

Tony says, "You know, the first part about loving someone genuinely is making sure they don't die in a burning car crash."

"Well what's the fun in that?" I reply, giggling seductively. I reach over and turn the radio on. I settle back down into my seat, put my seatbelt back on, and start scanning through stations. I find a big hair station, which is totally rocking Van Halen, so I crank it up and just get lost in all the noise. The music seems to calm us both down, which is a good thing.

As we continue making our way south, I keep thinking about what Tony said about me and Dad. Tony's right, Dad was the meanest, angriest little nice man you'd ever meet. He would do anything for anyone, but he knew how to maniacally fuck someone up if they crossed him or if he was just feeling like fucking somebody up that day. I think he and I share the same fatal flaw—the few times when we're nice, we're nice to the wrong people, and it costs us everything. I desperately want to change how I am. I'd rather be nice instead of paranoid and distrusting, but I don't know how. I don't know how to be nice, but I can be sweet—of that I have no doubt.

I seriously hope I can learn to be nice to Tony. I've been the bane of his existence for years. Maybe that's what love is all about—being nice to someone you don't have to be nice to—like I was with Vanessa. Well, maybe not exactly like with Vanessa because I was a real abusive shit to her, but she liked it and encouraged it, so I don't think that counts. I mean, she was really the scum of the earth, but I guess so am I in a lot of ways, so there's that. But she was really unapologetically good to me. She didn't judge me. We were good, and I miss that—I need that. Tony's right, I don't really "love him" love him, and I'm not sure I ever will, but from where I'm sitting right now—for a man who just saved me from my doom, kissed me passionately, and made love to me so tenderly—I can learn to be nice to him all day long and twice at night. *Practice makes perfect.*

Day turns into night faster than anticipated. Tony and I are still on the road. I keep asking him if he wants me to take over, but he politely keeps refusing my offer. Maybe he's really wired and has a bunch of energy to burn off. *Mama's sweet black pussy will do that to the average man.* I rest as much as my warped brain will let me, and when I'm not resting, I'm looking at Tony's handsome face and praying to God we make it out of this mess alive. I keep trying to convince myself I've fallen in love with this man, and whether that's actually true or not, who cares? I just want the opportunity to play it all out in real life—not just in the depths of my mind. I'm desperate to see if it actually sticks. Maybe, just maybe, Tony is the answer to my Blondie problem—hell to all my problems. Maybe I can find real love with him. And, maybe I can finally kiss that filthy, blonde slut in my head goodbye forever.

It all sounds good, but the reality is I'm stuck with Blondie, and she's stuck with me. Unless Tony's one to go back on his word, he's about to be stuck with her too. Sure, it seems silly for me to be sitting here riding in his freshly procured hooptie thinking I am with child, but with every tingling sensation in my body, I just know I'm pregnant. I want it too. I want it all with him. I'm going to force myself to be good for my man and for my baby. We Southerland women are fertile as hell. I'd have 17 babies by now if I weren't so crafty. Obviously, every time Bill stuck his baby dick in that fat whore—wait, what I meant to say is Bill and my sister didn't have any trouble getting pregnant. Theresa lost a baby and went on to have that little angel Angie.

Tony and I stop to use the restroom and grab a bite to eat. There's no one in sight, but we know Pearson's men are still after us, and surely by now they must be getting close. We have to pick up the pace. I'm guessing next time we stop they'll converge on us. We eat fast and hustle back to the car. Tony's been driving for hours, and though I appreciate his chivalry, I know he's got to be dead tired. He argues for all but 30 seconds before retreating around to the passenger side of the Taurus.

I hop in the car and buckle up. I start the engine, shift into drive and we continue making our way south on I-24. We're in Grand Rivers, Kentucky about three and a half hours away from Chattanooga. I see state patrol vehicles lined all up and down the freeway, so I take my time and keep my speed well under the posted limit. A few miles down the road and Tony is out like a light bulb. He's sleeping like a baby but snoring like my grandpa. Grandpa Southerland used to bring the house down at night. I think the neighbors called the police a few times for the noise violation.

I'm relieved Tony is actually finally resting. Between storming a castle like the Mission Impossible Force and putting up with me—which may be considered an even more impossible mission—I'm surprised he stayed awake this long. After about an hour and a half, I see the signs for Chattanooga/Knoxville. It's nearly one in the morning, and my eyes are starting to feel heavy. I look over at Tony and he is still out cold. I switch on the cruise control and stretch my legs a little bit as best I can in my seat. I put the A/C up on max because my ass feels like it's suspended in a sack of fluid. I wish I could at least kick my shoes off, but I'm not wearing any. This fallout suit conforms to your body in every way, hardening in certain places like your torso for armor or the bottom of your feet for shoes. It stays locked tight in place no matter which way you turn, but I guess that's a good thing. If it didn't fit so tight on me, I might be sliding around in it at this point.

I try to live my life without regret, but every time I lift my chin up, I can smell my own funky ass. *What on earth was I thinking not taking a bath back at the cabin? What a day.*

A few more hours on the road, and we're dipping down into Georgia to get back into Tennessee. It won't be long now, and we'll be ready to chase Tony's hunch in a place that's hours away from the place we actually need to be, Marietta, Georgia. At the same time, storming an Air Force base and seizing a nuclear weapon seems like a bigger stretch than finding one man on the Chattanooga Choo Choo.

I take exit 178 and continue following the GPS. I remember seeing a Motel 6 on the map, so I head in that direction instead of going straight to Billing's alleged location. After all, this is Tony's hunch, and he is still asleep. I need to wash, and we need to get organized before storming the historic train station. The way we both look, someone's bound to call the police on us the moment we step onto the property. Maybe Tony has a plan, but I sure don't, and since he is snoring loud enough to wake the dead, stopping at a nearby motel makes sense to me.

I finally get us over to Williams Street downtown and pull up to the front of the Motel 6. I park the car and dig around in the bags on the back seat. I find a poncho and a stash of cash. I pull the poncho over my head to cover my suit and take a few hundred dollars from the bag. I get out and head inside to the front desk. I reserve a room under a phony name and return to the car. I hop back in the car and pull around to the side of the motel. Then, I park and turn off the motor. I look at Tony for a few minutes. He's still sleeping peacefully.

"Tony," I say softly. I touch his shoulder and shake him gently. "Tony, wake up ... Tony...."

"Yeah...?" Tony sits up and rubs his eyes. "How long was I out?"

"We're here," I respond.

"Chattanooga?" he asks.

I nod. "I checked us into to Motel 6, so we can put a plan together on locating Billings."

"Okay, good deal," Tony says. He leans his head back and yawns. Then, he opens his door and hops out. He walks around the car to my door and opens it.

I stand up out the car and move in close to him. He kisses me softly. I kiss him back.

"Ewe," I say. "Your breath is horrible."

Tony smiles. "Well, you're not a beacon of air freshener either."

We both laugh.

"Yeah, that whole I don't wanna wash your sperm out of me for three days was just a bad fucking idea. I'm going in to get cleaned up. Sorry, but you're on your own with the gear."

"Come on," he says, touching my arm. "We don't need it. Let's get in and get settled. Here, I'll grab your helmet so you can get out of that thing."

Tony takes my helmet out of the car and closes the door. I hand him the keys and he locks the car up. Under normal circumstances, I'd be concerned about leaving a bunch of weapons unsecured in a civilian vehicle, but there are a few other cars in the parking lot, so the odds of someone even noticing are probably slim to none. At least the hooptie has an alarm system, which is better than nothing at all— provided it still functions.

We walk together to the front of the motel and go inside. The front desk attendant pays about as much attention to us as he did to me when I paid for the room, which wasn't much at all. We take the elevator up to the second floor and I use a keycard to access rom 224. Tony holds the door open for me like a true gentleman. I walk in and he shuts the door, locks the dead bolt, and slides the latch in place. I pull off the poncho and toss it in a chair. Then, I turn on a few lamps and sit down on the bed closest to the window. The air conditioner is already blowing, so that's a good thing.

Tony hands me my helmet, and I hold it in both hands and just look in it for a while. Tony goes into the bathroom and closes the door. This place is so cheap. The walls are thin as paper, and I can hear every drop of his pee going into the toilet. I can also hear him flush and wash his hands, which quite frankly is a good thing. I've never been around Tony in a domestic setting. It's good to know the man I mean to marry actually washes his hands' unless he's just in there washing his cock because he wants to fuck me again. Actually, that's fine too because in order to get soap on his cock he also has to get soap on the palms of his hands—it's a win for everybody.

Tony walks out of the bathroom, wearing only his boxers. I hear running water.

"Anybody ever draw you a bath before?" he asks.

I smile and nod. "Yeah, once upon a time."

"Well, I doubt they did it as well as me," Tony brags. "You need some help getting out of that thing?"

"No," I reply softly.

Tony turns to go back into the bathroom.

"Tony...?"

"Yeah?" He stops in his tracks.

"Will you...? Nevermind."

Tony turns back to me. "Spit it out, kid."

I smile and run my fingers through my hair, pulling all that sweaty mess up out the back of my suit. "I'm embarrassed to ask, but...."

"What is it?"

"Will you take a bath with me?" I ask.

Tony smiles back at me. "So, we're bathing together now?"

I throw a pillow at him. "You know what, fuck it asshole, I was just trying-"

"Yes!" he exclaims. "Yes, I will take a bath with you. I'd love to, but it might be a tight squeeze in there."

I giggle. "I like to live dangerously."

Tony laughs and returns to the bathroom.

I put my helmet on and boot up my display. I eject myself out of my suit and turn it as far inside out again as I can. I lay it over the chair in the corner near the air conditioner.

Unfortunately, Tony steps back into the room and catches me red-handed, sniffing both armpits and rubbing between my legs and smelling myself. I'm not sure what's worse—how bad I smell or how embarrassed I should be for putting on that horrible display for a man I want to spend the rest of my life with. I guess he should see the good, the bad, and the ugly as soon as possible though, so ... bygones.

Despite my antics, Tony doesn't seem one bit turned off because, even with all my rankness, he walks right up to me, grabs two big handfuls of my ass, and pulls me in for a big wet kiss. "Come on," he says, kissing me again, "let's get cleaned up."

He doesn't have to ask me twice. I take his hand, and he leads me to the steamy bathroom, where he'd drawn a very nice hot bath—bubbles and all. I was most impressed. Forget about the fact we were in a crappy motel—based on the events of the previous day, things were really starting to look up.

Chapter 8

After cleaning each other from head to toe in the most sensual manner I have ever experienced, Tony and I just soak in our hot bath for about an hour. My very first bath with a man in my entire life and it is turning out to be a picture-perfect experience. When Tony's not kissing my neck, he massages my shoulders and rubs my breasts. He periodically makes his way down to my tummy too, and I am loving every minute of being right there between his legs with his cock pressed against my back and his big strong hands making me melt into him.

We finish relaxing in the tub, get out and dry off. I blow dry my hair and lotion up. Tony steps out while I finish moisturizing my body. After a few minutes, he returns with some travel sized toiletries—toothbrushes, toothpaste, roll on deodorant, and baby powder. I feel like a little girl on Christmas morning. There's no way a man is this thoughtful—no way in hell. Bill could take a lesson. In fact, every man I ever been with needs to go to Tony Crane's school of how to treat a bitch right. Then again, maybe he's just trying to impress his new ... fiancée? *Wow. Like, wow. I have nothing more to say. I'm somebody's fiancée now. Brothas and Sistahs, I don't know what this world is coming to!*

I brush my teeth, stuff powder up in all the right places and roll on some deodorant—yes deodorant! It's the little things that make all the difference in the world.

I exit the bathroom and join Tony back in the room. He looks like he is trying to get into the bed near the bathroom, but I've already claimed the one near the window, and at this point, with his sperm swimming all around up in my womb, he most definitely needs to be sleeping with me.

"Oh no, Mr. Crane," I say, waving a finger at him, "I am not sleeping alone tonight. Get your ass in my bed, so I can get on top of you."

Tony laughs out loud but doesn't hesitate to pull back my covers and follow orders. He crawls in and positions a few pillows behind his head. I get right in on top of him and pull the covers up over my back. I lower myself down on Tony and push my ass back up to his cock, kissing him everywhere I can. He grips my ass and pulls me down onto him. My pussy lips instantly tighten around the shaft of his cock, and I am right back in heaven, breathing heavily and taking Tony's hard, long cock for the second time in 24 hours. If he didn't get me pregnant the last time, he will tonight—I'll make damn sure of it.

Tony grips my waist and bounces me to and fro, pushing deeper inside me with every downward motion. I want this to last forever. I feel the pressure building up between my thighs. I'm so hot for him I'm about to explode and squirt all over his cock when there comes a knock at our door. We freeze in our tracks, looking over at the door. Whoever it is, they knock again and again. The knocks are coming faster and louder by the moment. Tony sits up with me still straddling him.

I shake my head. "No, just ... it's probably the wrong room."

They knock again.

"Give me a second," says Tony.

I move off and he gets out of bed. He wraps a towel around his waist and slowly moves to the door, which is still being knocked on. I sit down and pull the cover up to my neck.

Tony nearly makes it to the door when it gets kicked wide open. Little shards of wood fly into the air. Tony drops to one knee and covers his head. He says something that sounds like *feelings*, but I can't quite make it out because I'm focused on the shadowy figure with the gun that just came, lunging into our room.

I spring into action, running full speed right past Tony, who tries to grab me, but I jump right past him onto the man with the gun, slamming my fists into the top of his head and screaming, "MOTHERFUCKER!"

"STOP!" exclaims the man, "STOP IT! IT'S ME!"

I hit him again, and he drops a moderately-sized black bag.

"IT'S ME, GODDAMNIT!" he yells.

I hit him again, this time with both fists, and he stumbles over to the left. He leans against the door and drops his gun down by his side.

"IT'S BILLINGS!" Tony blurts out, far more clearly than before.

I focus my eyes on the battered man. "Holy shit Stevo, what the hell are you doing here? You're supposed to be at the choo choo train!"

I lunge at Agent Billings again. He tenses up at first, but realizes what I'm doing this time, and gives into my signature bear hug.

"I'm so sorry, are you alright?" I ask.

"Uh, yes ma'am, I'm fine," he replies, checking the top of his head for blood. "Ma'am-"

"Alex!" I remind.

"Alex ... you're naked."

I squeeze him even harder. "Yes ... yes I am. I am naked. I am so very naked."

"We should probably move inside, don't you think?" he asks.

I shove Billings back against the door and stick my head out into the hallway. I look both ways. Then, I quickly duck back in and pull him away from the door, allowing it to slowly shut for the most part. Billings really tore the latch off the door, but I am still able to lock it, so I do.

Steve walks up to Tony and they shake hands. I step into the bathroom and wrap a towel around myself. Then, I join them in the room, where I hop up on the bed nearest the bathroom and start jumping up and down, clapping my hands and singing *Celebration* by Kool and the Gang. I can hear them talking about me, but I don't care, I just keep on having my moment.

"Is she okay?" asks Agent Billings.

Tony shakes his head. "She wasn't this happy to see me," he replies, standing very manly in his little towel.

Billings looks at Tony and asks, "Am I interrupting something here?"

Tony shakes his head again and grabs his clothes. "I'm going to get dressed," he grumbles. He slowly walks into the bathroom with his clothes as if a cloud of embarrassment has just moved in on his head and is now suffocating him.

I finally climb down off my high—and the bed—and step right up to my Secret Service man, smiling. "Are you okay? How'd you find us? Do you need some ice for your head? Are you married...?"

"No ma-" He shakes his head. "No, Alex, I'm not married and I'm-"

I plant a long, soft, unexpected kiss right on his lips. He just stands there until I'm finished.

"Alex, this is highly inappropriate. I saw you-"

"Hey, hey man, fuck appropriate!" I exclaim. "I'm free. And Tony's alive, and you're here and really alive, like I thought Tony was just off his rocker with all this shit like ... holy fucking shit I'm like wooowooo goddammit!" I nod my head rapidly, and then take a few fast, sharp deep breaths. "You wouldn't believe it Stevie, I swear man, like the last time I saw you, we were-"

"You shot my boss!" he interrupts.

I hold one finger up. "Yeah, about that ... he actually thanked me for it, and-"

"I know he's still alive, and he was with you at that other White House."

"How did you...?"

Tony comes out of the bathroom fully dressed, which I guess makes the situation a little more normal. He walks over to us, and I step back a bit because he looks confused as to why I'm pushing up on Steven, but I only halfway care because I'm just so happy to see him. I'm not even sure why, but I am. I feel like justice has been served by the Universe keeping the three of us alive. Maybe Blondie wielded her anti-matter and made it so, you know like she actually did some good with her infinite powers for once. I'm not sure why I thought Tony was just full of shit and we were coming to Chattanooga to chase our own tail, but here we are, and here Steve is in the flesh.

I stand there shaking my head and looking at Tony. "I swear I thought you were full of shit, but look Stevie is alive and well, and he's here!"

"How 'bout a little respect, Alex!" Tony exclaims. "I apologize Agent Billings, I don't-"

"Sir," he interrupts, "If Alex calls me anything other than some odd variation of my first name, I know something's wrong."

I giggle and give Tony my best neck roll. "Stevesie is my man! Woot woot!" Tony makes me sick. A few minutes ago, he was all, "You my bae, and this pussy taste so sweet," but now he's all, "I'm the Deputy Director and show some respect. *Fuck that shit!*

Tony says, "We were talking about the Chattanooga hotel before we got split up. I thought you would be there."

"Sir, I didn't know what you were doing, I just followed you here," says Billings.

Tony looks just as surprised as I am. He squints at Agent Billings. "What? I don't understand."

I sit down Indian style on the bed near the window, and Steve continues explaining himself.

"After we got split up, I started researching the Agency's financials," says Billings. "I found a line budget item for more than eight million dollars that just didn't look right. The only thing I could find on it was coordinates, but then I tracked some email communications to CIA Director Pearson, repurposing the facility, which turns out to be an exact replica of the White House. He changed its designation from a training facility to what seemed to me to be a black site. That's when I sent you the coordinates and I went off the grid. I knew if they had Alex there and Vice President Keller was alive, he'd be there too. I accessed the facility and verified Keller was there. I waited until they fueled those choppers up and moved the bomb and I was going to go in and get Keller out, but when you attacked the helicopters, they hardened security and I missed my window. I tracked you back to the cabin, and then I followed you here."

Tony stands in disbelief. "How the-"

"Respectfully Deputy Director, I'm Secret Service, not FBI. We know how to stay on target.

I can see right away my smiling and clapping is irritating the shit out of Tony as he is in complete "I'm the boss mode" so I try and calm down. Tony is acting like the man, but Steve is a total badass, and he knows how to cook chicken like black folks, so if I have to vote, I say Steve takes charge.

Tony scratches his head. "Okay, listen ... we have a dilemma here, and we're going to have to split up. Alex, fill Agent Billings in on what you know."

I'm still smiling. "Steve, I'm going to give you the Cliff Notes version ... they made me think I killed Vice President Keller, and they did this real but not so real military tribunal. It was all bullshit, but it was convincing enough that they made me believe I had committed treason. They tortured me for months trying to get me to take it to the next step and play ball with the bad guys, but I never broke, at least I don't think I did because I woke up in a bedroom in that White House in South Dakota. Pearson met me there and laid it all out."

"What were they trying to get you to do, and what does it have to do with the VP?" Steve asks.

"See that's the crazy thing," I reply, "All of this was cooked up by President Wood and Director Pearson to destabilize the global market and create a security panic. They have been sticking all the attacks on DEA raids and drug activity on Alluvion. Thing is though, Alluvion is not a terrorist group, it's a U.S. government led black bag operation to prevent what Wood believes will be inevitable. Saudi Arabia's market has been completely unaffected by the economic crisis, and they volunteered to bail everyone out, believe it or not, provided they had oversight on expenditure and payback. So, the world leaders planned this big Summit that's coming up in just a few days, but Wood wants to show the world how weak Saudi is on all fronts, so he's going to bomb Riyadh with that nuclear device and prove to everyone the U.S. is the only place we can trust to lead us out of the economic and terror crisis. Since they couldn't break me by making me think I'd killed the VP, they took my family ... if they are not dead, they are still back at the compound. Dr. Taylor, the man who created the prototype device they are using and, who obviously had something to do with these fallout suits," I point over to the chair in the corner where my suit is, "got word from Keller of what Wood and Pearson was up to, and he did what Keller asked him to do ... he reprogrammed the bomb so only I could arm it. I guess they figured I would never do that."

Agent Billings rubs his chin. "Tell me about the device."

"It's a smart bomb," I reply. "It uses the same type of nano bots the suits do. It's far beyond my technical understanding but they say they can configure it to manipulate forensics, so whatever material has to be released to make it look like Iran or Russia or whoever made it, it does it and burns up the rest. The trigger, wiring signature, hell I don't know how he accomplished it, I'm not bomb tech, but it's a sleeper bomb. They can set that thing off and blame anybody for it. The good news is I can track it with my suit when I go fully online."

Billings asks, "And the bad news?"

"Well, a couple of things, Stevsey, first—and don't judge me—but I armed it already."

"What?"

Tony speaks up. "She didn't have any choice, and unfortunately, I damaged the device used to interface with the bomb during the attack, so we can't turn the damn thing off."

"So, this bomb is going off no matter what?" asks Billings. Tony nods.

I put my hand up. "I know that sounds like the bad news, but when I come out of stealth mode and track the bomb, anybody with the same tech can locate us easy as using Google Maps, so they will pounce on us before we can ever get to this thing. Plus, we only have one suit against God knows how many others."

"Are there any other bombs?" asks Billings.

I shake my head. "Pearson claims this is the only one, and they don't know how Taylor put it together. I imagine they've been trying, but so far, no cigar. It sounds bad to say, but thankfully, Taylor is dead, so they only got one shot to pull this off."

Billings rubs the top of his head again. "Well, I've got some bad news of my own."

"What?" I ask.

He sighs. "I'm afraid we aren't the only ones here in Chattanooga. Pearson's men are here looking for you both. I took a radio from one of the men you left back at the cabin. They have ID'd you Mr. Crane and have orders to shoot you both on sight. I got word to your ex-wife to lay low until she hears from you or me. She and her family are safe. They contacted me a few hours ago. Right now, we need to gear up and get back up to South Dakota. I can't get in there on my own, but we have to get the Vice President out of there. He can stop this from-"

"No!" Tony interrupts.

"Sir, respectfully, I-"

"It doesn't matter what you do," says Tony, "you get him out of there and they will kill him and claim you did it. We've seen how these people operate."

Steve becomes frustrated. "Then, what do you suggest?"

"I confided in Director Carter," Tony says, "and Attorney General McNamara. They both have our backs. The AG is drawing up documents to impeach Wood based on our collective testimony. That puts some serious targets on our backs, so we have to hit them all at once. I need you to give me the intel I need to get into the real White House and arrest the President and Secretary of State. They are both tied up into this thing. I have a Navy Seal Commander willing to take two teams and storm the replica White House as soon as I notify them that I have Wood in custody. They'll go in, neutralize the threat, detain Pearson, and get the hostages out. Wood is forcing Keller to go to the Summit. Chances are the VP has already left South Dakota, hell we don't know he may already be out of the country, but we need to get him back here safely so he can invoke the 25th and take the oval back. We know Keller will be in Riyadh. I need you to back up Agent Southerland over there. Find the bomb, find a way to shut it down, and get Vice President Keller the hell out of there."

"My mission is the VP," Billings says. "I don't like this. We need more men. I can't secure the VP and help Alex deal with the bomb. I need to secure the VP immediately, and-"

"There's no other way, Agent Billings!" Tony exclaims. "I doubt we find help we can trust at this point. Alex can't get Keller out of Riyadh alone. Alex needs somebody watching her back, now that's either you or me. It will take at least a two-man team to get Keller out, unless you can you guarantee Keller's safety by yourself? Can you?"

Billings shakes his head. "No, sir. I cannot." He steps up close to Tony and gets right in his face. "Are you sure you can trust your boss and the AG?"

"I bet my life on it," Tony responds.

Billings turns and looks at me. "Where's the bomb now?" he asks.

"Dobbins Air Force Base," I reply. "I found the flight it's going out on, but I had to go online to get it. That's how they tracked us to the cabin. They were probably right behind you, Steve."

"Any chance we can get into Dobbins and intercept?" Billings asks.

I shrug my shoulders. "Maybe, but I doubt it."

Tony chimes in. "Security is going to be tight."

Billings' eyebrows shoot up to the ceiling. "Tighter than at the Summit?"

"It's us against the bad guys at the Summit," Tony reminds, "not us against servicemen. We need Keller alive. You can take him in transit to the Summit better than we can from a fortified armed location, and we can limit casualties on our side if we hit the bomb while it's in play off U.S. soil."

"Yeah, we may be able to exploit security better in Riyadh," Billings says. "Get the VP out safely."

"We have to take that chance," says Tony. "You get Keller out of there, and Alex can make sure that bomb detonates away from the city."

"We can't let Alex sacrifice herself," Billings says, "there's got to be another way."

"These suits are bomb-proof," I remind.

"Be that as it may," Billings replies, "how will you get out? No way you can get out of that blast site and not get captured by someone. I've seen the reports. You and your team were able to capture a man wearing one of those suits back in New York, so don't tell me it's impossible. You've gotta keep that suit on to survive, and it will make you stick out like a sore thumb."

"We have to take that risk," I say. I get up and walk over to them. I touch Billings' arm. "Steve, unless you have a better idea, we have to do this."

"Then, I'll go in for the bomb."

I shake my head. "No, I need intel, and that's what you do best. We get in there, and you find us a contact. Get us a helicopter, drop me in and lead me out of there with aerial support. I saw the bomb, and it's strapped up on some kind of motorized rig. One guy was able to move it up onto the chopper without Rodriguez's command interface, so I know I can get it into a vehicle and run it out of there as long as you have my back. I've been on the ground over there before and I know my way around. I'll find somewhere safe to drop that bomb, then I'll get back to you and Keller and we will escort him to safety."

"Okay," Billings responds. "I'll see what contacts I have over there. I have someone in mind if I can reach him. We'll-"

"Shhh!" Tony holds up his hand and listens for a moment. Then, he rushes over to the window. "We got movement!" he whispers.

I launch myself over the bed, drop my towel on the floor and start pulling on my suit.

Agent Billings draws his weapon and joins Tony at the window. "Yeah, that's them," he confirms. "They're coming in two-man teams. Can you get to the gear in your vehicle?"

Tony shakes his head. "We should've brought it in. Look, they're wearing suits just like Alex's. We won't even put a dent in them."

"I need my rifle," I whisper.

"Forget it, kid," Tony replies. He draws his weapon from his holster and chambers it.

I stand up and pull my suit up around me. It snaps into place. I grab my helmet and put it on as well. It seems to take forever for that thing to load, but finally my display is up, and my suit is shrinking back onto me. I squat and bend my arms, swinging them around to stretch everything in place. Then, I turn on my external audio. "I need a gun!"

Billings, still staring out the window with Tony, reaches behind his back and pulls out his backup weapon.

I grab the gun and check it. "Okay, what's the plan?" I ask.

"I've got a SUV parked one click south of here," Billings says. "Mr. Crane...." He hands Tony the keys. "There's a hardcase laptop under the seat. Keep it plugged up. If it runs out of power, you'll lose the VPN and you won't be able to access Secret Service protocols, schedules, and the like. Everything you need to get into the White House is on that machine. Alex and I will draw their fire. You wait till it's clear and I'll get Alex and I out of Chattanooga on a flight to Dallas. We can get to Riyadh from Doha. We'll find a friendly on the ground in Riyadh. I've got someone in Dallas, who can help us with ID's long as we can catch a flight here without drawing attention to ourselves."

"I'm impressed Stevie," I say.

Billings looks at me and gives me a half smile. "I do my research, ma'am."

"Alex!" I remind, whispering.

"Okay, okay, here we go!" Tony says, softly. He turns around and huddles in with us. "Two men near our car." He hands Agent Billings the keys. "How are you two getting out of here?"

Billings thinks for a moment. "Alex, can you go to the other end of the hotel and draw those two guys your way?"

I nod. "Hell yeah, I got this."

"Good," Billings replies, "I'll get the car and pick you up. My bag over there by the door has extra magazines-"

"I don't need 'em," I interrupt.

They both look at me for a second like I'm crazy, but then they suddenly seem to remember who they're talking to.

"Okay," says Billings. He heads for his bag at the door. He picks it up and cracks it open a little.

I stare into Tony's eyes, and he looks at my helmet.

"I want to kiss you," I say.

He smiles. "I do."

"Huh?"

He nods. "I do. Say, I do."

I tear up, and I nod with him. "I do, I swear to God I fucking do, and I will change for you I swear."

"We don't have time for this!" Billings reminds.

Tony grabs my hand. "You get back here safe, and we'll have a proper wedding and start making babies."

I hug him. "We're already pregnant, remember? But I need lots of pregnancy sex, okay?"

"Whatever you say, baby," he replies. "I love you."

"I know!" I reply.

"Come on!" Billings exclaims.

I rush over to him at the door. "You still got that radio?"

"Yes," he replies.

"What frequency you on?" I ask.

"Channel three."

"Hang on," I say.

Agent Billings sticks the earpiece in his ear.

I turn off my external audio and radio him. "Can you hear me?"

He nods and touches his ear. Then he presses the button on his radio and says, "Comm-check."

I can hear him in my helmet, so I nod.

He props the door open with his foot and waves for me to go. I stand up and take off running full speed down the hall to the right. When I get to the end, I look back and see Billings sneak out of the room, so I start making noise. I bang my way through the door and down the stairs out the back of the motel.

Outside I see two guards. I point Billings' pistol at the one farthest from me and tap off two rounds. He goes down, and his partner spins around just in time to see me fire two more shots. I hit him right in the helmet and he goes down too. Then, I get grabbed from behind and the gun gets knocked away. Next thing I know, I'm up in the air and being slammed down. I roll over on my back, and the big man in his fallout suit is crashing his foot down onto my helmet.

Even with all the armor and padding it still hurts. I feel like he's about to knock me out so, I kick him in the balls, but it has no effect. He draws back to stomp on me again, and I roll over and kick his knee from the front. He goes down. The suits are tough, but they still bend at the joints, and with enough force, you can still break someone's limbs.

I spring to my feet and so do the other two I just shot. They are back up and ready to fight. I look back over my shoulder, and the big man is still rolling around on the ground, so I rush the other two. They literally beat the shit out of me for over a minute until I accomplish the only mission I had from the moment I ran up to them—get their helmets off. I finally wrestle one of the men's helmets off and smash his face with it. Blood splatters everywhere and he goes down. The big guy limps over towards us with his gun pointed at me, so I back up quickly, and then we all look to our left, startled from an unexpected bright light.

Billings turns on the high beams just before the moment of impact, and then he spins the wheel and flings the car left. He hits the assailants, and they go flying. I run to the passenger side of the car and tug at the door. I have to put my foot up on the back door and pull with all my might along with Billings pushing from the inside to get it open. The impact from hitting those men must've bent the body on that side of the car. I finally get inside and Steve slams down on the accelerator. My door flings shut as we peel off around the back of the building.

Steve turns off the headlights and smashes through the back gate. The car bounces up and down, finally coming to rest on all four wheels out on the street, and we speed off into the distance. I spot headlights behind us, but Steve spins the wheel, makes a sharp turn, and pours on the speed.

"We're about 20 minutes from Lovell Field," he says.

I reach in the back and grab my rifle. I check it and push my seat all the way back. Then, I sit up and spin around, crouching down with my back against the glove box and my rifle pointed at the rear window. It's uncomfortable as hell, but I can watch our backs and engage the bad guys before they know we know they're coming. Oddly enough, nobody's coming. In fact, we make it all the way to the airport without incident, which makes me worry about Tony. They must have gone after him.

Billings flashes his credentials to access the rear entrance of the airport. I continue to worry about Tony, but then I hear a phone ring. It's one of the burner phones in the bag on the back seat. I set my rifle down and lunge into the back to retrieve the phone. There are at least 10 phones left in the bag, but only one is lighting up and ringing, so I grab it and accept the call.

"Hello?" I answer.

"Alex, it's me," says Tony.

"You okay?" I ask, frantically.

"Yes, I waited till they were gone. I thought they might pursue you and Agent Billings, but they didn't. They loaded up and went in the opposite direction. But, that's not why I'm calling. You thought they were sending Keller to Riyadh instead of Wood."

"Yes, with the security threat, that's what Pearson-"

"Wood is on his way to Riyadh right now," Tony interrupts. "I checked Agent Billings' laptop. They're on high alert for Riyadh, and Secret Service just posted a plan for Wood's security detail on the secure network."

"Shit!" I exclaim.

Billings looks over at me. "What is it?" he asks.

"I thought Keller was going to Riyadh, but Tony just told me he saw plans to get Wood into the Economic Summit. That means Keller never left South Dakota!"

"You've got to get the VP out of there!" Billings yells.

"You hear that, Tony...? Tony?"

"Yeah," I'm here, Alex. "I'm going to reroute and coordinate with the Seals. I'm headed back to South Dakota. Director Carter is sending two teams as well. He's got Justice backing us now. We'll hit 'em hard. Contact me as soon as you get on the ground. Be careful, Alex."

"You too."

I hang up, and the car comes to a screeching halt. I look up and we're in front of a hangar. The bay doors are open. A man walks out towards us.

"Billings!" the man yells in a strange accent.

Steve hops out of the car and greets the man. "Hello my friend," Billings says.

"What do you need from me?" the man asks, shaking Billings' hand.

"Just the gear we talked about," Billings replies. Then, he starts talking softly.

I can't hear what else they are saying, and I don't care as long as Steve's got us a way to Dallas that doesn't involve us being shot out of the sky. I get out of the car, snap my rifle to my back, and pin a gun to both of my thighs. Then, I pull all of the bags up onto my shoulders and hustle over to Billings, who shakes hands with the stranger one more time, and then moves towards the hangar. The man smiles and salutes me as I sprint past him. I give him a nod and catch up to Billings.

"We got a plane?" I ask.

"Yep."

"We got a pilot?"

"Yep," he replies, pulling the bags off my left shoulder.

"So, is he the pilot?" I ask.

"Nope."

We're inside the hangar near the plane now. I look around and it's just us. "Okay, so where's the pilot?"

"You're looking at him, Alex."

I drop the bags. "The fuck outta here, Stevo, you shittin' me?"

He shakes his head. "No ma'am. I can fly this thing in my sleep."

I drag the bags over to the steps of the small jet and start pulling them up into it. I take my helmet off and toss it up into the plane. "Steve, you are a bad motherfucker man. Secret Service teach you how to fly?"

He smiles. "No. I was a Navy pilot," he confesses.

"No shit?"

"No shit," he responds.

"You're Navy too?"

"Yes ma'am," he replies, proudly.

"I was crypto and intel before I did special warfare support," I say.

Billings nods and hands me the other bags. "Yes, I know."

"So, when were you in?" I ask.

"Vietnam," he replies, proudly.

I start moving the bags around a lot slower. "Uh, so, when was the last time you flew?"

He smiles at me, and hands me the last bag. "Vietnam."

My eyes grow big. "Oh hell naw!"

I start moving for the door, trying to get down out of the plane, but he pushes me back up and gets in too. He quickly pulls the door up and locks it. I plop down in the first seat my butt can find and start freaking out.

"Fucking Vietnam, are you serious, man? What the fuck, this shit is not like riding a bike! Do not say it's like riding a goddamn bike, Steve or I'm gonna fucking flip!"

"Alex...."

"What!" I yell.

"It's like riding a bike," he says, sarcastically.

My head drops down into my lap. "Jesus, just kill me now!"

He laughs loudly. "We're going to be okay. I promise. Now come on ... I need a copilot."

I start mumbling. "Okay, so now I can be a copilot. Nobody needs to know how to do their job, we're just going to wing it. Me, the untrained copilot and Agent Billings the senior citizen dog fighter from the 50's."

"I was there in 1965, thank you very much," he reveals as he climbs up into the cockpit.

"Steve, you're not making me feel any better, okay!"

He points to the chair on the right. "Strap yourself in right there and put those headphones on."

I shake my head. "This is stupid." I sit down and do as he asks. I put the headphones on, and I can hear him in them.

"A few deep breaths may help," he suggests.

I breathe really short, fast breaths, and shake my head again. "Okay...." I nod a few times and tighten both fists. "I'm good now ... let's light this fucking candle man!"

Billings laughs and flicks a bunch of switches all over the instrument panel. I have no clue what all that stuff does, but he seems to know what he's doing, so I just shut up and pray. He starts the engines. The lights dim for a bit and the air conditioning goes off. Then, I hear the engines fire up one by one, slowly coming up to idle. The air kicks back on, and I see the man we first met outside the hangar down on the ground offering guidance, which at this point, I'm not sure is worth the little glow sticks in his hand. *And who's fucking plane is this anyway?*

Steve looks cool as a cucumber—as if he's been waiting half his life to fly a jet again, which could be true based on his last-minute Vietnam confession. I'm trying to be positive, but the way he is rolling this jet out, it's hard not to imagine us crashing to our deaths well before Dallas. We taxi up to the runway, and Steve doesn't even radio the tower for clearance. He literally just takes off. I grip whatever I can around my seat and pray we make it off the ground. Amazingly, we do. In fact, he is flying this jet like a straight up boss, so I just relax and kick back. I turn and look at Steve, and then swat his arm.

"I really am impressed!" I exclaim.

"Wait till we land," he says in the driest tone imaginable.

I frown and shake my head slowly. Then, I point at him a few times and shake my finger at him. I settle back into my seat as we climb to more than 40,000 feet. We level off around 47,000 feet, our cruising altitude, according to Captain Billings, and my ear popping seems to disappear at least for the moment.

"We're two hours out from Dallas," he announces.

I nod. "Okay. You need me, or can I get some rest?"

"No, you're fine," he replies. "You can go back and relax. I'll wake you when we land."

I unbuckle and get up but stop halfway. "We are going to land safely, right?"

He gives me a thumbs up.

I hang up my headset, tap Steve on his right shoulder, and then make my way back to the passenger cabin. I take the first seat on the right and buckle myself in. Then, I recline the seat back as far as it will go, which was about six inches, but I don't care. At this point, any amount of recline is better than being stuck straight up. I close my eyes and fall fast asleep.

Chapter 9

"Alex," comes a voice. "Wake up, we're here."

I wake up to Steve, hovering over me.

"You alright?" he asks.

I nod.

"Time to switch planes," he says. "Come on."

I yawn and sit up in my seat. I unbuckle my seatbelt and look out the window. We're inside a hangar right next to a Gulfstream with a bunch of busy little people loading God knows what up in it.

"We in Dallas?"

"Yes," replies Billings as he gathers up our things. "Do you need all these bags?" he asks.

"I'm not sure what Tony has in them," I respond.

"Alright, we'll take them all," he says. "Come on, let's move."

I spring to my feet. "How did you-"

"We're sneaking into Riyadh on a private jet that belongs to a businessman, who shall remain nameless. He owes a buddy of mine in the CIA a big favor. We'll be able to get in undetected, and he has a contact for us on the ground."

"CIA...? And, what about Pearson?"

"My guy's retired," he responds, opening the door and lowering the steps. "He hates Pearson's guts."

"Well that's a relief," I reply. I snap my rifle to my back and grab as many bags as I can carry with my helmet in hand.

I carefully make my way down the stairs and around the front of our jet. I look back over my shoulder and Steve is right on my tail with the rest of our gear. A man standing at the stairs of the other plane waves us to him. I run over and greet him. He tells me to go onboard and go all the way to the rear of the plane, so I do.

Inside, the plane looks like a five-star hotel. I drag the gear to the back and sit down. Agent Billings follows suit and joins me. He pushes our bags all the way over to the side with his foot and motions for me to come closer, so I do.

He whispers, "When this gentleman comes on board, do not engage him—do not make eye contact. His representative will address us. Do not ask any questions. This is a highly fragile situation. We shouldn't be on this plane, and if we get caught in Riyadh ... just use your imagination. Now, I have watched you Alex, and I know you automatically believe you have latitude in every situation you're in, but I assure you there's none here. We will get thrown off at 30,000 feet without a parachute, and I don't know about you, but I cannot fly."

I look him directly in the eyes. "Understood."

"Alex, I'm serious."

"So am I, Agent Billings."

He smiles.

I smile too, but I'm nervous as hell. I was already nervous before, but now here goes Stevo talking about shut up or get ejected from the goddamn plane, midair, so now I'm shitting bricks I didn't even know I had to shit.

One-by-one, men in all white thawbs, wearing red and white-checkered headscarves, board the plane. They instantly fix their gaze on me, and I feel like I'm shrinking down to the size of a malnourished baby goat. One of the men walks straight up to me. I'm not sure whether to stand or stay seated, but Steve springs up, and so I do as well.

"My employer needs to speak with you, Agent Southerland."

I realize I'm staring him in his face, and I turn my gaze slightly in Steve's direction, hoping for guidance. He nods towards the man, and so I turn my head and nod to him. I guess it's enough because he smiles, thanks me, and asks us to remain standing until his employer is seated. So, we do.

A man, who for all I know could be the first one's twin minus the beard, comes back to us. He shakes Steve's right hand and touches his shoulder with the left.

"Salaam alaykum," he greets.

"Kaif hal ak," Steve replies.

Then, the man places his hand over his heart.

I hang my head low, trying to be respectful.

"Sir, this is Alex Southerland, FBI."

I give him a nod, and he smiles.

"Please sit," says the man.

We each sit down. I'm careful not to cross my legs or lean back in my chair. I sit up straight with my hands in my lap.

"Agent Southerland," says the man.

I look him in the eye, but then remember what Steve said and quickly avert my gaze.

"It's okay," he says, "what I must say to you, I must know that you have full understanding."

I slowly turn my head back and look at him.

He smiles. "My name and the name of my associates is not important. What is important is that ... when one makes what he discovers to be a terrible mistake, he does what is necessary to correct his error in judgement. It was my assets and resources that made this all possible. A man came to me, a man from your CIA along with a scientist, who told my advisors of a device that could reshape the future. This device was said to be able to be configured to match the threat of many faults in the earth's structure to extend the dormancy of fault line activity to stave off disasters, earthquakes and tsunamis, around the world. This life saving device would be my greatest contribution to mankind. It was not until recently I learned I had funded terror. I have done nothing but helped an evil man to make a sophisticated weapon of mass destruction and the means to manipulate a region post detonation. To think I could shape mother earth...." He drops his eyes for a second and shakes his head. "My good friend, Dr. Taylor paid the price for my hubris. The suit you are wearing exists because of me. This is an embarrassment to my people, but I have brought more than just shame. If the Prince is killed by this bomb ... this cannot happen, Agent Southerland. You need to know that the fallout suits, like the one you are wearing, are not indestructible. They are not designed to withstand the impact of detonation. You will die along with everything else in the blast radius. They are however designed for a team of scientists and engineers to safely enter a contaminated land, neutralize the atmosphere and make it inhabitable again in a short period of time. The man, who is sending you to Riyadh means to kill you and everyone around you."

"But, sir, I—I'm sorry ... I shouldn't-"

"Please, speak freely," says the man.

"President Wood is in route," I explain. "If he is behind this-" I stop mid-sentence. "It's not him is it? Pearson's trying to kill them all, the President and the Prince. He's holding Vice President Keller hostage and pitting us all against each other once again."

"Your Secretary of State and your CIA Director Pearson are exactly where they want to be," the man says, "far away from Riyadh. They mean to not just take over the U.S. government, but the world. Your suit is useless in the blast."

I sigh heavily.

"I am a man of peace, not war," the man confesses.

"How do we stop it?" asks Billings.

The man snaps his fingers and another man in all white rushes over to us with a box. He puts the box right in my face and opens it. Then, he closes it and sets it down on the seat beside me before quickly returning to the front of the plane.

"There were two control modules made for the device," says the man. "A primary and a backup. They both require your biometrics to control the device, Agent Southerland. When we land, I will go to be with my family in the city, and I will either come home for the last time ever or it will simply be the best time we have had together in many years, I will see to that. My fate, and that of my people, is up to you, Agent Southerland. Either way, we will never speak again. May Allah guide you."

He stands, and Steve and I spring up to attention.

The man moves in very close to me. I try not to move or breathe or anything.

"You must be within 10 meters of the device," he warns. Then, he gives me a head nod. "As-salaam 'alaykum."

"Wa 'alaykum salaam," Steve replies.

They shake hands again, and the man returns to his area at the front of the plane, far away from us, which was fine by me because his very presence, along with Steve's frightening threat about getting kicked off the plane, made me feel like the dog that should've been left out on the porch during supper.

"You alright?" Steve asks.

I nod. "I feel better now that I know Asad Alibabba isn't going to throw me overboard for speaking out of turn."

Steve bursts out in laugher like I've never seen him do before. Everyone up front looks back at us, and he covers his mouth.

"Jesus, Alex," he whispers, still chuckling.

"You better watch it with that Jesus stuff, Stevsie," I whisper, "They're not going to throw me overboard. He didn't say anything about you. Hide your crosses and your bibles buddy."

Steve shakes his head. "I don't know how you do it."

"Do what?" I spin the little box around and lift up the lid. I tilt my head to the side and look at the device controller for a moment.

He says, "We're probably not going to make it out of this alive, but you're joking about it. I remember you back in New York. You're a real hoot. I needed that."

"Stevsie...."

"Yes, Alex?"

"I think we just got a hail Mary pass," I say.

"We still have to find the bomb," he reminds.

I breathe in deep and roll my eyes. "You just gotta blow my high and bust my bubble, huh?"

He shrugs.

I pick up the controller. Underneath, it's made out of the same material that's affixed to our weapons which makes them stick to the suit. I carefully line it up with my forearm and lower it down until it snaps in place. I just stare at it.

Billings leans in. "Something wrong?"

I look over at him. "I don't know how to make it do anything." I tap the screen a few times. "Nothing." I've been walking around with my suit's holographic display minimized, so I maximize it and start scanning through the menu. I find an item labeled "Peripherals" and activate it. I get a message that reads, "Scanning for peripherals..." The control module lights up and comes online with a "Ready to Pair" message, so I tap the "Ok" button and it starts doing something. Finally, it connects and shows active on my display.

"Okay, I got it connected," I say, softly, "but I can't do anything in stealth mode. If I come out of stealth, I can track the bomb, but they will be able to track me."

"Well, just leave it for now," Billings recommends, "no sense giving the enemy a chance to blow us out of the sky. It's a long flight. We should try and get some rest."

I nod in agreement. He settles back down onto his chair and I move my ass around on my seat to get comfortable. I lean my head back and shut my eyes, hoping I just might be able to go to sleep, but my brain won't let me.

Listening for hours to the internal sounds of a jet flying high above the clouds, complimented by the ever so subtle sound of Agent Billing's snoring is about as suckish an experience as one might hope for. Whenever Steve's snore increases a few decibels, I crack open my left eye just in case he's drooling or making some YouTube-worthy face. A "Sleepy, the drooling Secret Service man" video might turn a pretty penny and based on the odds of our success on this mission, I may need to start looking for alternative forms of income. Hell, I'm sure my assets are all still frozen ... *Oh wait, that was all just an elaborate bucket of bullshit courtesy of Mr. Secret Agent man, Pearson. I'm not really one for violence, but I can't wait to fuck his ass up. Come to think of it, I also can't wait to go shopping. And, I can't wait to get out of this suit. And, I can't wait to go home. And, I need to see Tony again.*

This is crazy. I don't think I've ever been as into a man as much as I'm into Tony right now. It's hard to say whether what I'm feeling is real or not. It could be the whole "end of the world danger thing" kicking my hormones into overdrive—I don't know. What I do know is it feels like it was always meant to be. Somehow, through all our respect and care and caution, we missed opportunity after opportunity to have what we both want—each other. Maybe it was best to wait. Or, maybe things would be totally different had we thrown caution to the wind. Maybe I'd already be a mom. Maybe Tony would've succeeded in calming me down. I dunno.

I hope so much that I'm pregnant. And, even though I am pretty sure I should be drug out into the street and shot for having that thought in the first place, that's what's dominating my mind right now. I want to feel a little life growing inside me kicking and pushing all around, stomping on my spleen and bladder. As horrible as it sounds, the thought of it feels so right. Maybe I need to stop thinking about it and get back on the clock. Work always helps me ignore the most important aspects of my personal life.

So, let's recap. Keller hires me—no, the sumbitch actually blackmails me into going after a terrorist, who turns out to not be terrorist after all. Instead, he was working for Pearson, who is so talented, he makes the President and the Vice President—and hell even me for that matter—believe there's some evil, traitorous battle between them for the oval office. Meanwhile, by way of small attacks on the government—infiltrating agencies with spies and such—Pearson also manages to blackmail and bribe a slew of government officials. I mean this man screws up entire departments and makes law enforcement look ineffective, which in turn makes Wall Street nervous, the real estate market crashes and the whole world has a global economic meltdown. Now, I'd like to believe that last part is just coincidence, but either way, Spy vs. Spy took advantage, putting a bomb, that we now know was funded to stop earthquakes, into play to kill the President, the Saudi Prince, and my black ass too all in one setting. Granted, I've left a few things out in my summation, but the bottom line is Pearson is not a bastard—he's a fuckin' bastard, and that fuckin' bastard has manipulated us all.

What kind of sick shit is this? And for what...? Power? Money? Control? I mean, does he love his country so much he would fuck it apart to get it all going the way he believes it should be? There's no way one man could be the cause of all this. But I guess he isn't. He's had a shit ton of assistance along the way, and I seem to be his number one helper. I can be so stupid. Everything was right in front of my face the entire time, but I was too blind to see any of it.

Again, I try and change the subject of the conversation I am having with myself, about myself ... but, for some reason, I can't get it all out of my mind. I can't stop thinking about having a baby, and I can't stop thinking about how stupid I was. Let's face it, like Pearson said, had I just sat back and done nothing, none of this would even be possible. I should've just said no to Keller and took my chances with the tax evasion charges, but noooooo, I had to be the fucking hero.

I continue beating myself up, but then I start to think maybe that's what this is all about. Like Daddy always said, somebody's got to be the hero. I don't like the job much, but nobody else is showing up to interview. And, what should I do now? Sure, I have the backup control module strapped to my arm, but it's no good without the bomb, which just so happens to be on final countdown to nuclear detonation. The odds of us touching down in Riyadh, operating in secret, and locating a thermonuclear device nobody wants us to find is pretty slim.

The only good thing as far as I can see is these Saudi boys keep it cold on the plane. Finally, my ass feels so good and dry all twisted up in this little suit. Whoever designed these things did so with a horribly fatal flaw—they lack basic comfort. Clearly, they were designed by some man, with little shriveled up wrinkly balls, who had no fear whatsoever of a suit riding up his crotch and chafing him. Maybe it was Dr. Taylor and he felt the need to keep it high and tight, so you can count how many pennies are in his pocket when he was wearing this suit.

We're 11.5 hours into an 18-hour flight, and I'm still trying to find a way to get to sleep. I kid you not I've done everything up to and including counting sheep with no such luck. I wonder if my family is alive and okay. I'm also wondering why the thought of them being murdered is not bothering me. I mean, I can understand why Pearson torturing Bill brings a slight smile to my face, but the others ... I dunno maybe Theresa too, but the others ... they don't deserve any of this. Not being able to communicate with

Tony right now isn't helping either. I hope he is alright. I hope he makes it back to South Dakota, and I hope he finds my family alive. I just want them back home and away from all this nonsense. Speaking of nonsense, Tony better make good on his promise. Maybe we can move in together ... into my place? And just like that—after that last not so blissful thought, I fell asleep.

Chapter 10

I sleep soundly for hours. Finally, I wake up to Billings shaking me from side to side. I guess I really was tired. My entire chest is covered with drool. I just shut my eyes tight and shake my head. Of course, I am not too embarrassed to wipe my mouth and chin with the palm of my hand. Like the gentleman he is, ole Steve is kind enough to offer me a hanky. I roll my eyes at him and take the hanky, quickly.

"Thanks," I say, reluctantly.

"You're welcome," he responds.

I wipe my face and push Steve's hanky as far down the front of my suit as I can in a futile attempt to dry my tits off. The suit is just way too tight on me. "How long was I out?" I ask.

He looks down at his watch. "About five hours. You rested now?"

I nod. "I still feel tired, but not as much as before. I couldn't get to sleep for all the tea in China."

"Well, we'll be landing soon," he says. "I've been trying to think of a way we may be able to get a jump on things, but I'm coming up with nothing. Hopefully our contact on the ground can help."

"Yeah Stevesie, about that...."

"What...?"

"Well, I've got an idea, but you're not going to like it."

Steve automatically frowns. "Do I even want to know?"

I sit straight up and push my wet hanky down in the cup holder beside me. "A dream I just had made me think about this National Geographic episode. There was this snake that camouflaged itself in order to blend in perfectly with the rocks it was coiled up on. I mean it was just chillin' there, right? Then, this spider is crawling all over it, so this bird is like yo, its dinner time, right? So, the bird flies down to get the spider, not suspecting for a single second the spider is crawling on anything other than a rock, but it's actually a damn snake. Soon as the bird touches down, the snake does this lightning fast strike in less than a second and kills the fuck outta the bird. They called it a predatory lure … an elaborate predatory lure."

Steve rubs his chin. "So, you're saying, we make the bad guys come to us?"

I point my finger in the air. "Exactly!"

"And how do you propose we do that?" he asks.

"We've got the lure right here," I reply. "I'm wearing it."

"Yeah, okay," he nods, "but my understanding of how those things work, you can't turn them on until you're in them, so we can't just toss the suit out and wait for them to find it."

I think for a moment. "When does the Summit start?"

"Exactly four hours after we touch down," Billings replies.

"What are the odds there's a parachute on this plane?" I ask.

"Well, no, but even if we had a chute are you that good? To jump out of a speeding jet at over forty thousand feet?"

I smile and shoot him a bird. "Well, the only other thing we can do is turn this bad boy on and be prepared to come out of the plane shooting."

"And what about the civilians on this aircraft?" he asks.

"Move them all up towards the cockpit," I reply. "Lock your buddy up in with the pilots and barricade everyone else with whatever we can take down."

Billings shakes his head. "He's never going to go for this."

I lean in close, "Do you have a better idea, 'cause I'm all fucking ears?"

"No," he says, softly. "I don't have a better idea, but I know a really bad idea when I hear it, and this is a really, really bad idea. We'll be dead the moment we open the doors."

"Look Steve, if I go down first, I can block for you. You find cover, and we lay into those assholes. If they are wearing suits, and I guarantee you they are, maybe I can do just like Rodriguez and blow each one of them to hell." I lifted my arm up a little. "We can do this. We take them down, and then we take the bomb down too."

"And what if they don't have the bomb with them?" he asks. "What if their suits don't have explosives in them?"

I sit back and cross my arms. "I don't know." I shake my head. "We'll have to find the bomb, but I think it's worth the risk to try and draw them in to us. Matter of fact, I could just sit in one spot and draw their fire while you find the bomb."

"Yeah, provided they don't blow us out of the sky when we get in range. Alex, I don't know about this. I know you feel some level of confidence or you wouldn't suggest it but giving the enemy the advantage of early detection of our position is a bad idea. I think it puts too many civilians at risk. And, you heard him say it ... your suit is not indestructible. It won't survive a major blast. We lose that controller on your arm and it's game over."

I take a long pause. "Maybe you're right," I say.

"Yes, I am," he replies, confidently. "Just relax. We'll be on the ground soon and we'll figure it all out then."

"Okay," I reply. I maximize my heads up display one last time, click a menu item, and then minimize it again. "Let me know when we're getting ready to land. I'm going to try and rest a little more."

"Roger that," he replies.

I close my eyes and play possum for the next hour and a half until I feel the plane begin its descent. I open my eyes and see the man who first spoke to us on the plane walking back towards us again.

"We are landing now," the man announces, and then he returns to the front of the jet with the others.

I scoot to the front of my seat and start loading up my weapons. I check a few of the bags Tony gave me and consolidate all the compatible magazines into the one bag I could swing over my shoulder. Then, I put my helmet on.

"What are you doing?" Billings asks.

I ignore him and continue getting ready. I power up my helmet and attach my rifle to my back.

"Alex...?" Steve is starting to look worried.

I continue to ignore him. The man from up front comes back over to us.

"What is going on?" he asks.

Billings stands up and looks at him. "I'm not sure."

I take in several deep, long breaths, back to back, and then I pump my fists down by my sides.

"What is she doing?" asks the man, frantically.

"Alex!" Steve shouts. "Talk to me!"

I turn slowly and look at him. I switch on my external audio. "I'm sorry, Agent Billings, I switched off my stealth mode hours ago. They have been tracking us ... two teams are on the ground, all in suits, heavily armed and waiting for us to-"

"Oh my God!" exclaims Steve.

"...land." I finish my sentence and stretch.

The man runs full speed up to the front of the jet and starts shouting. Everyone immediately springs to their feet. Our frantic friend returns to us with the main businessman and the other passengers, who I can only assume are his security team because those particular men have somehow produced guns from under their little white dresses. They are all yelling at me in Arabic. The businessman is the only one in the bunch, who seems to be calm all things considered.

Steve turns to him and shouts, "Sir, we have to turn this plane around."

He raises both hands and everyone goes quiet. "And why should we do that, Agent Billings?" he asks.

"Alex- Agent Southerland has activated her suit and the enemy is waiting for us at the landing site."

"And why would Agent Southerland do this?" he asks, calmly.

"Sir, I do not know," Steve replies.

The man turns to me. "Why would you do this, Agent Southerland?"

"Your family," I reply.

The man looks puzzled, but curious. "I do not understand. Please explain yourself," he orders.

"We had precious hours to find these men, sneaking around the city to do the impossible. Doing what I did, they found us ... they found me, and I will talk to them, or I will fight. I will save your family, I swear. On my life I swear. I swear on my unborn child's life I will save your family. When this plane lands, I want you and everyone, Agent Billings included, up at the cockpit. Block yourselves in with luggage or whatever you can find, and when I exit the side of this plane, I want you back in the air. Do not return until I clear the area, or they carry my dead body back to Pearson." I turn to Billings. "You keep them alive. If I fail, get him and his family out of the city, okay?"

"Alex, this is crazy," says Billings.

I nod. "Yeah, I know, but ... this is what I do. You tell Tony I love him, and he will always have my heart." I touch his shoulder and squeeze it. "Thank you for everything my friend."

He stands there shaking his head.

"No," the businessman says softly.

I turn and look at him. "No?"

"No, this is not ... I will meet these men you speak of. You will stay onboard, and you will do nothing I do not approve of. You are a guest on my private jet no different than if you were in my home. These men must honor my wishes."

"These men are killers!" I exclaim.

He turns to Steve. "Agent Billings, I know you understand our customs and traditions. Please take your seats and do as I wish. Do you understand?"

"Yes, sir I do," Steve responds.

"Good, then ensure that Agent Southerland understands," says the man.

I just stand there watching this macho Arab bullshit.

"Yes sir, I will," says Steve.

"Good," the man says. He waves his hands around in the air. "Please everyone take your seats."

His men all comply. They scatter, sit down, and buckle up. I draw my rifle and sit down, holding it, ready to run out and fire. Steve moves over and sits right up beside me.

"Alex, you don't want to do this," he warns. "They will kill you. You are our best chance of-"

"I know," I interrupt. "Trust me, whatever you are trying to say, I know. I get it, but I know something you don't."

"And what's that?" he asks.

I pull back the slide on my weapon and release it. It snaps a round into place. "I can do this."

Steve stops trying to argue with me, and he starts gearing up. "You're not leaving this plane alone," he tells me.

"You wearing your vest?" I ask.

"Yes ma'am, I am!" he replies.

I nod. "Stay behind me and use me as cover. If I go down, prop me up, and stay sharp. If a round knocks me out, hold me up and use my suit as a shield till I come back to, okay? We go straight up the middle and break right. I can see them on my display. They are holed up on the left behind a wall or something. You take cover, and I will draw them out. Hit 'em hard, try and knock them down, and I will try and get their helmets off, then it's headshots, got it?"

Billings says, "Got it."

"I'm sorry," I tell him.

He gives me a stern look. "No, you're not."

"No ... I'm not."

"We're landing now!" comes a nervous voice from the front.

I push back into my seat and Steve braces himself using the seatback of the chair in front of him. We hit the runway hard and the wheels chirp as we touchdown and roll to a stop. As soon as the plane stops moving, Steve and I get up and head for the door, but the men with the guns pop up and draw down on Steve.

"Stop!" I command, but they ignore me about as well as I ignore other people. "You don't wanna do this man!"

The businessman casually walks over to the door. "Keep them here until I return. No one leaves the plane."

Another man opens the door and lets the stairs down.

"Do not shoot!" the man says as he makes his way down the stairs.

I rush over to the right side of the plane and look out a window. It's hard to tell but it looks like there are more men out on the ground than my display shows. A cloud of nervous anxiety begins to choke me from every direction. *What the hell are we doing here?* I think.

"Take it easy," says Billings.

I look over my shoulder and he is backing up from the men with guns. They tell him to sit down, so he makes his way over to me and sits.

"What do you see?" Steve asks me.

"Hard to say," I reply. "I see our friend walking, but I still can't see the assholes. We're going to get this guy killed, Steve. We gotta get off this plane."

"No, we sit tight," he advises.

"Steve, I can't-"

"You can, and you will," he interrupts. "You played a dangerous game of chance with all our lives, and this man has called your bluff. I'm not even sure that's the right way to describe this situation, but for now all we can do is sit here and wait."

I see a shadowy figure move out from the darkness and approach our guy. He is armed to the teeth and wearing a fallout suit. He points his weapon at the businessman and walks up to him slowly. He aims his gun right at him, and they exchange words. I cannot hear what they are saying, but the man lowers his gun. The businessman turns and waves at us.

"He wants us to come out," I say. "Look, come here!"

I wave one of the armed guards over. He comes to our side of the plane and takes a look out the window. He mumbles something I don't understand, and then he grabs my arm, pulling me towards the door.

"I'm coming with her!" exclaims Steve.

The other armed men move in and try to block Steve, but he makes sure they know he means business and they cave in and let him pass.

We move down out of the plane. I strap my rifle to my back again. Steve is gripping his pistol and moving forward, but I don't have a gun in my hand. I don't care anymore. I take my helmet off and hold it down by my side and breathe in fresh shitty Saudi Arabian air. It totally stinks, but that's the least of my concerns because more than 50 men creep out from the shadows, some wearing fallout suits and others in normal tactical gear.

Steve and I get within a few paces of the Saudi businessman and the bad guy in black. The businessman spins around and reaches out for me with both hands.

"Come, he says," reaching and grabbing my left hand. He pulls me over and extends my hand out to the bad guy. "As-salaam 'alaykum," he says. Then, he puts my hand right into the bad guy's.

The man squeezes my hand and I squeeze his back.

"As-salaam 'alaykum," the businessman says again, nodding at me.

I repeat him. "As-salaam 'alaykum."

He shakes his head in approval. "As-salaam 'alaykum," he says again.

"Wa 'alaykum salaam," says the man in black.

The businessman smiles and steps back a few feet. He waves and motions for us to come together, but I am not a fan of embracing the enemy. The man pulls his hand back quickly, and I step back, expecting the worst, but he doesn't attack. No one does. He reaches up with both hands and removes his helmet.

"Agent Southerland," we meet again, he says.

"Holy fucking shit!" I exclaim. "Mr. White!" I can't believe my own eyes. I feel like I am going crazy. He was the last person on earth I expected to see.

Billings holsters his weapon and stands in amazement that we know each other.

Mr. White turns and points at his men. "Alex, meet team Bravo."

One-by-one, they all remove their helmets, and the men not wearing suits step up into the light as well.

Mr. White turns back to us. "Rodriguez is dead. Pearson has been detained. Your family is safe, but one sustained a minor injury."

I cover my heart.

"Do not worry, Mr. Chris took a bullet in the arm. He was very brave, protecting his niece, little Angie. He will recover just fine. They are all safe and surely, they are in Langley by now for debriefing. You will be with them soon."

"And Secretary of State Clarke?" I ask.

Mr. White replies, "Arrested. Keller is free and preparing to take office. The Secret Service agents guarding President Wood are not on our team, and we cannot reach them. We are on high alert. POTUS is in danger here, so we must act fast."

"I don't understand how-"

"Alex, it doesn't matter," says Mr. White. "There will be plenty of time to understand why and how. Right now, we have work to do. We are with the President, Alex ... we are with you." He salutes me.

All the men behind him stand at attention and salute me as well.

I'm so excited I slam my helmet into Steve's chest like right in the vest. Steve grunts upon impact, and then grabs hold of my helmet with both hands.

"Steve! Steve!" I yell.

"Yeah?"

"Steve!" I yell even louder.

"What!" he replies, angrily.

"I have fucking Storm Troopers, man!" I step to the side and pump my fist in the air.

The men drop their salutes and sound out with a chilling, roaring battle cry.

I turn back to Mr. White and lunge for him, wrapping my arms around him and kissing his cheek. "I fuckin' love you man!"

He struggles to break free. "I ... I'm very fond of you as well, Alex. Now, there is a small issue of an atom bomb we need to tend to most urgently."

"Oh, shit!" I exclaim. "I almost forgot." I held up my arm. "You know how to work this thing?"

"I do," Mr. White replies. "This way. The bomb is here."

"Wait!" I run over to the businessman and jump all over him. "Thank you!" I say, hugging him with my face pressed against his chest. Then, I stop and realize he is completely mortified. "Oh my God I- oh shit, I mean shoot, I mean Allah ... I'm very sorry." I just step back and cover my mouth.

The man runs his hands down the front of his clothing to straighten it out. "It is alright," he says. "I am okay. You are okay. For now, we are all okay. Now, go stop the bomb!"

I nod and bow, which I'm not sure is appropriate, but I figure it was better than me kissing him. I drop to my knees and say a quick "thank you Lord" prayer, and then I spring back up and run over to Steve and Mr. White. The night before was hell, and the early morning seemed like it would be the longest ever, but we're going to be alright thanks to one secret businessman, a Secret Service Agent, a team of bad asses in black, and a shit ton of luck.

Chapter 11

The sun is beginning to rise literally and figuratively. Agent Billings and I are walking side-by-side CIA operative Mr. White. Now, I know his name really isn't White, but why do I care? He's got the bomb, and well he is the bomb. Today is going to be a good day—no bloodshed and no battles to win—just shut the bomb down and rescue the President. Seeing as we outnumber the bad guys two to one, and the local police officers augmenting Wood's detail probably don't give two shits one way or another whether he lives or dies, this should all be a cakewalk.

Mr. White and the rest of my Storm Troopers lead us to the far side of the airfield, where they have several heavy-duty vehicles parked. The men secure the perimeter while Mr. White, Steve and I move to the biggest truck in the bunch—the one carrying the bomb.

We all climb aboard and move around to the control panel side of the bomb. The display read "00:01:12".

"Is that the countdown?" Steve asks.

"You're kidding me, right?" I say.

"I'm afraid not," says Mr. White. "And, I know what you're thinking, but Pearson didn't care. Doesn't matter where the President and the Prince are, when this thing goes off it will level the city."

"So, let's stop the timer," I say, eagerly.

Mr. White sighs. "It's not that simple. There's nothing we can do to stop the timer. However, we can destroy the materials inside using your control module."

I cross my arms. "Okay, that sounds pretty straight forward. What button do I press?"

"Not that simple," White replies.

I cock my head to the side. "How long?"

"About an hour," White replies.

Steve looks up and rubs his face with his hands.

"Jesus Christ!" I exclaim. "What the fuck was this gingerly walk across the airport and shit. The fuck are we doing assing around goddammit, we need to-"

Mr. White gives me the hand. "Alex, biometrically you're the only one who can do this. I need you calm. There's a very long procedure to neutralize the nuclear material in this device. We can do it, but we cannot prevent its detonation. The bomb will still go off, but it won't go nuclear. We have to work swiftly and accurately so we can clear the bomb site before it explodes. Understand?"

I nod. "Okay ... okay... I need to sit down."

"Over here," says Steve, pointing to the bench running along the side of the truck.

I move over and carefully sit my butt down. Mr. White joins me. I position the command console atop my knees and tap the screen to wake it up. The screen illuminates and icons appear all over. Mr. White pulls out a pair of glasses and pushes them up on his face. Then, he takes out a manual.

I look right at him. "Are you serious, man?"

He smiles. "Patience, Alex. The device has a massive generator, which makes up the majority of its size. This generator uses a high-powered beam of neutrinos to destabilize the ordinance. Essentially, we're going to scatter the neutrons in the plutonium and turn the bomb material into mush ... are you ready?"

"Yes," I reply, nervously. "Wait!" I interrupt. "Shouldn't we have on some, well, shouldn't we be wearing our helmets and shouldn't Steve be out of here."

"I'm not going anywhere, Alex."

"We're shielded from the radiation, but truthfully, it won't matter where he is if we don't succeed," says Mr. White. "Those of us with suits will make it with our helmet on, but-"

I shake my head. "No, we won't. The man you saw earlier, he was behind the suits. He told us they are only designed to survive nuclear winter. He says the blast will kill us, suit or no suit."

"Well that's the worst thing I've heard all day," replies White. "I say we get on with it … Alex, you're looking for menu item number 42," says White.

I scroll down the endless sea of icons. "Got it." I tap the icon and a security screen appears.

"Fingerprints, please," he says.

I press my thumb and four fingers down on the screen and hold them in place.

"Now, repeat after me … Horse…."

"Horse," I respond.

"Church," he says.

I repeat it. He says "spectrum" and I repeat that too. I continue repeating, word after word, until he stops.

I pull back my hand and the display reads, "Access Granted."

"The fucking numbers are in Japanese!" I exclaim.

"They built the device, and the suits and the beam," White replies in a calm, dry tone. "The first number, is-"

"Wait!" I shut my eyes tight and try to remember what the numbers look like because on the digital keypad on the display, they are not in order. I nod, nervously, and say "Okay, I'm good, no wait, why don't you punch them in, and I'll read them off to you?"

Mr. White shakes his head. "I don't read Japanese and besides, it only works with your fingerprints. I press my print down and we detonate."

I mumble, "If that sumbitch Taylor wasn't already dead…."

"What was that?"

"Nothing!"

"Are we ready?" White asks.

"Yes," I whisper.

White looks at me funny. "Why are you whispering?"

I tip my head forward towards the bomb. "So, it doesn't know we are fucking with it."

He gives me another funny look and then starts giving me the numbering sequence. "Eight," he says.

"Eight, eight, eight … hachi … got it!" I press the button and it remains lit.

White gives the next number. "One."

"Okay, ichi...." I find it on the number grid and press it too. It also remains lit.

"Five," says Mr. White.

"Hmm ... five, five, five ... got it." I press "go" and the colors from the three numbers all combine together in the middle of the screen and move to the top.

"How many groups?" I ask.

"Sixteen total," he replies.

"The fuck man!" I exclaim.

"Focus, Alex," Billings says.

Mr. White gives me the next group of numbers, and I put them in as well. They lock in together and join the first group at the top of the display.

We continue working, taking as much time as we feel we can to get each number group in correctly. Finally, we get to the last group and I punch it in. A continue button appears. I take a deep breath and press the button, but instead of continuing, group number nine blinks red at the top. I tap it and it drops down to the middle of the screen. There's an invalid number sequence according to the display. Mr. White and I look at each other, and I'm pretty sure he's holding his breath just like I am, bracing for the worst, but nothing happens. He flips back and finds the right group and gives it to me again. I punch it in—more carefully this time—and the "continue" button appears again.

"That's it," says Mr. White. "Press it, and the sequence is supposed to begin."

I hover my finger over the button for a second, and then I pull back. "Is your name really Mr. White?"

He nods. "Benjamin White, CIA Case Officer, London. I wasn't born there, but it has grown on me."

"Well that explains the shitty accent," I joke.

We both smile, and then without skipping a beat, I press the button and a progress bar appears.

"That's it," says White.

"That's it?"

"Yes, Alex. Now, we wait and watch from a safe distance."

"So, if this works, we'll just see the truck get scattered all over the place?" asks Steve.

"Yes, and if not, all bets are off," White replies.

"Understood," Steve responds.

We climb down out of the bomb truck. All the other vehicles and all the men are gone except one man in a jeep. As soon as he sees us, he hops into the driver seat and cranks up. We all pile in with him and he speeds off towards the runway. He makes a sharp left and pulls up to a building across from the tower. We hop out and follow him inside. The men are all lined up in a big room. We walk in, and Benjamin addresses them.

"Gentlemen, thank you for your efforts today," he says. "We have done our best to neutralize the nuclear capabilities of the device, but it is a race against time. One of two things will happen ... either we beat the clock and we lose a truck, or the clock runs out before the process is complete and we lose the city ... perhaps our own lives. You may put on your helmets and hope for the best, but if the device goes nuclear, as I understand it, based on recent intel, you will burn up along with everyone else anyway."

The men groan and talk amongst themselves briefly.

"Alright," White continues, "Now that we've got that out of the way. We have approximately 37 minutes before detonation." He turns and points to Steve and me. "I imagine you all know by now this is Agent Alex Southerland of the FBI and Secret Service Agent Steven Billings, who is tasked on Vice President Keller's protection detail. He has intimate knowledge of Secret Service protocols, and if we make it out of here alive, they will assume command for Operation Wolf Pack to neutralize the threat on President Wood's life. Target location is the King Abdulaziz International Conference Centre, Radisson Blu Hotel, Riyadh. Questions...? Good then. Godspeed, gentlemen."

Benjamin pulls out a satellite phone and walks over to the corner. I slowly make my way to the windows on the left side of the room. Steve follows.

"You know you're not assigned to me anymore, right?" I ask.

"Yep," Steve replies.

"You could be spending your last few minutes on earth mingling with evil charismatic assholes you may never meet where you're going," I say.

Steve chuckles. "Yep."

"Alright," I reply. "I'm just checking."

We both stare out the window right at the bomb truck.

"Alright, Agent Southerland, it's my turn," Steve announces, in a tone I'd just as soon avoid during the end of days.

I shake my head a bit. "Awe shit, Steve, I know what that tone of voice means."

"I haven't even said anything," he replies, calmly.

"Go on," I say.

"That was reckless back there on the plane," he says.

"Uh huh."

"You could've gotten us all killed," Steve says.

"Yep." I nod.

"And, you lied to me, Alex."

I frown. "I do feel ever so slightly some kind of way about that, but you would've tried to talk me out of it, and had you succeeded, which the way I was feeling at the time you would've, we'd miss this glorious death by light show we're about to experience. Besides, I didn't smell anything. Honestly, I don't smell anything now either."

Steve turns and looks at me as confused as ever. "Smell what?"

"I don't smell Carla-"

"Agent Southerland," comes White's voice from behind.

I turn around, and he's shuffling towards me, waving his sat-phone directly at me.

"Call," he says, energetically.

I point at myself. "For me?"

"Yes!" he exclaims, pushing the phone into my hands.

I raise the phone to my ear and say, "Hello?"

"Alex," comes a familiar voice.

"Tony!" I tap Steve's shoulder and cover my other ear. I walk off to the quietest corner in the place. I was totally calm before, but now my heart is pounding inside my chest like some wild beast. I cannot contain my excitement. "Fucking shit, Tony, how the-"

"Alex," he interrupts, "White told me everything ... about the bomb and all."

"Yeah, I kind of—look Tony, I don't care. I just want to spend these last few minutes with you, and I don't want to talk about all this bullshit."

Tony gives me a long "okay" and clears his throat. "What do you want to talk about?"

"What are you wearing?" I ask.

"Well, I was wearing a suit, but I took my jacket off ... and my tie...."

"Which suit?" I ask.

"The dark navy with pinstripes," Tony replies.

"Ooh, I like that one it makes you look like a sexy banker. And, where are you?"

"Alex, this is crazy, we need-"

"Ump! NO! These are my last minutes. We do this my way."

"Fine," he agrees. "I'm back in New York ... I'm at your place."

I smile. "Our place," I say. "I want you to move in with me, and ... I wanna make you breakfast."

"Alex, you can't cook for shit!" He laughs. "No, I'll make us some pasta baby. We can have some wine. A nice bottle I been saving."

"No, I'm not drinking," I reply.

"What?" he responds.

"The baby, silly," I say.

"Alex, you're-"

"Hey, don't fuck this up, Tony!" I exclaim. "I need this. I need you. I need you to put your cock in me again in every hole and fill me up with your hot fucking cum." I notice a few of the guys staring suddenly, so I slump down onto a chair and spin around in the opposite direction. I think about talking softer, but at this point, who gives a damn. We're nearing the end. "I want you to tie me up with your necktie and eat my pussy until I'm almost ready to cum, and then I want you to get up and walk out of the room."

"Really?" he responds.

"Uh huh." I lick my lips and spread my thighs. I can't feel a thing through this suit, but again—*end of world—hello!* I touch between my thighs and close my eyes. "I want you to come back in and keep bringing me close to orgasm. Tony...?"

"Yeah?"

"Stroke your long cock for me."

"What?" He sounds shocked.

"Pull your goddamn cock out and stroke it while I talk dirty. Keep up white boy!"

"Alex-"

"Shhh! I'm wet!" I close my eyes again and continue rubbing my thighs, imagining how it might feel if I wasn't wearing a futuristic girdle made of high-tech Kevlar. I try to rub my clit up against it, but the suit kind of just moves with my hips, so there's nothing happening. I just have to rely on my imagination. "I wanna taste it, and I want you to stuff your balls in my mouth, I wanna taste them. I love that they are nice and smooth and big and heavy."

"Hair removal cream," he says.

I can tell he really is stroking his cock and it's making me wetter, but so are the men, who keep casually trying to get closer. I can see them over my shoulder and even though I know we're all about to die, I also know they are just like me, naked under their fallout suits. And the ones who aren't naked, I just want to cut their clothes off and force them to suffocate me with their cocks. Death by cock before the nuclear bomb de-atomizes us sounds so fucking hot to me right now.

"You fucked me so deep and hard, Tony, and you knocked this dirty bitch up. I have your baby in my womb right now. I love the way our bodies feel. I want you so bad. Momma needs some more cum in her pussy, can you do that for me?"

"Yes, baby."

"Can you fuck me balls deep and shoot your load up in this pussy? I wanna die riding your cock baby. Will you fuck this hot pussy really good like you did at the cabin?"

"Yes, oh yes, Alex, I ... I love-"

The phone goes dead, and so does everything else in the room, inside and out. I drop the phone and instantly look at Steve. He looks back at me, and the room lights up. The red ball of fire that erupts from the bomb truck is bright enough to cast a shadow from behind the sun and the room is illuminated with the blindingly hot sensation of death.

Have you ever been to Vegas and hit the tables hard? I remember once, Bill and I went to gamble, and the whole plane ride over, he's giving me this big long speech about how we're on a budget, and we have only so much to play with. I just sat back and listened to him, keeping quiet and pretending I was going to follow his boring ass guidance, but what he didn't know is I had my own money, and I was going to rock the Bellagio like a big hair concert in Kansas City—like, them corny wheat harvesting motherfuckers would have no idea what to do with all that rock and roll, right? So, we get there, and Bill's pansy ass goes straight for the slots. *Bitch ass.* And, what do I do? I plop my fat, sexy ass right down at the roulette table, pockets on swole. I was wearing some expensive shit too I'd bought just for this occasion, so everyone knew I was a high roller. There I was, betting like crazy, and losing like a lunatic. I get this feeling like I'm doing all I can to stay positive, but I know it's going down. And that it does. It goes down so bad I end up five grand in the hole between betting the tables and betting on the game. I was sure some big Italian dude named Guido would break my legs before I left there, but it didn't happen. Bill bailed me out. Yes, Bill. A man so cheap he squeaked when he walked. I don't know how he did it, but he did, and we went on to have a good trip.

I'll never shake that feeling of hopelessly holding out hope. And, that's how I feel right now, watching the fire being hurled right towards us is like watching myself lose bet after bet in Vegas to no avail. I never thought I'd die this way, obliterated at 10,000 degrees-.

"Wait? What the fuck...?"

The men all turn and look at me. I start walking slowly to Steve, who seems just as shocked as I am.

"Mother ... fucker ... son of a bitch!" I exclaim, speeding up and walking faster towards Steve.

I get over to him and, at the window, parts of the truck and other debris, landing and banging up against the thick glass. The other end of the airfield's lit up in a bright amber, and whatever's left of the truck is a smoldering mess, but we're alive. The men erupt into the loudest roar I've ever heard—so loud I have to cover my own ears to scream along with them without blowing my eardrums out. I grab Steve and hop all over him, hugging without remorse. He wraps his arms around me and buries his face into my shoulder.

"I don't know how, but we did it!" he exclaims.

"Steve, we are totally fucking alive. Wait...." I push him back and look into his eyes. "We are alive, right?"

He nods. "As alive as ever, Alex."

I let go of Steve and run around the room, shaking hands, hugging, and slapping high fives. *We did it. We fucking did it.* I get around to Benjamin and he is in tears.

"I never doubted you for a second," he tells me.

I smile and pull him in for a hug too.

"Alex Southerland, you are the huggiest thing ever!" he exclaims, embracing me like a long lost relative.

We hold each other for a while, and then he gets back on the clock. "Alright, time to fight the next battle." He says. "Gentlemen, evidence response, check the blast site. Put your helmets on just in case." Then, he points right at me. "Southerland, you're up."

I raise both hands and nod. "Okay ... okay ... Jesus! We're good. Okay evidence response? What are they-"

"Checking for radiation," White interrupts.

"Gotcha! Okay guys. Listen, President Wood is in trouble. We don't know who's on his detail, but we have to assume they are compromised. Same for the Saudi police officers augmenting his security detail."

Steve joins me by my side and speaks up. "Security protocols suggest the President may be here in his limo. It is bullet resistant. Our best shot is to engage the agents and the police with non-lethal force—even if they are traitors, we still have to take them in. They may have additional intel that will help us exit Riyadh safely with the President. Again, non-lethal force when engaging the President's security forces. If for some reason we cannot get President Wood back in his limo, we will surround him ... I want fallout suits on every corner of him on the way back to the convoy. The rest of us will lay down covering fire and do our best to make it back to the vehicles. Mr. White already has us set to extract from what's left of this airfield, so if you get separated, make your way back here. We've got a C135 fueled and ready to go. We get President Wood on board and change call signs."

"I don't need to tell you, we have to get the President home alive," I say. "This is what we do. We protect America and her interests, and Wood is her interest. I don't know all of you men, but I can tell you believe in honor and doing what's right. Agent Billings here has been trained to give his life for our President. You may not have received similar training, but today, we will all pretend as if we have. If it comes between one of us or the President, we ride home with the President in a body bag."

"We've been unsuccessful getting word to the royal family," says Mr. White. "Protect President Wood but watch your fire. We shouldn't be on Saudi soil. If we kill—I don't even want to say it. Watch your fire. We're on our own, and the Saudis will hang us out to dry. They can't appear for a second that they cannot control their own country or vipers will consume them from the north, south and east. If we do our job right, we'll be in and out and on our way home in no time. Questions...?"

A man in a fallout suit steps forward. He has a full beard and a slight New England accent. "This is hardly a plan," he remarks. "What if they know we're coming, and we're ambushed?"

"Soldier, did you just get a new lease on life?" asks Mr. White. "I mean, did we just avoid nuclear obliteration?"

The man laughs.

White says, "Let's split in two teams. If you are wearing a fallout suit, you are Alpha team and you're with Agent Southerland. If not, you're Bravo, you're our backup and you're with Agent Billings. Alpha team goes in to secure the President. Bravo team sets up a perimeter with the vehicles around the Radisson. If we're ambushed, Alpha team crowds around the President as a human shield. You get hit, get back up and get back in position. Alex will get Wood back into his limo and Agent Billings will guide us back out to the perimeter using his knowledge of Secret Service tactics. Alex, drive as slow as the situation permits, and we can use the car as cover. Remember, this is not a State Department sanctioned mission. If you are caught, you're on your own. A wise man once said it always seems impossible until it's done."

"Nelson Mandela," comes a voice from the crowd.

White points towards the back. "Exactly. Now, link into my coms and give me a moment...."

The men comply. One-by-one they pop up on my display.

"We're all clear," comes a voice over the radio.

Benjamin looks around. "Alright, Alex ... it's your bag."

I put my hands up a little. "Let's roll!"

The men rustle around and collect their gear. I do the same.

Then, I walk back over and pick up Benjamin's sat phone. It's live again. The shockwave from the blast must've temporarily knocked the signal out. I hold it up in the air. "Can I keep this?" I ask, yelling across the room to Benjamin.

He gives me a thumbs up, so I stuff the phone in Tony's bag I still have strapped across my chest. I walk over to Steve, who's talking in a huddle of men without fallout suits. He sees me and finishes up with them. Then he turns and taps my right arm.

"You ready for this?" Steve asks.

"You want to trade suits?" I ask. "It's going to feel weird not having you protecting me."

He smiles. "Alex, of all the women I ever met, you are the one, who needs the least protection. I probably need protection from you."

We both laugh loudly. I notice from the side of my eye the men are starting to file out of the room.

Steve walks over, picks up my helmet. "I've been standing in the line of fire for Vice President Keller for a long time now," he confesses. He walks back over and offers me my helmet, which I take. Then, he tells me, "Life is finite, Alex. You can try and avoid death with all your might, but it doesn't matter. No matter what you do, one day you will die. How you live is up to you. How you go out is up to you. Remember that and get President Wood out of there safely. I'm hoping we're not going to run into any resistance.

Remember, these guys in here with us now were with Pearson, and they chose to do the right thing. Whatever these agents have going on, hopefully, they will be reasonable too."

I reach up and squeeze his right shoulder. I tilt my head to the side and smile. "It's been a pleasure knowing you, Steven. Watch your ass out there."

"Don't worry about me, Alex ... I'll be fine. I'll see you back here after."

I give him a nod. And he turns and walks out. I stand in the room alone, thinking about everything that's transpired up to this point, and one thing is certain—I can't remember a single operation that was easy. My little voice says this morning there will be war in Riyadh, and it will be hell for all of us brave enough to do the right thing.

Chapter 12

It's been a long time since I was around trigger pullers on a daily basis, but every now and again, I remember some of the lessons they taught me. In my heart, I am forever grateful—not just for their service, but for the way they beat me, mentally, physically, and spiritually. I miss my Xavier Slade. He kept me safe when he didn't have to. They all could've played stupid and been like, "Alex? What Alex? We don't know why she was with us. We thought she was on vacation." He was my boy, and now he's gone because he was trying to serve his country the best way he knew how. It wasn't until the end that he knew it was all a lie, but he didn't have an ounce of regret in his eyes when he told me to kill every last one of these sons of bitches. I owe Slade my life. But I owe Riggs too. Believe it or not—even though I hated the living shit out of that asshole—he hardened me. He told me a distracted soldier is a dead soldier. I believed him then, and I believe him still. Right now, the only thing that's distracting me, is the last thing I ever thought would—my love life.

As I stand in an empty room, watching my new team outside through the window as they load up in the few vehicles that survived the explosion, I realize if I don't talk to Tony now, I won't be able to focus on the mission. I reach back in my bag and fish around for the satellite phone. I radio the team and tell them I will be out in five and offline. I mute them and redial Tony. He doesn't answer at first, so I call back again and again. On the third try, he finally picks up.

"Crane," he answers.

"Tony...."

"Alex."

"I love you too."

"I know," he replies.

"I-"

"Alex...."

We both pause.

"No, you go first," he says.

"You're such a fucking gentleman," I tease, smiling like a little girl.

"Yeah, and you're such a fuckin' lady," he says, chuckling a bit.

"You go first," I say.

"Okay ... Alex, save the President and bring my baby back home safe. Can you do that?"

I stand up straight at attention. "Yes, sir!"

"Then, do that!" Tony exclaims, forcefully.

I pull the phone back away from my ear, and I look at it, smiling. That's all I needed to hear. I hang up and stuff it back in my bag. Then, I walk towards the door with a strut that would make the kings of the 80's movies quiver. I'm certain if Steven Segal, Sylvester Stallone, or the Terminator could see me now, they'd shit in their goddamn Depends. I'm fierce. I'm angry. I'm focused. I kick the door open and step outside. I look over the men, and then stomp towards the lead vehicle—a desert-colored, armored Humvee. A man is standing, holding the passenger door open for me. I walk up, give him a nod, and climb in. He goes around and gets in the driver seat, and I turn my coms back on.

"Daylight's burning, gentlemen!"

A sea of "roger that's" comes over the radio. My driver shifts into gear, guns it out back across the runway, and heads for the exit.

As we rip through the streets of Riyadh at more than 100 miles per hour with only a few feet between each vehicle, I get a call on the sat phone. I mute my suit's coms.

"Southerland," I answer loudly.

"Alex, it's me again."

"Tony, I can't talk right now, I-"

"Alex, shut up and listen ... can you access your Bureau email?"

"Yeah, I think so," I answer.

"I'm sending you information on the Summit, attendees, everyone. Should be helpful. It's in your box. Go get 'em kid." He hangs up.

I immediately access the browser from within my suit and locate the FBI secure portal. I log in and see a new message from Tony in my inbox. I open it, and there's an attachment. The file opens wide right in my face. This holographic display is insane. I scan through the file, and open coms again.

"Gentlemen, the Deputy Crown Prince is already on site with the U.N. Secretary General and President Wood is scheduled to arrive within the hour. Delicate touch," I remind. "Mr. White's plan is still a good one. Bravo team set up the perimeter and clear the area. Chances are the President's motorcade will beat us there, so Alpha team will move in on my command and secure him. Remember, non-lethal force. We do our job and we try not to make a scene. Agent Billings thinks we may not have any trouble, and maybe he's right. If there's no danger, we detain the Secret Service and Saudi police. Take them out to the perimeter. Then, we'll assume responsibility for President Wood's security. Whoever takes the men back to the perimeter, you clear the area and bring Agent Billings back to me. You don't just send him out amidst the wolves, you cover him all the way back to me. He will lead the security detail. I imagine the Prince will be pissed about all this, but we gotta do what we gotta do. Defer him to me. Any questions, cause now's the time?"

"We're all good," Benjamin radios.

"Roger that," I reply, "over."

I get shaken nearly out of my seat as my driver swerves into the left lane to avoid a slower vehicle. I grip the seat and the door to hold my hind parts in place as we fly like a bat out of hell towards the conference center. With 10 American military vehicles balls-out racing down Makkah Al Mukarramah Road, you'd think we'd attract the attention of Saudi police, but we don't. In fact, aside from a few nervous patches of road, we make it off 522 and onto King Abdul Aziz Road unscathed.

We slow down and make our way around traffic. We stop short of the Radisson on Al Qayruwani and step out of the vehicles for a brief huddle. Steve asks for the phone, so I give it to him. He steps away from us and makes a call.

"Looks like it's pretty thick down there," I say. "Any ideas?"

One of the men steps forward. "We push in there with Humvees and we're going to get nowhere fast."

I look around and think for a moment. Steve runs up to me and hands me the phone.

"President is already on site," he says. "He's at the front of the hotel."

I give him a strange look because I'm wondering who the hell he called for that information and why the hell he didn't just tell them we were coming, but I didn't have time for a lesson in Secret Service. We had to act fast.

"You got your credentials?" I ask.

"Yes," Steve replies.

"They may kill us if we walk in there together, me in this big black suit and helmet and all." I hold my helmet up briefly.

"Ma'am, it's a chance we have to take," he replies.

I hand my helmet to the man to my right. "Okay, guys, hold the perimeter here. Close off that street and wait for my command. Agent Billings and I are going in."

Together we walk towards the crowd at the front of the hotel. The property is beautiful, and the building is absolutely stunning—just the way a five-star hotel should be. However, there's no time to take in the awe of its architecture. We need to get to President Wood and this bold walk we are doing with me in all black and a rifle strapped to my ass doesn't seem like the way to go.

We make our way to the back of the crowd and start pushing through to the front past a mix of Saudi and American civilians and the press, who are too busy taking pictures, reporting, and trying to ask questions to notice our presence.

By the time we get to the front of the line, we see President Wood, smiling and waving behind his security detail, which as expected is a mix of more than 60 Secret Service and Saudi police. *Outnumbered my ass!*

"Put your hands up high like this," Steve orders.

I do. "So, since this may be our last breath here Steve, who the hell did you call back there."

Advancing past the press with his hands extended high, he says, "Vice President Keller." Then he starts yelling, alternating between English and Arabic, "HORIZON! AL'UFUQ! HORIZON! AL'UFUQ!"

I stay right on Steve's tail, looking over his shoulders at a host of agitated security folks, who either don't know what's going on or know all too well and are getting ready to engage. We take a few more steps and those, who are not drawing their weapons and aiming at Steve and I, are jumping on the President, trying to pull him inside, but for some reason, he doesn't budge. Wood points at us and says something, but I can't make it out. We freeze in our tracks and I can hear the people behind us panicking. I try to step around Steve to protect him, but he holds me back with his arm and tells me to wait.

Steve shouts, "Horizon! Horizon!" Then, he yells, "Reinhardt! Wolfpack."

The Secret Service Agent in the middle orders everyone to hold their fire, and then he cautiously walks towards us. He stops in front of Steve and offers a handshake.

"Bob Crawford, Secret Service."

"Sir, if it's all the same to you, I prefer to keep my hands up," Steve responds.

Crawford smiles. He drops his hand and casually asks, "How do you know the operation designation for today?"

"Sir, I'm Agent Steven Billings, Secret Service, and-"

"I know who you are," Agent Crawford interrupts, "I don't know why you're here. Why are you here?"

I move to my right ever so slightly, so he can see me.

Steve keeps his hands up high. "I'm ... we're ... FBI Agent Southerland behind me and I are here under orders of President Keller."

Crawford gives him a strange look. "President Keller?"

"Sir, your COMSEC is compromised," Steve tells him. "I have credible intel your security team has been infiltrated by rogue members of our government ... possibly Saudi police as well. They're going to make an attempt on Wood here at the Summit."

Crawford gives Steve an even stranger look. He briefly looks back over his shoulder, and then returns his attention to us.

Steve continues. "You are not in contact with Washington. Your communications are being intercepted by the CIA and I assure you this is true. We don't have much time. I have 50 men establishing a perimeter. You've been completely out of touch with the White House since your wheels were up, and Keller was being detained by CIA Director Pearson. He and Secretary of State, General Clarke, were planning a coup. A team of FBI agents and Navy Seals took their compound in South Dakota and brought Keller safely back to Washington where he invoked the 25th Amendment. You and I are under orders from President Keller now. I need to replace every member of your security team with my men, who are holding a perimeter one block away."

Crawford shakes his head. "This is an incredible story, but ... I'm going to need you two to come with me." He turns and puts his wrist up to his mouth.

"Wait!" Steve yells.

Crawford turns back. "What?"

"Talk to Keller," he suggests.

Crawford holds up a finger and speaks into his radio. Then, he waits a moment. Then, he turns back to us. "Everyone here is authorized, except you, I'm-"

"If you are using your coms, you are not talking to the White House," Steve warns. "Agent Southerland has a sat-phone. You know the number. Use it. Bypass your coms and call the White House. See if they verify what your support team is telling you."

Crawford stares him in the eyes for a moment. "Give me the phone," he orders.

I reach into my bag and retrieve the phone. I slowly slide it up and over Steve's right shoulder. Crawford snatches it from me. I watch from behind Steve as Crawford takes a few steps back and makes a call. I can't hear what he's saying, but he keeps looking up at us after almost every other word. After a few more nail-biting moments, he hangs up and steps right back up to Steve.

Crawford leans forward and says, "Don't move." Then, he radios, "I need Reinhardt back in the limo immediately, I repeat move Reinhardt back to the Presidential limo now!"

I watch as Secret Service rushes President Wood back to the car. Crawford points the phone at us. "Don't move!" he orders again.

Steve and I stay put, nervous as ever as Crawford makes his way over to President Wood's limo. He knocks on the window, and the window goes down a bit. Then, he passes the phone into the car. I see Wood reach out and take it, and then the window goes back up.

With Secret Service agents and Saudi police still drawing down on us, and the only way for us to talk to Keller is locked inside an armored luxury tank, I'm not feeling very positive about our chances here. It seems to take forever for that window to roll back down, but it does, and Wood hands the phone back to Crawford, who talks a little more on it and then finally hangs up. Crawford leans in and says something to the President. Then he backs up and the car window rolls up again. Crawford turns to the security detail and addresses them.

"One block to your north, there are men in armored vehicles." Crawford draws his sidearm. "Drop your weapons, report to the perimeter, and surrender to those agents, or you will be shot!"

Based on his stance, I could tell he meant business, but one man against more than 50 just seemed like he was pushing his luck. Amazingly, they all complied. They put down their weapons and slowly moved past Crawford beyond the other side of Wood's limousine. Crawford storms back over to us. I move to Steve's right, and we both finally put our arms down.

Crawford gives me the phone back. "Send five of your men over to secure the entrance. You two are on me. We'll protect the President inside and when we come back out half of your entire team will move in and help me get the President back to Air Force One."

"So, he's going ahead with the Summit?" I ask.

"Yes ma'am," Crawford replies.

I just give him a blank stare.

"Come with me now," Crawford orders.

I radio the perimeter while Steve and I follow Crawford to the President's limo. "Mr. White...?" I radio.

"Go for White," he replies.

"You got a gang of U.S. Secret Service and Saudi police on their way to the perimeter. Detain them. Then, I need you and four more guards on my position immediately."

"What?"

"Yeah, believe it or not, the President is going to do the Summit anyway."

There is a long pause. "Roger that," White finally radios in a very frustrated tone.

Billings, Crawford, and I reach the Presidential limousine and Crawford opens the back door. He motions for me to get in.

"The President would like a word with you, ma'am," he says.

I detach my rifle and guide it into the limo butt first. Then, I slowly and cautiously climb inside. This car is about as luxurious as the jet we flew in on earlier. The President's seated in the back. He waits and watches every move I make as I get in. I back up and sit on the seat directly across from him, but he pats the seat to his right, gesturing for me to sit beside him. I sigh heavily and stare at the seat ever so briefly. Then, I move over and sit down. As soon as my ass hits the seat, this man grabs my hand and puts it in both of his. He pulls my hand over and rests our hands together on his leg.

"Agent Southerland ... may I call you Alex?" he asks.

I nervously reply, "Yes, please."

"Good," he responds. "Very good. How are you?"

There's no point in me being anything other than honest now. "Nervous and scared out of my mind, Mr. President. I mean, are you going to hang me?"

He lets out the most ridiculous, loud laugh I could ever imagine would come from a president. "Alex, you know what I just sat in this car and did?"

"Sir...? No sir."

"I talked to my friend," he confesses, "my best friend as if there was never any bad blood between us. Because, I'll be honest with you ... I don't know where things went wrong. I tell a lie ... I do know when they went wrong, and it was shortly after I appointed Pearson Director of the CIA. Tell me something, Alex...."

I just sit there, stiff as a board with the President holding my hand. "Sir?"

"How is it that one man ... not 10 or 20 or an entire army, but how can one man cause this much chaos on a global scale. How did it get to this? How'd it get past me?"

"Sir, may I speak freely?" I ask.

He tightens his grip on my hand. "Yes."

"Well, at this point, I'm pretty sure the Saudi Prince is ready to behead me for pulling this stunt, and I'm pretty sure someone is trying to kill you too, so if you are looking for me to give you a goddamn ... I'm sorry, a pity party, you've pulled the wrong person into this limo, and I just as soon get out and-"

"Point well taken, Alex."

"Sorry, sir—okay, I'm really not sorry, but your best buddy Keller entrapped me and put me at risk, and I'm still stewing about that because the only reason he did it is because you two were both acting like a horse's ass-" I turn and look at him. His face is a little red, but not too much, so I just keep at it. "And, now, you want me to tell you how Pearson was able to fuck you and me and him and her and everybody? You dropped the ball Mr. President ... you let the enemy in the front door ... you turned your back on your friend and the only one who seemed to ever have your back and my fucking friends died!" A tear streams down my cheek. "So, if you want to know how it happened ... hubris ... that's how it happened. You were so concerned about being important and forgot about what was important. Me? I never forget. I'll do anything for my friends, and I don't care what they do to me, I love them for who they are and not who I want them to be. Nobody comes between us, not even family members. I just as soon throw 'em off a bridge and keep driving. Bottom line, you fucked us all ... sir ... and it's unforgivable. And it was all unnecessary. If you can't see past slimy sumbitches like Pearson, what are you doing in Washington?" I turn completely to him and snatch my hand away. "Did you know they built another White House under your nose and were kidnapping and torturing people in there? Building goddamn secret nuclear weapons!" I've lost track of my hands, and finally realize I've reared back to punch the President of the United States of America, and as soon as I do realize it, I almost fall off the seat. I drop my fist and cover my mouth with both hands. "Oh my God," I say, my voice muffled by the palms of my hands. "I am soooooo sorry, like I didn't mean to do that-"

"Alex-"

"Oh, Jesus, oh my God, you're gonna-"

"Alex!" President Wood exclaims.

I stop and lower my hands just enough to make a few clear, reasonable excuses for my behavior. "I just ... it's like I'm tired, and I'm sweating in this suit, and I ... I may be hungry too, and-"

"Alex, it's okay," Wood interrupts. "You're right. More than you know, and I needed a wakeup call." He sighs and rubs both hands down his pants leg. "You believe this threat today is credible?" he asks.

I nod.

"Keller told me everything," says Wood. "...about as much as he could, given our short window of opportunity to speak. But he told me about you shooting him...."

I drop my head.

"...and the trial Pearson orchestrated along with all the charges, some of which seem to be appropriate-"

My head automatically pops back up, and I get defensive. "Sir, I-"

"My advisors told Keller to accept the recommendation to sentence you for treason."

My jaw drops. I just shake my head.

"I've asked Keller to grant you a pardon," Wood says. "If we make it out of here alive, we both have a lot of changes to implement. Can I count on you?"

I give him a confused look and grasp the bag across my chest with both hands. "I don't know what to say, Mr. President."

"Say I can count on you," he responds.

"Am I still allowed to speak freely, sir?" I ask.

"Please."

"Then, respectfully sir, you can count on me as long as you don't treat me like your bitch." I tighten the grip on my ammo bag and shrink down in my seat.

"Say again," he says calmly.

I clear my throat a few times. "Sir, Vice President Keller would've gotten more out of me if he didn't come at me cross-eyed and hanging stuff over my head, treating me like his bitch as if I had to do what he said or else. I love my country. I volunteered, and I'll volunteer again and again. I don't need anyone to coerce me into doing anything and besides this is America. We're better than that. We know better. Look at what Pearson did in the dark. Look what we did in the dark. We all made a terrible mess of things. If you want me on board, I'm there, but put me all the way on board and not just have me under the table at your feet." I give him a sheepish expression and then softly say, "And ... I think I've said and done more than one idiot should for two lifetimes, so I'm not going to say any more ... and I feel like I need to say sorry, but ... ... yeah, I'm not going to." I sit tall and put my palms down on my thighs. At this point, I'm really done, possibly more literally than figuratively.

"What you ask ... though, I've never had anyone speak this way to me before ... what you ask of me is reasonable." Wood ruffles his perfectly styled silver hair and sighs heavily. He slowly rolls his head around on his neck a few times and takes in a long deep breath. "Now, I have to ask something of you."

I sit up tall and straight. "Yes, sir?"

"Get me in this Summit, get me a private meeting with the Prince ... and get me back home alive."

"Yes, sir."

I reach over to the door to exit the vehicle.

"Alex...."

I turn back to him.

"Thank you," he says, offering a handshake.

I give him a firm handshake. "Thank you for not hanging me."

He smiles.

"Wait here, Mr. President."

I step out of the limo and look around. Benjamin and four of his men in fallout suits have joined us at the car.

"What's the deal?" Steve asks.

I move in close to Steven and Crawford, and wave off Benjamin, who instantly gets the clue I need some privacy. He moves with his men back a few feet.

"President is not going to do the full Summit, but he wants a private meeting with the Prince," I tell Steve and Agent Crawford. "We get him in safely, we get him out past the perimeter and back to Air Force One ASAP."

"It's been all quiet out here," says Crawford. "I think we're going to be fine, but are you going to be the one to ask for the meeting?"

"You got a better idea?" I ask. "And, don't give me any of that "you're a woman" bullshit."

Crawford looks at Steve and back at me. "Well...."

I cock my head to the side and roll my eyes. I point to the limo. "Keep him safe, I'm going in. Steve I'll radio you if they don't kick me out."

Steve nods and says, "Remember what I shared with you back on the plane?"

I give him two thumbs up, and then I turn and walk towards the front entrance. Inside the extraordinarily immaculate lobby, I spot the Prince with his entourage crowded around him back near the elevators. I walk straight towards the Prince. I don't even get close to him and his people all but jump on me, screaming and yelling. I'm pretty sure his head security guy was about to slap me silly before the Prince intervened.

"Khalass!" Prince Mohammad yells. "Let her through."

I pry both arms away from his men and slowly push my way up to him. I stop a safe distance from the Prince and stand straight, moving my hands behind me and lowering my head a little to avoid eye contact. "Your Royal Highness,

Minister of Defense Mohammad ... on behalf of President Wood, I humbly request an audience with you."

He moves in closer to me. And closer. And then even closer. "Yalla, yalla," he says, waving me into him.

Next thing I know the Prince is touching both my arms, and I feel like I'm going to drop to the floor. My stomach is flipping in all directions. Steve's crash course in Saudi etiquette sure as shit didn't prepare me for anything like this. I don't know what to do, so I just freeze.

"My security forces tell me you and your team of men detonated a bomb in Riyadh," Prince Mohammad says in perfect English.

"Yes, your Highness," I reply, meekly.

"A bomb that would've killed me and everyone in Riyadh, yes?"

I remain still. "Yes, your highness."

"In a land, where a woman cannot drive a car, a woman has saved us all." He pauses a moment. "Only King Salman himself can grant permission for you and your men to be here in Riyadh. And only your President was invited. Our relationship with America is fragile. No matter how your efforts will be interpreted by the King, and despite the fact you may never be acknowledged as a hero, your actions today will be rewarded by me. Now ... how may I repay you?"

I thought carefully. "A private meeting with President Wood ... and safe passage back home."

He lifts my face with his hands and looks into my eyes. "Of all I may grant you, this is all you ask?"

"Yes, you're highness."

He smiles. "Wherever you go, you will be known for your actions and humility. My security forces will accompany you back outside. They will know where to bring your President, and he and I will meet in private now before the Summit." He taps both my arms at the same time, and then squeezes them simultaneously. "As-salaam 'alaykum."

"Wa 'alaykum salaam," I reply.

Prince Mohammad releases me, and I immediately lower my gaze and take several steps backwards. I spin and walk back across the lobby with his security team trailing behind me. When I walk out of the hotel with all his men, Steve and

Crawford look up as if they just knew I'd fucked it all up. *Men are such sexist assholes!*

I walk up to them with my new team of Storm Troopers in tow. I stop and motion for them to get the President out. "We're going in now," I say.

The men behind me form lines on both sides to protect us. President Wood gets out of the limo, and Steve and Crawford, rush him towards the door. I go with them. As we move, Prince Mohammad's security team crowds around us, covering us from all angles. We make it to the door without incident. When we get in, the Prince is standing in the middle of the lobby, arms extended towards the President.

The President and the Prince embrace, and then we all follow them to a private room, where they disappear, and we have the uncomfortable pleasure of standing around looking at one another. Eventually, Steven and Crawford mix and mingle, but I just stay in my "womanly lane" for fear of collecting even more evil stares.

Two hours we stare at that door. I imagine each of us is wondering just what the hell is going on in there. If only I could be a fly on the wall. I'd probably start buzzing and interjecting myself. I think I lack the capacity just to sit around and do nothing, but that's exactly what I'm doing. I'm crouched down with my back against the wall. Steve keeps giving me "looks", so I guess he'd prefer I stand, but I don't give a tinker's damn—I'm tired, and I'm hungry. I wasn't lying to Wood when I said that. I shouldn't have said what I did, but I really wanted to kick his old ass. If it wasn't for his pansy ass playing school yard games with Keller, Vanessa would still be alive. Then again, if Keller hadn't swindled me, I may never have met her.

I think that's the worst thought I could've possibly allowed to creep into my head. And, where the hell is Blondie? Did she die in the blast back there? With all the action, I should be feeling horny and tingly all over, but I got nothing. I'm starting to smell myself again though. The smell is not as bad as when I didn't wash in order to make sure I got pregnant, but it's bad enough for me to want a shower. The hell of it is I left my damn helmet back in the Humvee. I can't take this thing off even if I wanted to. I'm pretty sure we can classify this as another design flaw. What if you lose your helmet? They'll have to cut you out of this thing with the Jaws of Life or something. I start fumbling through my suit's menu and come across an item labeled "Emergency Eject". Foolish me, I tap it. My suit decompresses, spewing air out in all directions like some wrinkly old man farting in front of the TV. All I could do was grab it wherever I could to keep it from falling off.

I jump to my feet and drape my baggy suit up over my breasts in the front. My only saving grace is the suit got caught on the ammo bag I still have draped around my chest because the weight of my guns are dragging this thing straight to the floor.

"Ahem…! Ahem…! Ste … Agent Billings!"

Finally, he turns around and just stares at me. Then, he bursts out laughing. He quickly regains his composure, and rushes over to me.

"What happened?" he asks.

"I don't know," I reply. "It doesn't matter! I need my helmet." I feel like my head is on fire, I'm so embarrassed. All the men are just staring. I try to shift around and hide behind Steve, but he's just not big enough.

Steve looks over his shoulder and back at me.

I lean into him. "I'm going to get a room and take a shower. Can you get my helmet and bring it to me?"

He looks down at his watch. "We'll have to be fast. President may be back out soon."

"I swear I'll be lightning fast," I say, shuffling my feet and moving backwards down the hall.

Steve covers me, literally. I drag myself, baggy suit and all, back to the front desk to the receptionist.

"Welcome to the Radisson Blu Riyadh," he greets.

"I'm with the-"

"Yes, I saw you with the Prince and the U.S. President. You're American?"

I nod. "I am."

He looks over the counter and down at my clown-looking garb. "How may I help you?"

"I need to get cleaned up," I reply. "I need a room."

He immediately starts clicking keys on his computer and wrestling with the mouse. "Prince Mohammad says to take care of you all. I have a suite ready for you." He removes a keycard from the drawer and swipes it through a little machine. "Room 2012." He puts the card down about halfway across the counter. "Is there anything else I can help you with?"

I stare at the card for a moment, wondering how to grab it without my suit falling off and me causing yet another international incident. "Can you push it to me a little more?"

He pushes the card closer to me.

I continue looking at the card. "A little further."

He does.

"A little further."

He moves it until it's hanging off the edge of the desk. I look up at him and I give him a half smile. He smiles back. I inch myself all the way up to the counter and bend over, carefully. I'm holding my suit up with both hands, so I have to grab the card with two fingers. Then, I stick it between my teeth so I can move unrestricted. I nod at the man, and he smiles again. I mumble, "thank you," and scurry off to the elevators.

It takes forever for an elevator to get down to the lobby, and when it does, the door opens and a pile of Saudi businessmen freeze in their tracks, staring at me, half dressed with a room key in my mouth. I do my best to shrink over to the left, and they empty the elevator, moving slower than molasses. *Fucking pervs!* As soon as they're done eye-raping me, I zip into the elevator, press two and start jamming on the button to close the doors. Thankfully, they close before anyone else decides to take a ride with me.

Being in Saudi is a bit crazy. It's like being on the dark side of Beverly Hills. Everything is weird, and what's worse is no matter what you do, you have this constant feeling you don't belong—like you just need to stay out of their way or they will crush you with their boot heels and you will be compelled to thank them for doing so. The culture is so anti-female it's almost sickening. All I want to do is just get cleaned up, get dressed, get my goddamn helmet from Steve, and get back home. Even though I'm a hot mess, I have a good feeling about everything. Far as I can tell, the mission is accomplished. We're totally done here. Bomb is literally dust. President Wood is safe, and I bet he's ready to get back stateside to fuck Pearson up. He's got a good poker face, but even I can tell he's mad as hell, and when we get back, it's gone be some smoke in the city.

Chapter 13

I get off the elevator on the second floor and rush to my room. I open the door and use the latch to keep the door propped open. I'm not sure where Steve is, but hopefully he'll be here soon with my helmet, so I can go from clown suit back to badass ninja.

I drop my suit and shoot straight to the bathroom. We'd been at it so long, and everything had been so intense up to this point, I totally forgot I had to pee, which brings me to another very interesting question. *Can I pee in my suit? Like where does all my sweat go? I mean, if they are designed to withstand Armageddon, I wouldn't be able to remove it or I'd get radiation poisoning, so maybe I should just go in the suit. Yeesh! Now that I think about it, were all those men standing around peeing like dogs?* Suddenly, that whole sexy orgy fantasy I had back at the airfield just went straight to hell.

I plop down on the toilet and pee like never before. *Thank you, Jesus!* I sit there forever and take a deep, long sigh of relief after the very last drop comes out. Then, I start thinking about my life, which is usually never a good thing, but today seems different. Even with all the foolishness going on, things couldn't get any better. I still have sadness in my heart over the losses I've experienced, but I'm forever happy and grateful my family is okay. And Chris taking a bullet for his niece...? We will never hear the end of that war story. I'm not a bible thumping, praying gal, but I actually prayed for them, and I feel like God answered my prayers.

Speaking of bible thumping, Dad was all in. I mean that man knew every word of the bible. He was like Jesus, only the version of Jesus that kicked ass in the temple, turning over tables and smacking the shit outta the scribes and the

Pharisees like, *not in my house, bitch!* If only he was so forceful with Momma, but he was a complete punk when it came her. Like I always say, that good ole sweet black pussy will make you go from roaring lion to punkass kitty in 60 seconds. He was such a good daddy to me. He was a devout religious man and a total badass all at the same time. I loved it. I love him. Everything I do, I tend to think of him. I don't really follow what I know would be his advice, but at least I think about it, and that's gotta count for something.

One of the things that sticks out in my mind is how Dad used to tell us to pray. He would say that most people don't know how to pray at all—they pray for things and money or to get better when they're sick, but that's not what prayer is for. He'd say most people pray to the wrong person too. Here's how he explained it—he said God lost confidence in man when Adam and Eve screwed it all up over an apple, a snake, and a fuck. *Yes, he actually said that.* And, since then, God doesn't listen to man anymore, so if you're praying to God it's like dialing the wrong number and expecting to talk to the right person. When Jesus died on the cross, he opened up a channel of communication, but we have to go through him to get to God. So, he said when you pray, you have to pray to Jesus, and when you do pray, don't ask for anything just honor Him. Just pray and give thanks. He always told me to be useful and kind and thankful and satisfied. He said that's the only way to tap into the power of abundance in your life. I believe him too, now more than ever. I'm trying my best to finally start practicing some of the things he taught me.

I'm in the shower now and giving more thanks in a matter of minutes than I have my entire life. It feels good. I soap up and wash all over and then work some hotel shampoo in my hair. It smells musky and manly, but I don't care. It feels clean, and the hot water is like heaven pounding against my chaffed-up body. That suit is a helluva thing to wear. I usually go and get all my dead skin scraped off by those little Asian ladies down the street from my place, but I don't think I have to this month. This thing is totally rubbing me the wrong way in every direction.

I finish washing my hair and just stand under the shower stream, leaning my hands against the wall and moving my head around under the hot water. I'm thankful Tony is okay as well, and I don't want to seem like a bitch, but even though I totally loved being with him sexually, it was nothing like being with Vanessa. I think I'm still infatuated with her. Just thinking about being with her and … well, the hot water isn't the only thing wet in here right about now.

I wonder how Tony really is, or at least how he will be with me. People change when you finally get with them officially. They court you and be all nice, but then they change. I dunno, I think he's being sincere and will actually go through with it. I'm totally engaged, I guess, but I wonder if he will change once he knows he has me. I wonder how long he's been thinking about sticking his dick in me because he was acting like he wanted to ram-fuck my ass. *Filthy bastard.* I hope that feeling was true though because I cannot deal with boring sex. It will absolutely kill me.

Vanessa was far from boring. After a while, she started talking about BDSM, which is bondage and angry violence and all sorts of other fuckery. I was hesitant to even listen to her talk about it, but I was also shamelessly turned on by it. She'd been into it for years, but the crazy part about it was— even with her Amazonian stature and strong personality— she was a submissive. She wanted me to beat her and punch her and choke her while we were fucking, and I was horrified at first, but it didn't take long for Blondie to give me courage. I swear, just forcing that big woman down on her knees and full on slapping her face 10 times in a row, making her count each strike, brought the goddamn beast out of me. When we stayed with her wicked, psycho gay and lesbian kink buddies, it was hard to contain myself. I would walk Vanessa around with a collar and leash and she'd wear these little numbers that would make a nun's bible spontaneously combust. I don't think I will ever want to be with another woman, but if I could find one who looks just like Vanessa— body and all—and she is a nun—to hell with Tony—I'd break her into sinful submission.

I know it sounds really bad, but I crave hurting someone special in my life now, and it's all Vanessa's fault. I knew the moment I laid eyes on that tramp she would corrupt me, and she did. I loved it too. I love her.

I hear a knock at the door. "Hello...?"

"It's me, Alex," comes Steve's voice into the room.

"I'm just going to lay this here and go," he says. "I'll see you back down there."

"Okay," I yell.

I hear the door shut, and I stop fantasizing about my dead girlfriend and my husband to be. I turn off the shower and reach for a towel. I dry off and step out onto the cold floor. I reach over and wipe some of the fog off the mirror and admire myself for a while. Satisfied, I'm still a foxy bitch, I get to the business of my hair, which must be dealt with immediately. I can't go another minute with my hair pulling my head back because it's getting jammed around in the back of my suit. I look around to see what's available to me, and there's nothing useful in the bathroom, so I go out into the room to check around. The only thing I can find is an old rubber band that looks like Moses himself used it back in the day, but it's all I've got so I make it work.

I stand in front of the big mirror in the room to do my hair. I roll it up in the back, twist it, flip it, and do every other trick I can to get it up in that rubber band to the point where it actually stays on its own. I'm good now on hair, so I go back into the bathroom. There's no deodorant anywhere, but there's lotion, which smells just like a man bought it and some powder on the counter. I smack powder all over my body up in every crevice God saw fit to give me. Then, I rub lotion all over too, trying to stay focused and not get horny, but it's a battle.

I successfully ignore all my uncontrollable urges for once, thank God. Hell, the President is right downstairs, and I don't think it's appropriate for me to be up here trying to stuff a little shampoo bottle in places I'm sure the manufacturer didn't intend. I grab my suit off the floor and drag it into the bathroom. All in all, it's not as wet as I thought it would be. When the helmet is snapped in place it maintains its own air conditioning, but when I walk around without my helmet I sweat like a pig. I grab the blow dryer off the wall and jam it down into my suit. I put it on high and push it down the arms and legs and hold it there to get it as dry as I can before I put it back on. It's awkward trying to hold the suit up and dry it with my guns still attached to both hips. They just keep banging around and hitting my legs, but I'm in a bit of a hurry, so I just keep at it.

A few more minutes, and I'm good to go. I take my suit back into the room and pull it up as best I can. It shrunk a few sizes back down while I was showering, so it was pretty much back to normal, and I was able to snap it back into place enough to get my helmet back on. I pull my helmet over my head being careful not to screw with my little hair bonnet. Thankfully I get it down, just barely. My helmet attaches to my suit and all the light between the bottom of the helmet and the top of my suit disappears. It's pitch black now, and my display boots up. Then, my suit starts squeezing the fucking breath outta me again. Each time I do this it feels like someone is taking my blood pressure all over my entire body. It hurts. *Again, design flaw.*

The discomfort subsides, and I'm able to breathe again now, so I take off my helmet and minimize my display. I put my helmet down on the bed and check my guns. I'm locked, loaded and ready to go. I strap my ammo bag back across my chest and stuff my helmet under my arm. Then, I exit the room and head back towards the elevators.

Back downstairs everything was calm and business as usual. I rejoin Steve and the Saudi crew outside the room President Wood and Prince Mohammad are meeting in. I return to my self-assigned position and continue waiting, hoping the men have a short memory and are not looking at me side-eyed for losing my clothes in public. I'm sure they think I should be trussed up in a burka, but those towel-head bastards can kiss my black ass up, down, and back and fucking forth. I'm not even going to look in their direction.

I check the time more and more as time goes by. Finally, after a little more than two hours, the door opens. I take a few steps towards the men surrounding the door and can just barely see Wood and Mohammad embracing one another. I hope that means it was a good meeting.

As soon as Wood is out the door, Steve and Crawford are on him, and so am I. Steve tells me to take point while he and Crawford cover the President from both sides.

We make our way back out to the lobby, past the front desk and to the glass doors, where we stop to get our game plan together.

"Mr. President, we're going to get you back to the car and to Air Force one," says Steve. "Are you ready?"

Wood tightens both fists and gives him the nod to proceed. I put my helmet on and maximize my tactical display. Then I radio Benjamin to let him know we're coming out.

"Agent White is ready at the car," I tell Steve.

"Good deal, Alex, stay on point, and-"

There's a flash of light, a loud crashing sound and Steve knocks me to my left with the force of a 300-pound linebacker. I barely move a few inches before a cloud of blood impairs my vision. I wipe my helmet with my right glove enough to see the President shocked at the sight of Steve's body dropping to the ground. His entire left side was covered in blood and I couldn't tell whether his arm was still attached or not.

"Get Wood out of here!" Steve yells.

Crawford lunges for Wood, but I hear another blast from behind and this one hits Crawford square in the torso. It knocks him clear across the room. There's so much blood. All I can do is grab Wood, run, and pray. I all but clinch the President into a headlock, pulling him down and breaking left. As we run full speed, more shots are fired inches behind us, literally blowing holes in the furniture. I see the people behind the desk take cover, but I don't look for long because the long gun rounds keep coming. My heart feels like it's about to implode. I get the President around the corner and kick the door in that leads behind the front desk. I push him down.

"Stay put, Mr. President," I yell, bullets zipping past us.

"What are you doing?"

I shake my head. "I can't leave him out there!" I exclaim.

Wood squeezes my forearm. "Be careful," he warns, gravely.

I squeeze his hand and crawl back to the door on my belly. Then, I drag myself up to my feet and look around the corner. The sniper is still firing, trying to hit Steve, who's literally pulling himself with one arm towards me. I stick one foot out, but another shot hits the floor near Steve. Then, another and another.

"Fuck this shit!" I yell. I take off, sprinting to Steve. I do a power slide on the floor like I was running for home base and grab him up with all my might. His left side is so wet and sticky with blood, and I'm afraid I'm further injuring his arm, but I can't stop. I drag, pull, and then push him across the floor as far as I can throw his heavy ass. I'm getting ready to jump back to safety when I feel like I've been hit full swing by a hot iron.

My screen goes dark right about the time where my head rings like a bell and my arm feels like it's on fire. I see daylight through the top of my helmet as the high caliber round spins me down to the ground.

I'm fucked up, and so is my suit. My arm feels numb, but I manage to reach up with both hands and remove my helmet. Bullets are striking the ground, one after the other all around me. This bastard is firing a 50 caliber or something big enough to tear right through this suit. My display flickers and then I get an error message that says the battery has critical failure. Then, my tactical display disappears. In fact, everything stops working except the emergency eject button, which I know better than to push.

I drag myself over to the side, leaving my crippled helmet behind. I don't have my rifle. All I have are my side arms, and my best targeting aid is laying over on the floor with a hole in it.

"Fuck!" I scream. "Steve, are you alright?"

"I don't know," he replies, his voice is weak and low. "I'm losing a lot of blood."

The bullets keep zipping by.

"Hang on buddy, I'm coming to you!" I yell.

"No!" he replies, forcefully. "Stay there goddammit!"

Of course, I plan to ignore him. I back up to the wall, so I can get a good push off, but then I see an arm reach out of the room and around to Steve's leg. It's President Wood, and he's dragging Steve to safety, thank God.

I pull both my guns, keeping my back pressed against the wall. The sniper has no target, but that doesn't stop him from firing rounds into the lobby. I creep to my right and peek around the corner. I look at the President's limo, and it's still in one piece, but our guys are down all five ... wait, only four of them.

"Hey, you back there behind the counter!" I yell.

Everyone yells "yes!"

"Is there another way out of here?" I ask.

"Yes, through the back," comes a voice.

"I'm coming in!" I yell.

I crawl around back behind the counter. Everyone is laying as low as they can. The president is wrapping his tie around what's left of Steve's arm to make a tourniquet. I pull myself all the way in and past them.

"That it?" I ask the man to my right, pointing at the door on the far left.

"Yes!"

I pull my feet up under me and sprint as low as I can back and out the door. There is a long corridor leading to an exit, so I run full speed and kick the door open. I peek around outside, being careful not to stick my head out into a bullet. It's all clear, so I slowly creep outside, periodically looking down at my arm that still feels like it suffered a third-degree burn. That fucker hit me twice—in the arm and my helmet. Thank God the bullet didn't go through my arm, but it sure hurts like hell. I don't have time to worry about a little injury though. Steve is bleeding out, and if I don't shut this sniper down, he's not going to make it.

I get to the edge of the building and look carefully across the street. I can see the muzzle flash from the sniper every time he fires. He's literally across the street on top of a building. I suck in about five deep breaths, and then I take off running. I don't even look up, I just run as fast as my long, slender legs will carry me. It seems like with every other step, I hear a new gunshot, and I hope it is not the end of me.

After a grueling trek across the street, I make it to the building and kick the front door in. I point my guns inside, check the lobby, and move in. The stairs are to my right, so I open the door, and move in slowly.

I can hear shots as I run up several flights of stairs. *Bang!* I take a few steps. *Bang! Bang!* I take more steps. I hear at least one shot per flight. All I can hope is the sniper runs out of ammo by the time I get to the roof.

My legs are burning, and my heart is racing faster than it ever should. My damaged fallout suit is still holding on by a thread, but I can feel it slowly beginning to loosen up.

Finally, I reach the top floor. The shots are coming one after the other, and now I can hear small arms fire too. I push the door open a little, and then a little more. I stick my head out just enough to have a good look at the roof in both directions. I spot the sniper to my right. The door creaks and squeaks, but he's too busy firing what indeed appears to be a 50-caliber sniper rifle. *Jesus!*

I creep out of the door and hold onto it until it closes quietly. Then, I sneak all the way over to the edge of the building. I look over the side. There are so many bodies laid out and only a few moving. One of the men in a fallout suit fires at the sniper but can't get a good shot off. The sniper, who also is wearing a fallout suit returns fire and blasts a hole straight through our guy's torso. The sniper is one of us—a traitor. I can't let another man die. I have to engage.

A few more deep breaths and I take off running full speed. My clever rubber band had failed me, so the wet ends of my hair slap me in my face with every forward. As I near danger, I point both my guns forward and open fire. I yell *MOTHERFUCKER* at the top of my lungs and nail that son of a bitch and his long gun that's poised atop a tripod. I can't be sure, but I think I've put at least 10 rounds in his ammo box and the other 26 in his ass. He doesn't know what's hit him, but he's still standing so I throw down both my empty guns and execute a full-on flying kick dead in his chest. His back hits the wall and he goes down hard. I kick him while he's down, and then I reach down, twist his helmet, and pull it off. I throw the helmet right off the roof, and then proceed to kick him in his skull. I kick and kick and kick and kick and would keep on kicking only this bastard rolls left and sweeps my feet.

As soon as I hit the ground, I shuffle backwards and get back to my feet, but unfortunately so does he. He stands tall and cracks his neck from left to right. Then, he stares me square in the face and I get a good look at his mug. My mouth hits the floor.

"You goddamn, evil, crooked, ass fucking son of a bitch!" I exclaim.

"I can't imagine you addressing your mother with such language, Alex," Mr. White replies.

"Benjamin, you motherfucker! Why! I mean, what the fuck man?"

He puts both his fists up and starts circling. "President Wood should not have met with the Prince," he tells me.

I put my guard up. "Keep talking asshole!"

He smiles. "I'm sorry, Alex, I truly am. You seem like a good woman—a good agent, but it's time for Wood and Keller to go. I have to complete my mission."

I shake my head. "But why all the shenanigans. Why help me shut that bomb down?"

He responds, "We want to shape the future, not destroy it like Wood wants to. He's weak. That bomb should've never made it out. Pearson's a fool, but he is a patriot and his heart was in the right place."

"So now, you're the man?" I nod my head.

"I'm afraid so, Alex. I'm going to kill you ... then, I'm going to kill Wood ... then, I'm going to go home and kill Keller. When we set the record straight and paint the three of you like the traitors you are, they will release General Clarke, he will take office, and I'll be right by his side—a goddamn hero."

I stop moving and plant my feet down on the roof in a fighting stance. "Well come do it, motherfucker!"

White runs full speed at me and swings. I duck and kick him right in the ribs. Sure, he has a suit on, but so do I and suit to suit, it feels like getting hit by a baseball bat. White is big, but I'm fast, so I kick him everywhere I can, but then he hits me with a right and I go down. Asshole almost knocks me out. Obviously, his suit is still functioning because his fist feels like brass knuckles. My vision is blurry, but I can still see his sick ass, walking around me.

"It's time," he says. "I know everything about these suits, and you know one thing they neglected to tell you...? They will stop most low caliber rounds, they really are bulletproof, but knife proof...? Well, not so much." He pulls out his knife and tosses it from hand to hand.

I zoom in on him and watch his hands carefully.

"You're such a beautiful woman," says White, "I wish we had more time together."

"Yeah, so I could stuff your balls up your ass!"

He jumps right down on me. I try and move to my right, but he still manages to stab me in my left side. The blade breaks off and he pulls back the handle of the knife and looks at it for a moment. Before I black out, I can hear him say, "Goodbye Agent Southerland."

Chapter 14

Life's a trip. One minute you're smiling and thinking about pie and the next you are the pie, and someone takes a big bite out of your ass. Speaking of pie, I feel like I'm baking in an oven. My eyes instinctively crack open at first, and then all the way. The sun is so bright it nearly blinds me. I'm not sure how long I've been out, but I'm pretty sure I remember what just happened and I'm wondering why my side doesn't hurt. I'm also wondering why I feel so breezy, but it all starts to come together when I hear the door to the roof exit slam shut.

"GODDAMMIT!" I exclaim as I sit up. I look down and touch my side, which is bleeding but not by much. The knife wound is superficial. Apparently, I didn't die. I guess the mere thought of being stabbed to death was enough to make me pass out. The knife did more damage to my suit than me, and I'm ever so grateful. Problem is that the suit completely died and it's back to clown city. It just looks like a big black tent and there's nothing I can do about it. Amazingly enough, the control center on my wrist is still intact, detached from the suit, and functioning.

"Fucking son of a bitch!" I exclaim, standing to my feet, butt ass naked, holding the control panel and contemplating my next move. I stare at the door for a second, and then down at my feet. "Fuck it!" I take off running to the door, swing it open and peek inside. I wasn't out for long at all. I can hear Agent White running down the stairs, so I tear off after him.

Running downstairs as fast as you can, having been punched out and attacked with a knife, while trying to figure out how to fry somebody in a fallout suit is a lot for a girl to deal with all at once. However, I plan on turning that bitch into a Bloody Mary, so I'm grinning from ear to ear.

I hear the door on the first floor open and then close. I try my best to speed up, but the rugged concrete stairs are hard on my feet. I finally make it downstairs and kick the door open. I jump out into the light and see White in the distance, hightailing it past Wood's limo and to the front of the hotel, so I pursue him.

I run as fast as I can straight to the limo and crouch down beside the driver side back tire of the car. The surface of the limo burns my bare skin, but I ignore it. I put one hand over the screen of the controller to block the sun and keep scanning through menu items. Finally, I see exactly what I'm looking for. I light up White's icon and press execute, but I can't see if it worked or not, and he's already inside. I have to get in there too.

I take off running again straight for the front entrance, which is full of tennis ball sized holes. Not a single pane of glass is intact. The street burns my feet with every step, and my tits are flying all around, clapping together and damn near smacking me in the face, but at this point, who cares? I lean in, shoulder first, and crash through the doors. I zoom right in on White. He has the President down in the middle of the lobby on his knees with his head lowered. He's pointing his gun at the President's head and he's saying something, but I'm not close enough to hear.

I stand up tall, my legs spread wide and yell, "Hey asshole!"

Agent White, President Wood, and everyone else turns and stares at me.

I hold the wrist commander up high and press the kill button. Again, nothing happens. I press it again, and again, and still nothing. I lower it down and yell, "Shit!"

White laughs a hideous laugh. "Oh Alex, you slay me. There's no bomb in my suit. Don't worry, I'll be with you in just a moment." He turns his weapon back to Wood's head and then I hear a shot.

If I didn't see it, I wouldn't believe it, but even if I didn't actually see it happen, White's brains all over the floor is proof enough for me. My pride swells as I stare at Steve, who's still pointing his gun with his good arm at the lifeless body of one Agent Benjamin White. White's done for good, face down on the marble floor next to President Wood, who doesn't have a single scratch on him.

Steve tries to walk, but he stumbles. I run over to him.

"Holy shit man, you're a lefty!" I exclaim, grabbing him under his right arm and wrapping my arm around his waist.

"You're naked again," he replies, his voice even weaker than before.

President Wood jumps to his feet and comes over to help me with Steve. "Let's get you to the car, Agent Billings," he says.

"You got him?" I ask Wood.

"Yes," he replies.

"Keep moving," I say. I let go of Steve and walk over to White's dead body on the floor. I kneel down and place my controller on his chest and press the eject button on his icon. The suit starts to decompress. I sit there and fight with it, tugging and pulling. *What a mess.* His brains are all over the floor. The smell is awful, but I need his dead ass out of this thing. As the suit expands off of him, I pull it completely down and away from his corpse. The hotel staff seems horrified, but I don't care. I'm almost out of this place for good. I get the suit completely off of White and drag it to the door by one leg.

I walk right up beside Wood and Steve.

"Agent Southerland...."

"Yes, Mr. President?"

"...You're naked."

"Y'all keep saying that," I reply, standing tall with my head held high.

I hear footsteps behind and we all instinctively turn to see who's coming. It's a woman ... in a burka ... carrying a burka. I don't know what's wrong with me, but for some reason that qualifies as the strangest thing I've seen all day. The woman runs right up to me bowing and saying something I just don't understand. I speak a few languages, but they just totally miss me with this Arabic shit. The woman repeats herself several times and then holds the burka up. She nods and shakes it at me, and finally it clicks.

"Oh, thank you!" I say, lowering my head.

The woman puts the burka over my head and lowers it down over my naked body. I smile and thank her several more times. She bows again, and backs up, then turns around and retreats, being careful to avoid the mess on the floor.

I turn and look at President Wood. "How about that," I say, smiling.

"Can we go now?" Steve asks, before Wood even has a chance to respond.

"Can you get him to the car?" I ask the President.

"Yes, I've got him," he replies.

"Okay gentlemen, I'm going to step out … provided I don't get shot, I'll open the back door, and then I'm going for the driver seat. You guys get in, and-" I look back over my shoulder. The Prince is approaching along with more of his security forces. I turn around and face him.

Prince Mohammad is waving and pointing, commanding the men around him. He sends two men over to us and they grab Steve. Another man props open the front door. I hear vehicles approaching behind me and I look back over my shoulder. Several armored vehicles come to a screeching halt all around Wood's car. I smile. The Prince is making good on his promise—safe passage home.

One of the Prince's men walks up to us. "These men will help you leave Riyadh safely," he says.

I shake his hand and reply, "Thank you."

Mohammad's men help Wood and Steve into the back of the Presidential limo while I drag my bloody mess of a newly acquired fallout suit to the trunk. We all load up, and I climb into the driver seat. I crank up, and circle out onto the street.

"Wait!" I spin the wheel and pull into the parking lot across the road. Just as I suspected, Mr. White's helmet was still sitting right there down near the front of the building. I stop the car and put it in park. "Hang on a second," I yell back over my shoulder. I hop out in my big black burka and run over to the helmet. I pick it up and take it back to the car with me. I toss it over onto the passenger seat, close the door and put the car back in gear. I pull forward and roll down past the building, where I see body after body. None of our team made it out alive. That bastard White killed every last one of them from his elevated position. They didn't have a chance. They were fish in a barrel. Hopefully the State Department will send a team to investigate, but the way the Saudis do things that could take months. All I can do is concentrate on getting me, Steve, and President Wood back home safe. For now, that's my only mission.

To say today was tragic is a severe understatement. Once again, I've managed to escape death with only a minor cut as a memento. Perhaps it's not so minor though. My side is wet, and it stings something awful. I think I'm going to need stiches. *Focus, Alex. Drive.*

We hightail it towards King Khalid International Airport, our convoy speeding down the highway with the Saudi police vehicles performing a rhythmic, strategic dance of taking the lead and then shuffling back behind us. I guess it's standard procedure. Who knows? All I know is I'm doing all I can to keep up with them. I can't say for sure, but it's a good possibility the Presidential limo took a few rounds. Of course, I am no expert on bullet proof vehicles, but I'm guessing the smoke billowing from under the front of the hood suggest it's more bullet "resistant" than it may actually be bullet proof. Maybe the same Japanese assholes, who made the fallout suits made the President's limo. Those 50-caliber rounds tore through them like a hot knife through butter, God rest those men's souls. If it weren't for their bravery, Wood would be dead in the ground.

I continue driving, playing leapfrog with the Saudi Secret Police, and doing my best not to run into the back of one of them. Something tells me they would not take that too kindly, even if it was by accident. Besides, they are bravely escorting us back to Air Force One, so I guess it makes sense for me to do my best to see through the big cloud of smoke that's effectively serving as the worst visual impairment on planet earth. I use the windshield wipers, but that's a waste of time, so I just sway back and forth, working my vision around the thick, white smoke and hope for the best. Even with the current distraction, all I can think about is that bastard Benjamin White. He murdered those men in cold blood and was going to assassinate President Wood like it was just on his "to do" list. *Asshole!*

It almost seems impossible to believe Pearson and General Clarke could actually try and pull a coup on sovereign American soil. It sounds like something that only happens in the movies or a climactic episode of *24*. I can see Jack Bauer now, kicking terrorists' ass and using his field knife to cut off their toes to make sure he saves the President's life ... then, the President arrests Jack for performing illegal toe surgeries in the process of saving his life. Gotta love prime time television, but it may not be that far from the truth. I pop my eyes back and forth up to the rearview mirror. I can see President Wood in the back, applying pressure to Steve's mangled arm, but just as soon as he's finished playing Nurse Betty, he'll be all over my ass like white on rice on a paper plate in a snowstorm. *What the hell was I thinking going off on the President the way I did? I wonder if they're going to put me back in that replica White House ... that wasn't so bad—good food, nice tapestries—wait, what the hell am I saying. I ain't never going back to jail. I'll fucking defect first. Russia, here I-*
"Oh shit!"

I swerve just in the nick of time to avoid slamming into the vehicle ahead. I bring the Presidential limo to a screeching halt. I turn around and look back at Wood and Steve.

"Stay put," I order.

The President nods.

I jump out of the car and move in to meet a very large Saudi Police officer, who is walking briskly towards me. We stop at the front of the limo. He pauses for a moment and thinks about what to say.

"Uh, the car is very bad," he says, pointing at the hood of President Wood's limo and shaking his head. "We take you in my vehicle?" He nods a few times. "Your President, will be safe, yes?"

I look at the hood of the car. It does look bad. I can smell coolant and oil and something else I cannot readily identify. I see the holes in the top of the hood too. Mr. White put a hurting on the Beast. It may still be running, but just barely, and we have at least 10 more miles to get to the airport. The Saudi is probably right, and there's no time for me to stand here and think it out, so I make a command decision.

I put both hands up and say, "Wait here."

He nods. I do a 180 and run to the back door of the limo on the driver side. I yank the door open and stick my head inside. "Can we move him?" I ask.

President Wood looks over Steve carefully. Steve is weak, and he's lost a ton of blood.

"I don't know if we can," Wood replies. "Why?"

"Your car is toast, sir," I say. I shake my head. "No way we're going to make it to the airport, and there's a possibility more of Mr. White's men are in pursuit. I think we need to dump your car now."

The President stops and thinks about it for a moment. "Okay ... here, grab his legs and-"

"No, wait, sir let me get one of the-"

"No!" Wood exclaims. "He's our man, and we take care of our own."

I don't know what desert bug crawled up his ass back at the hotel, but the old man was giving me mad attitude.

"Sir, I think it would be-"

"Grab his legs!" he yells. "That's an order."

"Yes, sir, Mr. President." I immediately reach down and grab under Steve's legs.

"I can walk," Steve mumbles, trying to pull away from me.

President Wood says softly, "Pride before the fall young man. Let us help you."

Steve replies, "Sir, I'm here to protect you."

"OH, SHUT THE FUCK UP AND GIMMIE YOUR GODDMAN LEGS STEVE!" I yell.

They both look at me with their mouths wide open.

"We don't have time for this shit!" I exclaim. "LEGS! NOW!"

Steve moves his legs over to me and I grab his ankles and start pulling. Wood's old ass and I barely get him out of the car, and thankfully the Saudi police officer runs over and lends a hand. We get Steve up in the vehicle in front of the limo, and the President climbs halfway in, but then he stops and looks back at me.

"We can't leave the car open it's a security risk," he warns.

I look up in the sky and sigh really hard and long. I turn to the police officer and ask, "Grenades?" I make an explosion gesture with my hands, and he gets what I'm asking.

He nods several times. "Come with me," he says.

I follow him to the back of his vehicle. He opens it and has an arsenal back there. I grab a few hand grenades and tell him to move the convoy up a half a click and I'd catch up with him. He radios to his team and runs around and hops in the driver seat. The vehicles speed off, leaving behind a cloud of smoke. I turn around and stare at the President's limo for a moment.

"What a fucking waste," I mumble. Then, I walk to the driver side, open the door, and pull the pin on one grenade. I toss it in the back. Then, I pull the pin on the other grenade, and drop it in the driver seat. Then, I run like fucking hell.

I don't even look back, I just run, following the trail of smoke the vehicles left behind. A few seconds later and the grenades blow—first one and then the other. I can feel the heat from the blast on my back, so I keep running as fast as my long legs will carry me. I get several feet up the road and can't feel the heat on my back anymore, so I slow down and look over my shoulder. The grenades did the trick. That limo's a twisted heap of trash now.

"Awe shit, I blew up the last fallout suit." I pause for a moment, and then shrug. "Eh, probably more trouble than it's worth." I take off running back towards the vehicles. I can see them stopped on the side of the road ahead. Two men are standing on each side with their guns pointed in my direction.

The men start waving and yelling at me. As I get closer, I can hear them telling me to get down, so I take a nosedive, me and my burka straight into the dirt. I realize bullets are zipping all around me and kicking dirt up. I roll over and start crawling backwards. There are two vehicles in front of the blazing fire that used to be President Woods limo and I count at least six men firing at us from a distance.

With me down on the ground, the Saudi police officers return fire. I roll back over to my hands and knees, staying as low as possible, and double time it back to them. One of the men is reloading. I crawl right up to him and draw his side arm. Then, I turn and fire a few rounds back down the street. I can hear their bullets striking the back of the last car in our convoy, but they are not coming close to hitting us.

I run back to the lead vehicle and hop in the back with Wood and Steve. "Driver, we gotta go!" I yell.

The driver stomps on the accelerator and we speed off. I turn around and look through the back. Our two guys have hopped into their vehicles and are firing out the window and the rest of the cars catch up with us. I can't tell what's going on back there, but I can tell those men are in pursuit because our drivers are driving even more aggressive than before.

A few more clicks down the road, and I hear an explosion. We all look back to see what happened, and our worst fear is realized. Out of the smoke comes a vehicle, and it's not one of ours. I check the weapon I took off one of the guys back there. I have 11 rounds left in the clip and one in the chamber. I put the magazine back inside and grip the pistol with both hands.

"Get him down," I tell President Wood.

As uncomfortable as it looks, Wood manages to get Steve down to the floorboard, and he takes cover too. I move over to the right side of the vehicle and wait to see what happens next.

I keep looking back, and it looks like the vehicle can't catch us, but it keeps gradually getting closer and closer, and I keep gripping my pistol tighter and tighter. I don't know about the others, but I don't have much ammo, so I'm running scenario after scenario through my mind on what to do if this bastard gets any closer. "Goddammit," I whisper. They're almost on our bumper. We're moving as fast as we can, but the road is rough, and our driver slows down a little to avoid a slower moving civilian vehicle. That gives the bad guys the window they need to pull right up beside us.

They don't take any time slamming into the side of our vehicle. The jolt skips us over to the left, but our driver has skills and he keeps us on the road. They swerve back over and slam into us again. It looks like they're trying to pull a pit maneuver on us, but they're unsuccessful. The front passenger in our vehicle rolls his window down and sticks his rifle out. He fires off several rounds, but it has little impact. They're vehicle is armored too, and they do what any savvy operator behind the wheel of an armored vehicle would do—they ram us again even harder. This time we spin out of control and come to a stop. Our motor shuts off. The driver tries to start the truck again, but it's not happening. I see the other police officers getting ready to get out and fight. I don't know what the hell my problem is, but I jump right out of the vehicle before they have a chance with my one little handgun.

The men in the other truck are stopped about a hundred feet back. They see me and they exit their vehicles, pointing their weapons and yelling at me. I just stand there, my black burka fluttering around in the hot, dry, dusty wind and my pistol down by my side. The men slowly start moving towards me, but I stay dug in right where I am. They're still yelling, but I'm not saying a word—I just stand and wait. They take a few more steps, and I wait some more. Behind me, I can hear the sound of the starter motor on the truck as our driver desperately tries to get the engine going again. The men take a few more steps towards us, and the one in the front waves his arms left and right. They spread out in both directions.

I continue watching the six of them advance until I hear the sweet sound of our vehicle's motor turning over. And, that's not all. In the distance behind the bad men, I can see two of our trucks barreling down the road towards us.

"Gotcha, bitch!" I yell, simultaneously drawing down on the head honcho and squeezing off two rounds. The little cloud of pink smoke blasting out from his head makes for the prettiest thing I've seen all day.

Before his body hits the ground, our guys in the two oncoming trucks are on them. The assailants turn and immediately get sucked into a vicious firefight. There's nothing in the world sweeter than seeing the bad guys lose.

One by one, they go down. I just stand there and smile, until I hear Wood's voice behind me ruining the fucking moment.

"ALEX, COME ON!" he yells.

I turn and jump back in our truck, which is already rolling a bit. Wood has Steve back up on the rear seat, so I strap myself in and say a quick little prayer. Of course, I never want to lose another man, but whatever happens, I can't lose Steve. I need him in my life, so we've got to get him back to the airfield and stabilize him.

We continue speeding down the highway under bridges and underpasses out of what seemed to have been the dark side of Saudi Arabia into something that more closely resembles reality. I see armored vehicles and police car after police car, parked and lit up at every highway ramp. A few more clicks down the road, and I can see the outline of the ubiquitous Air Force One in the distance. The lines of blue waving down the fuselage blurred by the heat surrounding it bring a smile to my face. There's a unanimous sigh of relief inside our truck. We're so close, it seems I can almost reach out and touch that plane. We're home free. I look back and the only thing I see is two Saudi police vehicles riding so close the driver could be sitting in our back seat for all I know.

King Khalid International Airport is locked down at every turn. We gain access and make our way to Air Force One, which thank God is thick with Secret Service. I look over and Marine One is on the ground too. Why? I don't know, and I don't care. I just want to get the fuck outta Dodge, and I'm willing to bet Steve is too. We can't get out of Riyadh fast enough. Hell, we shouldn't've been here anyway, but let's face it, this isn't the first right thing I've done all wrong, and it won't be the last wrong thing I do right either.

We park near the runway and exit the vehicle. Saudi police secure a perimeter and President Wood and I walk behind two officers, who are kind enough to carry Steve to the plane. Off in the distance, the rest of Wood's motorcade and a ton of other things are being dismantled and loaded up in a military cargo plane. We get close to the steps that lead up to Air Force One and I stop short. The President realizes I'm no longer by his side and he stops and turns around. The Secret Service agents surrounding him stop and turn as well. Wood gives me a strange look.

"I don't think-"

Wood interrupts me. "She rides with me!" he exclaims. Then, he repeats himself. "She rides with me! She doesn't leave my side!"

One Secret Service agent in the bunch steps forward and grabs my arm. "This way ma'am," he says, ushering me towards the President, who spins and hustles up the stairs.

The Secret Service agent rubs up and down and all over my burka, but I don't have anything on me. I left that gun back in the Saudi police truck. Satisfied I'm clean, he nudges, pushes, and shoves me up the stairs. I get to the top and stop on the platform, which looks to have red carpet if you can imagine that. The pilot is standing at the door. I guess I should be excited about going on Air Force One for the first time in my life, but honestly, I don't even want to fly on it. I just want to find some kind of goat herder and sneak off to a boat that will take maybe six months to get back to New York. I stare at the pilot for a moment, and then I look around, peek inside, and step on in.

Onboard, there's more Secret Service and a ton of staff everywhere. My escort moves me to an area that is pretty much empty and asks me to take a seat, so I do. He tells me to put my seatbelt on, so I do, and then he disappears around the corner after telling me someone would be around later to check on me after takeoff.

We were airborne in minutes, and if I'm not mistaken the pilot's got this thing on full throttle. It feels like we are flying vertically, straight up into the sky. Although I'm sitting alone, the plane's busy as hell. I see people running back and forth up and down on both sides. I'm starting to get worried about Steve. I couldn't see where they took him. As soon as we level off, I unbuckle my seatbelt and stand up. I don't know his status, but I can't sit idle for another second without knowing he's okay. I need to talk to Tony too. I'm sure they don't want me wandering around, but I can't just sit and do nothing.

Chapter 15

The plane finally levels off high above the weather, and I see this as my opportunity to go all Batman on Air Force One. I mean, what else is a girl supposed to do when she needs information? So, naturally, I get ready to get my detective on. I count about two seconds after I pop out of my chair before some random Secret Service super-agent is up my ass with a poker.

"It's best if you stay in your seat, ma'am," the agent suggests, strenuously.

I think about how to respond, but since I can't think very fast right now, I do what I do best—I get hood ratchet on him. "Do you think it's best for me to be sitting around smelling like a goat's nut sack in this goddamn thing?" I pull my burka out on both sides with my fingers. "I mean, am I a prisoner on this bus or am I FBI Assistant Special Agent in Charge Denise Alexandria Southerland?"

The agent tries to keep a straight face, but he slips ever so slightly. "Ma'am, I didn't ... I'm sorry, I-"

"Save it!" I snap. "Find me some sweatpants or something so I can get out of this gown, and then I need you to find Secret Service Agent Steven Billings. He's injured. I need to know his status."

"Yes ma'am, but-"

I jam my finger up in the air. "No buts! Just do it!"

"Yes ma'am." He mumbles into his sleeve and then looks back at me. "Come with me please."

I follow him back around the plane to a small room. We walk in together and he opens a bin. He grabs two navy blue sweatshirts with both hands and holds them up one by one in my direction as if he's sizing me. The sweatshirts have the

Presidential Seal on the left side of the chest. They are still in the package.

"Are they men sizes?" I ask.

He studies the packaging closely. "Ma'am, I'm not sure," he admits.

I think about it for a second. Sometimes, I can go for a small, but if they are cut for women, small might be too little. I'd rather not walk around in a tight shirt on Air Force One, looking like the Presidential whore. Besides, Wood is no Bill Clinton. "You have a medium?" I ask.

He puts one shirt back in the bin and then grabs some pants. Then, he spins back around and looks down at my feet, seemingly confused. He places the items down on a chair and then squats down and starts rummaging through a drawer.

"All I have that might fight you are slippers," he says.

I walk over to the chair and tear open the pants. "I'll take them," I say. I pull the pants up under my burka and then, remove the burka.

The agent stands up and turns back around, holding up the slippers. His mouth drops as he instinctively stares at my smut covered big breasts. He's frozen in his tracks, but he doesn't excuse himself, so I don't excuse him either. Hell, thanks to Vanessa I'm quite the exhibitionist these days, and aside from all those unappreciative assholes back on the ground in Riyadh nobody seems to be noticing my figure. I really don't care what anyone thinks—well, actually I do, but what I'm saying is I have the body of a goddess and people should be in awe of it as often as time permits. So, there it is.

I take my time tugging and tearing at the plastic encapsulating the sweatshirt, putting on a very good peep show for the young agent. By the time I finally decided to tear it open, I figured it was high time I dealt with all the grime on me from where I ran naked through a war zone. I drop my sweatshirt down by my side and look at the agent, who's eyes were permanently glued to my nipples. You'd think they hadn't let him home to fuck his wife in six years. Oh, the hard life of a Secret Service Agent.

"I need a wet towel or something," I casually announce.

"If you like, there's a shower you can use," he replies, without looking up.

I snap my fingers up near my face and whistle. "Up here cowboy," I say.

His eyes jump back up to mine.

"I don't want to take a shower," I say, "I just want to wipe off and find Billings. Can you help me?"

He puts both hands up. "Yes." He looks around in all directions. "Wait here." He scurries out of the small room, trying to hide his hard on.

Too bad his suit is all buttoned up. I want to see it.

"Wait, Blondie! What the fuck!" I run my fingers through my hair and shake the dust and junk out of it, and a shell casing actually falls down and hits the floor. I giggle a little, and squat down to grab it. I pick it up between my index finger and thumb, hold it up and just look at it at eye level, thinking *At least it's not a bullet.* It probably flew into my hair when I shot at those guys out on the road. That or when the Saudi Police officers were firing at them from inside our car.

The agent reappears with two small towels in hand and a small package of baby wipes. I look up at him and smile.

"Thank you."

"Yes ma'am," he replies, "one is wet and the other is dry

I smile again this time really big. "Well aren't you helpful?"

"Is there anything else you need ma'am?" he asks. "I will wait outside for you to-"

"No," I interrupt. "I need you to watch me."

"Ma'am?" He nearly jumps out of his Kevlar.

I giggle a little and take the wet towel from him. I start rubbing the black smears of grit off my breasts with it. Slowly, I say, "What I mean to say is I'm not cleared to be on this aircraft." I cup my left breast with my left hand and push it up, rubbing it slowly with the wet towel. "I shouldn't be walking around without an escort, should I?"

"Uh ... well, I...."

I rub my nipple and let out an ever so slight moan. "With all the attacks and security breaches of late, I'd prefer we be as careful ... and thorough as possible." I rub my other breast clean, and wipe around my neck, then between my breasts and down the front of my tummy. "Shouldn't we follow protocol?" I take several steps forward until my fully erect nipples are millimeters from the front of his coat.

"M... Ma... ma'am, I'm ... I have orders to take you to the President, and...."

"And what?"

He whispers, "I'm married, I-"

"Don't flatter yourself," I interrupt. "I just need a dry towel, and I need for you to follow security protocols. Without clearance, you can't leave my side." I smile and reach down for the dry towel. I pull it from his grip and stand looking up into his face for a moment. Then, I sigh heavily and spin around in place so my ass brushes across the front of his pants. *How about that. He was hard after all. Married my ass. Men are full of shit.*

I step back over to the chair completely satisfied I still have it. Married or not, I'm sure if I pulled my pants down and bent over the back of that chair, he would shove his cock in me and ignore an active shooter in plain sight. The President would be shot dead and this fucker would be trying to cum in my ass. Men are so weak. Easy to distract. Easy to fool. Just the thought of being able to so easily manipulate a fully trained federal agent with just a flash of my tits gives Blondie a thirst for power that is unquenchable. If I were a terrorist, I'd be flying this plane to my private island and parking that bitch behind the house. I bet a sitting U.S. President would pull a pretty ransom. *Let me stop before I say some shit like that aloud.*

I lay the wet towel on the back of chair. Then, I rip open the baby wipes and start rubbing them between my thighs and cheeks a lot slower and sensually than I probably should. Satisfied I'm clean enough, I drop the used wipes in the trash and grab the sweatshirt. I pull it down over my head and turn back around to my horny little agent.

"Okay, I'm ready," I say. I move the slippers around in position down on the floor and stick my feet into them. "What's your name?" I ask.

"Greg," he replies.

I shift my weight to the left side and cross my arms. "What's your last name?"

He looks me up and down again a few times. "Price."

"Take me to President Wood, Agent Price," I order, emotionlessly.

He looks completely confused. Then, he straightens up and gets back on the clock. "I'm sorry about-"

"Forget it," I say in the worst tone ever.

He nods, spins, and says, "Follow me, ma'am."

I take off behind him and smile to keep from laughing. Of course, it's all part of our game. Blondie and I make a guy damn near lose his job wanting to bust his load in my pussy and then we act like he is a strange moon rock on the far side of Saturn's rings. We love it, and there's no place that's the wrong place to do it, especially with this young fucking hottie. He's tall and dark—about the only brother I've seen on board, and he looks well built under his starched up black suit. I could see his machine gun poking out a little in the back and that just made my pussy even wetter. I want him to take me right up to the cockpit and plant his cock in my wet little pit while he's wearing only his shoulder rig and that high powered gun—maybe his dress socks and shoes too so he can really dig in and thrust deep. I want to feel the controls bruising my back as he rams me over and over while the pilots watch.

We stop at a door, and he sticks his head in. I hear President Wood tell his caller to hold on a moment.

"Yes?" says Wood.

"Mr. President, I have Agent Southerland here as you requested, sir." He steps to the side to reveal me.

I give Wood a little nod.

"Thank you," Wood says. "Come in Agent Southerland."

I walk in. Agent Price shuts the door behind me. The President is seated at a long table.

"Jim, Mack, our girl is here," says Wood. "I gotta go." He hangs up the phone and turns his attention to me. "Agent Southerland...?"

"Sir?"

"Why did Agent Price look so nervous?" he asks. "I've never seen that before, and he's my youngest, brightest star, so what are you doing to my agents?"

I instinctively cover my mouth with both hands to try and disguise my sadistic laugh, but I'm not sure it's working. I shake my head. "I didn't do anything, sir. He was very helpful. He got me clothes." I run both hands down the front of my sweatshirt. "Very helpful," I repeat.

Wood squints at me and pauses for a moment. "Well, you leave that man alone, he's a good man. Very nice wife, Lori. Three fine kids. Don't be corrupting my agents!" He smiles really big.

"Sir, I'm dirty and my hair is a mess," I say. "I doubt anyone is interested in seeing me like this. I'm actually a little embarrassed."

He smiles again, even bigger this time. "No, you're not."

I smile too and shake my head a little. "No, I'm not," I say slowly.

"You didn't seem one-bit embarrassed standing around stark naked in the middle of a city where women can't show much more than their eyes. I don't know whether to scold you or promote you."

I look around the room a little and then look back at Wood. "Secretary of State seems to be a recently vacated position," I say, jokingly.

President Wood laughs a lot louder than I think he should in response to the thought of me being Secretary of State. "Alex, you are something else," he says, still laughing. He waves his hand at me. "Come on, sit," he says.

"Yes, sir." I walk a few feet down and pull back a chair. I sit down right across from him.

Wood is still chuckling. "Well, I may not be able to promote you, but I can pardon you."

"Sir?"

He gives me a stern look. "Cut the sir shit, you've saved my ass at least three times today. We're beyond sir."

I squint at him. "Mr. President...?" I smile.

"Call me Charlie," he says. "Let me guess ... you want to know about Billings, right?"

I nod.

"My medical team is working to save his arm now," he replies. He takes a long pause. "Steven is a good man. He saved us both today." He shakes his head. "I don't know how extensive the damage was, but it's a good chance his trigger pulling days are over. Whatever he needs, I will make sure he has it—anything at all. As soon as they are done with him, I'll take you right to him. For now, I want you to keep me company. You hungry?" he asks.

"Yes, but...."

Wood leans back in his chair a little. "But?"

"Honestly sir I don't think I can swallow," I reply. "I'm not sure what's wrong. I need to eat, but I don't want to."

"I understand," replies Wood. "So, tell me something ... how did you two make it into Saudi without an invitation from the State Department and get all those boots on the ground with no sponsor ... just what exactly did you do?"

I smile. "It was all Steve. He had a plan to get us in and link up with a CIA operative on the ground. Unfortunately, that man betrayed us. He killed our team members ... men I barely knew, but they put their lives on the line for the mission. It's strange sir-"

"Charlie," he reminds.

I smile again. "Well, it's just strange, Charlie. This guy was loyal to Director Pearson, and he helped me disable a bomb that would've leveled Riyadh. But then he turned right around and murdered all those men, every last one of them. He hurt Steve and he tried to kill you and me. What could drive a man to do that? Someone who's sworn to protect us?"

Charlie sighs. "Compartmentalization, frustration, and chaos can drive a patriot like him to make bad decisions. To think diplomacy has failed. To no longer trust in his Commander in Chief. Jim and I are close, but Pearson and I were far closer. We came up together. I appointed him Director of the CIA. Knowing what I did at that time, if I didn't know better, I would do it again. I thought there was no one else in the world we could all trust more with our intelligence apparatus. I felt he could've easily run for President and won. He told me he didn't want to be a politician. Said he wanted to serve his country not run it. He has a lot to answer for." He rubs his face with both hands and lets out another big sigh. "So, tell me … why'd you do it?"

"Do what…? I have to admit, I'm very uncomfortable talking to you and calling you Charlie, sir."

He chuckles a little. "Just relax, Alex. Why did you become an FBI agent? Was it because your dad was a policeman?"

I look directly into his eyes and smile, uncontrollably. Then, I shake my head a little. "No … I needed a job, and no one would hire me."

"After you came home from serving?"

"Yes. No one was willing to hire me, and I mean no one. I was too proud to ask for help. My dad was already gone. I couldn't go to my mom. A magazine with a lady FBI agent on the cover came in the mail, and I went all in. Turns out, my dad and his friends were pulling strings for me behind the scenes. They sent that magazine to me. I guess to prompt me in the direction they wanted me to go in."

"To help you succeed?" asks Charlie.

I roll my eyes as subtly as possible. "To keep an eye on me I suspect."

Charlie smiles and crosses his arms. "No matter the reason, we are all fortunate you are here. There are going to be some changes in my administration. I think it's inevitable at this point, given all that's transpired. I'd like your help with that."

"Mr. Pres—Charlie, I'm just an FBI Agent."

He chuckles and says, "You are far more than just an FBI Agent, and I intend on using your skills."

"I'm not sure how I can be of use to you, but-"

The door swings open and an airman sticks his head in. "Mr. President, Dr. Crawley would like you to know that Agent Billings is now in recovery."

"Thank you," Charlie replies, "that'll be all." He stands and points to the door. "This way, Alex."

I jump to my feet so fast I lose a slipper. I reach down and slide it back on and follow Charlie out the door and down the hall towards the rear of the plane. The airman leads us back towards a room with several Secret Service agents guarding the door. One steps forward.

"Mr. President," he greets, "Agent Billings is in stable condition. Dr. Crawley is inside waiting to speak with you."

The agent steps aside, and his teammates make a hole for the President.

"Thank you, Mike," Charlie says, touching his arm.

Charlie takes a few steps forward and I try to follow but they block me.

"Please step back, ma'am," Mike warns, extending his arm to prevent me from moving forward.

"Let her through," Charlie yells back over his shoulder.

Mike looks confused. "And, who are you ma'am?"

I frown a little. "FBI Special Agent in Charge, Southerland."

"I apologize ma'am," he replies, "go right in."

Mike drops his arm down by his side and allows me to pass. I enter the room. My Agent Billings is in a chair with his injured arm elevated and his feet propped up. Charlie is standing right beside Stevo, holding his good hand. He's saying something but I'm not close enough to hear.

Charlie stops whispering and looks up at me. "There's our hero now."

I slowly approach them. I smile. "How you feeling Stevo?"

He shakes his head a little.

"That bad, huh?" I giggle.

"I don't have much mobility in my lower arm," he says softly. His speech is a bit slurred, presumably from medication they gave him.

"You saved our asses back there," I say.

The right corner of his mouth shoots up ever so briefly. "Well, I think I've taken my last bullet." He tries to laugh but it doesn't get much past a grin.

I move in closer and touch his leg. "Yeah but it was a gargantuan one."

Charlie smiles and so does Steve as best he can. The doctor enters the room.

"Mr. President...."

Charlie replies, "Hey Doc."

The doctor moves right up to me and reaches for my hand. "I'm Doctor Crawley."

I spring to my feet and shake the hand of the man who saved my Secret Service man. "Alex Southerland," I greet.

He squeezes my hand tighter and leans back a little. "The FBI Agent Southerland?"

I give him an odd smile and ask, "Have we met?"

"No, but I've reviewed your medical file," he says, staring into my eyes. "I find it hard to believe you're still standing after what I saw in your file."

I squint at him. "I don't understand...."

Charlie speaks up, "Let's not talk business in front of the patient."

Crawley looks to his left, still holding my hand and then promptly changes the subject. "Agent Billings, how are you feeling?"

"Not well, doctor," he replies. "My arm hurts pretty bad and my mouth is dry."

Crawley finally lets go of my hand, and I step back out of the way. He leans over Steve and listens to his heart with his stethoscope. "We can make some adjustments to your pain management," he tells Steve. "I'll see what we can put together, but I want to make sure you're keeping as still as possible. We've stopped—wait, are you okay discussing your treatment in front of company?"

"Yes," Steve whispers.

"Okay good," replies Crawley. "We've repaired your artery. Frankly, I don't know how you made it as far as you did with the damage you sustained to your brachial artery, but we repaired it and we have used some plats, screws, pins and other materials to treat your fracture. This was a total fracture and I don't know any other way to say that you have a section missing from your humerus, which is your upper arm bone right here...." He waves his hand up and down near the area of his arm he's referring to. "You also sustained a tear in your distal biceps tendon on this same arm. We were able to reattach the tendon to your bone, but we do not expect you to regain full arm function and strength. Agent Billings, you are lucky to be alive. I want you to follow up with your physician upon return immediately to consider options for further treatment and physical therapy. Do you have any questions?"

"Yes, the pain...?"

"I can give you a combination of oxy and Motrin. You can take the oxy every six hours and the Motrin every four, but I cannot give you refills so it's important you get back home and get to your doctor. I'll send one of my staff back in with your meds." Crawley turns to Charlie and nods. "Mr. President."

"Thank you, Doctor Crawley," Charlie replies.

Crawley turns to me. "Agent Southerland, I imagine we will talk later."

I tilt my head to the side a little. "Nice to meet you, Doctor Crawley."

"After Agent Billings receives his medication, I have to ask you both to leave and let him rest. We don't want our patient getting too excited. My staff will tend to him. I promise he's in good hands."

"Not a problem," Charlie assures. "Thanks again."

Doctor Crawley leaves the room, and Charlie stands up. "You need anything from me, Billings? Anything at all?"

Steve shakes his head.

"Then, we'll leave you to it," says Charlie, motioning for me to head for the door.

I blow Steve a kiss and turn around.

"Alex," comes Steve's weak voice from behind.

I stop in my tracks and turn around.

Steve mouths the words *thank you.*

I smile so big. I run past Charlie over to Steve's good side and kiss his cheek. I see the nurse walk in with a small cup and a bottled water. I kiss Steve again and say, "I'll see you back home."

I leave with Charlie, who is then pulled right into a meeting, so I'm on my own again—the one thing I love and hate the most. When I'm by myself, all I do is think, and it's rarely good because I overthink everything. I sit back down in the same spot I was directed to when I first climbed aboard, and all I can think about is how Steve's career is over. You'd have to be a lizard or an ill-tempered starfish to recover from tissue loss like that. His arm was in a splint and he was all wrapped up, but even I could tell his arm is in bad shape. It may have to be amputated. I can't imagine what it would be like to lose a limb, and I don't ever want to find out.

Chapter 16

I'm not sure if it's the high altitude or the luxurious comfort Air Force one offers, but even after my head finishes taking me for a spin, I fall asleep, and boy do I sleep. I wake up briefly—just long enough to see the decoy Air Force One flying right beside us, and it's back to the sandman for me. I'm lights out and based on how tired I am, I'm probably snoring like an old man with a beer belly. True I only snore when I'm drained but trust me, and the partners I've been with, Homer Simpson could take a lesson.

Hours pass. The flight home seems longer than the flight out. I guess the adrenaline rush is officially over. I get up a few times to use the bathroom and stretch my legs, but I try to rest as much as my mind allows. Charlie talked a good game, but I've heard it all before. No telling what I'll be facing stateside. I take one last stretch break and then settle back into my seat for another long nap. I pull my blanket up to my neck and get comfortable, and then I fall asleep again.

I sleep the rest of the way over. The jolt from touching down on the runway startles me awake. I spring up in my seat and look around. I'm not sure what time it is, but it's definitely morning because sunlight is pouring in from all directions. I move closer to a window to have a look out. Andrews Airfield never looked better. We slowly creep off the runway, and in the distance, I see a huge show of force on the ground. There are armed airmen and Secret Service Counter Assault Team members on every corner, ready to strike. It's good they aren't taking any chances after what went down in The Kingdom.

The pilot brings the plane to a stop and the cabin gets busy again. I stand up and stretch. Before I can get my arms back down, I'm greeted by the same Secret Service Agent, who tried to keep me away from Steve.

"Ma'am, we're on high security," says Mike. "You won't be able to move with the President. He has asked to meet with you, but someone from the White House will reach out to you to setup that meeting. For now, we ask that you wait for the President to deplane, and then one of my colleagues will escort you to security. You'll need to register as a visitor while they arrange transport for you."

"Thank you," I reply.

Mike turns and disappears towards the back of the plane.

Despite my various naps over the course of 18 hours, I still feel tired, so I just sit back down in my seat and wait patiently for someone to come and get me. I rest my head back and close my eyes, hoping to find my safe, peaceful place where I am not haunted by six million "what if" questions.

I'm confident I do my best work when chaos is all about. Want someone to disarm a bomb in the middle of a tornado? I'm your girl. Need someone to perform laser surgery during a plane crash? Look me up. But, when it's quiet—when I can hear myself breathe, I'm just the worst.

I don't have to wait for some dangerous situation for my life to flash before my eyes. My life flashes every day, a constant reminder of what a horrible person I am. If it wasn't for Tony, I'd be dead by now, and I think he really wants to marry me and have a family again—I can tell. But I don't even want to see him. I just want to go to work, settle back in with my team, go home, get drunk, and get some cock or cocks or some good pussy—yes, Alex Southerland knows what good pussy is now, and, newsflash, I love good pussy. The feel of soft flesh on top of me, pushing against me, between my thighs—Jesus I'm wet just thinking about it. Settling down with Tony seems like a death sentence to me now. Having said that, it's all I want to do. *Why can't things be easy for me?*

I've got nothing. I've got no phone, no PDA, nothing, and I ain't mad at all. If I was on the grid, Tony would be blowing me up, and as much as he treated me like a little girl before, I know he's going to be riding me like a rodeo clown now.

I'm not even sure what kind of boyfriend—eh, husband—he is. Is he overbearing? Is he some kind of wife-beating asshole when he drinks? I guess I should know these things, but frankly I don't. Whenever his wife and I talked, I was too busy hating on her to even ask if he was any good at being a husband. Now, I'm wondering why they really broke up. He says it was all about me—he was obsessed with finding me—but that doesn't make sense. It's got to be something else. I may be lined up to marry a modern-day Jack the Ripper, pretending to be a good looking smooth white boy with a black man-sized cock.

I realize most of my adds and takeaways end up equaling cock or pussy at the precise moment the finest airman I've ever seen steps to me. He's pressed from head to toe in his tight little navy-blue uniform. *Isn't that ironic? I say black cock, and BOOM here we go!*

"Agent Southerland...?"

I smile and tilt my head to the side a little. "Yes?"

"Ma'am, if you would come with me please, I can get you access to the base and any resources you need. Do you have any bags?"

I shake my head slowly. "No, it's just me."

His gaze drops down to my slippers for a moment and then back up to eye level. Then, he offers a hand. "This way, ma'am," he says.

I reach out and take his hand. I pull and he pulls me up, but it feels like he's pulling my side off.

"Ouch," I say.

He leans in with his other hand and braces me by the arm. "Are you alright?" he asks.

"I think so," I reply. "I think I may have bruised something."

"I can take you to see the medic," he offers.

I think about it for a second. "No, that's okay. I may just be a little stiff from the flight." I'm not, but there's no way in hell I'm sitting at the nurse's station instead of hanging with this fine ass brotha. I'm finally up on both feet. I exhale and run my hands through my hair in hopes it looks as good as it can all things considered.

"Follow me please," he says, politely.

I walk behind the airman and out of Air Force One. Charlie is long gone from what I can see, but the men with the big guns are still on the ground. We walk down the stairs and I follow him to a jeep parked a few yards away. He leads me to the passenger side and helps me climb up. He's not afraid to put his hands on me either, so either he is extremely helpful, or he is looking for a nice warm place to rest his cock temporarily. I'm hoping it's the latter.

I watch this handsome Air Force boy circle around the front of the jeep, and with every step, his little young ass is making my pussy vibrate. He steps up and sits down in the driver seat. Then, he puts his feet on the brake and clutch, cranks up and shifts into first gear.

"Your seatbelt ma'am?" he says, staring into my eyes.

I smile. "Yes, of course." I take my time and slowly snap my seatbelt in place, glancing back up at him a few times as I wonder how big his cock is, and if he is going to throw me a curve or not, because I haven't had a nice big curve in years. I like to lie on my side and let a man with a curve push in just like that so every time he strokes it makes a left turn and slams right into my g-spot. *This little boy is going to become a man today,* I think, but then I stop dead in my tracks because I'm doing it again. I'm deliberately, willfully trying to fuck things up with Tony because I am running away from commitment. *Wow, I am a horrible person.*

"What's your name?" I ask.

"Jared," he replies.

"Like the diamond store?"

He smiles really big. "Yes ma'am."

"How long you been Air Force?"

"Three years," he replies, proudly. He checks to make sure it's clear, and then he pulls off. "And you?"

"What's that?"

"How long have you been FBI?" he asks.

I shake my head a little. "Too long, but I've been away for a while. I'm looking forward to getting back to work."

"You Army?" he asks.

I frown. "Do I look like someone who would join the Army?"

He laughs loudly. "Yes ma'am, you do."

"No. I was Navy."

Jared nods. "My granddad is a World War II Navy Veteran.

"Good man," I reply, "does he get a headache every time you punch the clock?"

He chuckles. "Oh, you got jokes!"

I smile. "What do you do here?" I ask.

"Tactical Aircraft Maintenance," replies Jared.

"That's a mouthful."

He makes a right, circling us around a building. "It's not too challenging," he confesses. "Besides, when I'm not actually working, I'm driving brass around the base so I-"

"Avoiding KP, huh?"

He stares at me briefly. "How'd you know that?"

I smile really big. "I'm FBI."

He stops right in front of a building. "We're here ma'am. Just go right inside and they will verify your identity and get you sorted. I'll wait here for you to come back out."

I can't help it. This young man is just lighting up all my feminine senses. "You don't have to wait for me," I say. If I need a ride, I will just ask. I'm sure someone can swing by and pick me up."

"I don't mind," he says.

"No, I'll be fine."

"Is there anything else you need me for?" he asks.

I stop Blondie from getting cranked back up again and reply, "No, thank you Jared."

He gives me a nod. "Ma'am."

I climb down out of the jeep a bit slower than normal. All that running, jumping, and kicking in Saudi combined with the long flight was a recipe for disaster. I can't see it all, but the way I feel I know I'm marked up with bruises all over. Vanessa would be proud—dirty, violent slut. I take a few steps and his voice comes from behind.

"Ma'am...?"

I turn back to him. He looks as if he wants to say something but can't quite get his thoughts together.

"I'm sorry," he says, waving his hands around.

"Take your time, Jared," I say.

"Ma'am ... Agent Southerland, I-"

"Alex."

He smiles the sexiest smile ever. His teeth are perfect, and his lips look so tasty to me.

"Alex, I know this is not, because, well, and you see-"

"Spit it out, son!" I say, hoping to encourage him to speak English.

"I'm wondering if I could take you out for a drink...?"

I smile even bigger than before. Then, I quickly stop smiling. "See that wasn't so hard."

"Well, how about it?" he asks.

"No," I shake my head.

"May I ask why not?" he asks politely.

I take a few steps backwards away from his jeep. "Because if you take me out for a drink, I wouldn't want you to wear a condom, and then I wouldn't want you to pull out, and I am insanely fertile."

Good thing he's gripping the steering wheel, because I think that comment could've made him fall out of his jeep. His mouth drops to the ground. His eyes blink fast.

"I ... I honestly don't know how to respond to that," he says.

I tilt my head to the side. "Exactly. Besides, I'm three times your age. Bye Jared." I turn around and walk as fast as my sore ass will carry me. I can hear Jared trying to say something, but I don't give a tinker's damn whatever it is. I have to get the hell away from that boy or else. All I want to do is fuck him like his momma never thought he'd be fucked in his life and get it all on tape so Tony could "accidentally" find it. But I'm not going to do it. I'm going to stop running from the good God sees fit to give me in my life. I'm going to put my big girl panties on and do the honorable thing for once. Tony may have not taken my shotgun wedding proposal seriously, but if he did, then I'm pretty sure I have to as well.

I walk in the building and go to the front desk.

"How may I help you?" asks the woman behind the desk.

"I'm Special Agent Alex Southerland, FBI. I came in with the President on Air Force one. I don't have my ID as I was in the field, but I need a visitor badge and transportation back to New York."

She pushes a small peripheral towards me. "Please place your hand palm down on the fingerprint reader."

I carefully line up my fingers and press the tips down on the green lit glass surface.

"Hold it right there please," she commands.

I stay as still as I can.

"Thank you," she says.

I pull my hand back and watch her as she watches her computer screen.

"Says here your name is Denise...."

"Yes," I reply, "Denise Alexandria Southerland. People call me Alex." I think I almost see her roll her eyes. It was on the sly, and it was subtle, but I'm pretty sure she just gave me attitude.

"Wait one," she says without any personality. She looks up at me and then back at her computer screen. Then, back to me, and then back to her screen. This goes on for at least three minutes.

After a few more moments of silence, she slides a visitor badge across the desk without even looking up at me. I take the badge and clip it to my sweatshirt.

The young lady looks up at me with her yes. "You're asking for military transport to New York...? I can't authorize that, not even for the FBI, so-"

"How about a ride to the airport?" I ask.

She rolls her eyes. "How about a ride to the gate and you take Uber?"

I smile really big. "Have a nice day." I spin and start walking.

"You'll need to surrender that badge to the gate before leaving."

"Bitch," I say clearly and loud enough for her to hear.

I walk back outside and guess who hasn't taken his horny ass on somewhere?

"Ma'am," he says, standing beside his jeep and waving at me.

I walk up to him. "How have you made it this long here? You don't follow orders well at all."

He grins. "I was ordered to drive you around, and I'm not finished doing that job."

I roll my eyes. "Come here." I wave him in with my finger.
Jared takes a few steps forward and leans down.

I whisper in his ear. "Can you hear me?"

"Yes," he replies softly.

"One—you hear me? One drink, and then you take me to the airport, can you do that?"

"Yes, ma'am," he whispers.

He tries to stand back, but I grab his shirt and pull him back down.

"And, I am not fucking you, understand?"

"Yes ma'am," he replies.

"No, I really need you to understand and agree to my terms, Jared."

"I agree."

I let him go and then nod a few times. "So, I can count on you, right?"

"Yes ma'am," he responds.

"Good then," I say, "now, get out of my way cause I don't need you rubbing all up on me to help me in this jeep. I can sit on my fat ass just fine by myself, okay?"

He smiles that perfect smile again. "Ma'am your ass is many things, but fat is not-"

I thrust my right index finger up in the air. "Jared! Drive!"

He laughs a hilariously loud laugh and makes tracks around the jeep to the driver side while I climb up on the passenger seat. We both buckle up, he cranks up, and we're off again."

"Thank you for waiting for me," I say, "although I think you just waited to see if you can get some easy pussy."

"Ma'am, I-"

"Alex!"

"Alex, I don't think anything with you is easy. Besides, I'm a virgin. I'm saving myself for marriage."

I burst out laughing. "The hell you say, are you serious?"

"Well, the way you reacted, I'm not sure I want to say I'm serious, but yes, I am saving myself."

"Fuck me!" I exclaim. "You some kind of wacko bible thumper, dragging me off base to burn me on a cross?"

He laughs harder than ever before. He can't seem to stop laughing. "No ma'am," he finally gets in between laughs. "It's just how my dad raised me."

"Oh my God, I haven't had sex in like forever and I get stuck with the 40-year-old virgin? This is not going to work for me. I am supposed to act like I would never have sex with you, and you are supposed to pull out all your little tricks to convince me otherwise. Just what the hell is wrong with you young people these days? I mean, do you spend all day in your jeep, so your buddies don't kick your ass?"

"You really are Navy, huh?" he says, still laughing.

"Smart ass! Jared, I don't believe you, you do something."

"What do you mean?" he asks.

I make a stroking motion with my right hand. "You jerk it, right?"

"Not as much as you probably think," he replies.

"You never penetrated a woman?" I ask, all up in his personal business.

"No ma'am." He turns a sharp corner and speeds up to beat a slow-moving oversized truck.

"Never fucked her mouth?"

"No."

"Ass?"

He is taken aback. "Uh, no!"

"You gay?"

"Hell no!"

"You eat pussy?"

He got quiet.

"Ooooh, so you're a pussy eater, huh?" I tease.

He seems very distracted now. "I didn't say that," he says, looking over at me.

"Hey, eyes on the road flyboy!"

Jared swerves back onto our side of the road.

"Sorry, about that." He tries to regain his composure.

"Jared, is your cock hard?" I ask.

He rolls his eyes. "Cock?"

"Yes, your cock, your dick, your Johnson, your man meat!"

"Miss Alex can we just change the subject?" he asks.

"Wait, you wanna eat my pussy?"

He doesn't say a word.

"Oh my God, you wanna eat my pussy, Jared?" I ask, loud and ghetto.

"Sssssshhhhhhh! We're at the gate."

I stop trying to see if his cock is hard and I look up. We're next in line at the exit. The security arm goes up and the car in front of us goes through. Jared pulls up and stops.

"I'm taking a civilian off post to the airport," he tells the guard.

The security officer leans over and looks inside the jeep at me. I unclip my visitor badge and intentionally drop it down on the seat.

"Just a moment, officer," I say looking down and spreading my thighs. "I dropped it between my legs. Let me just get it for you." I slowly retrieve the badge and offer it to Jared. "Would you kindly take my badge and give it to the officer?"

Jared tries to keep a straight face. He takes the card and hands it to the officer. Then, he grips the steering wheel as if he cannot get out of this place fast enough.

I just sit and stare at him. He's so cute. The guard finally opens the gate and we drive on through and off the base.

"Where are you taking me?" I ask as we speed down the windy road.

"I have a place in mind," he replies.

"No!" I exclaim. "I don't want to go to some bullshit uniform bar. Stop at a store, buy a six-pack of beer and take me to a park or some random cliff where you take girls to lick."

"Ma'am, I-"

"Alex, and yes the fuck you will or else."

He laughs. "Or else what?"

"I just got out of the field, and I have bruises all over my body. Who's to say you didn't drag me off base just to bust me up."

Jared slams on brakes and pulls over to the side of the road. "Wait are you serious?" he asks.

I pause a few moments. "Nah, I'm just fucking with you about lying on you, but I'm serious about the drinks. Just go in the store, get a couple of beers and find a spot we can get to know each other at."

He nods and starts thinking it all over. His eyes light up, and then he spins the wheel left and makes a U-turn. It's midday, and there's a little traffic, so it doesn't take long for us to get to a store just a few miles away. He pulls into the lot, and there's a big yellow sign with red letters that is right up my alley—it just reads *Liquors*. Whoever made that storefront is clearly my soulmate.

Jared parks the jeep and hops out. He looks at me and says, "I'll be right back don't go anywhere."

I smile and reply, "Just get something good and none of that light bullshit if you get that shit, I will be inconsolable."

He busts out laughing again and takes off jogging towards the front of the liquor store, looking back over his shoulder at me after every few steps. Jared disappears in through the front door, and I lean over to look at myself in the side mirror. I'm a hot damn mess. Boy was Momma right—men will fuck anything. I stick my fingers down between my thighs and hold them up to my nostrils briefly. Thank God I actually wiped myself off back on the plane, but I have zero makeup on and I'm wearing FLOTUS's sweatpants that frankly seem to be two sizes too big. My hair is not done, and this little boy is just giving me all sorts of good attention. But, do you see me asking why? No, you do not. And why do you not see me asking? That's simple. Assholes back in the service always bragged 40 ways from Sunday about fucking a virgin, and I think it's high time I found out what that's like. *Eating pussy only my ass, Jared!*

I run my fingers through my hair on both sides to help it look a little more "normal", but hell I don't care if he don't care. I'm not even wearing lipstick. Just goes to show you the power of women. A man will take a life-threatening chance just to get a chance at some good-good. The biggest, fattest, ugliest woman can get a man to chop his own arm off as long as she promises he can have some pussy after. He'll be sitting there bleeding to death, with his one-armed ass, holding his dick out, hard as a motherfucker, with his one good hand. *So pathetic.*

Jared reappears with a brown bag, hustling to get back to me. He leans in and puts the bag down between our seats. I peek over into the top of the bag as he climbs in. There's a six-pack of Corona in the bag, but I don't complain. They're cheap and go down easy. Should be enough to get my little Blondie pilot lit. I'm tempted to pop one open right now, but I don't have my ID, and no one would believe I'm an FBI Agent with the transgressions I'm about to commit.

"So, where we headed, flyboy?"

Jared replies, "I know a place not too far."

I lean over closer and touch the back of his neck. He shivers a little.

"Okay, so what are we waiting for?" I ask.

He smiles and shifts into reverse. He turns and puts one arm on the back of my seat, looking over his shoulder. He backs up out of that space in record speed, jams the jeep into first and pops the clutch.

Jared drives a few miles down the street and pulls off of the main road onto an unnamed dirt road. We go about a half a mile down south and cross the tree line into the woods. The unpaved road narrows and the trees get thicker as we continue heading south. The morning is nice and warm, and the sun is peaking in ever so slightly from the tall, thick, shadowy trees above. There are bugs everywhere, but I don't care. The smell of the woods is enchanting. I want this boy to show me he can be a man. Slam me down in the dirt. Mess my hair up and fuck me angrily till I cum. I start wondering if he has condoms because I didn't see any down in the bottom of that bag. I think I shouldn't have unprotected sex with an enlisted service man, but then Blondie vetoes that thought right away. Yes, she is back in the driver seat again.

Jared starts to slow down, and I see a small clearing ahead on the right. It looks just big enough to park, and as we draw nearer, it's clear to me we are not exactly pioneers. I see tire tracks, so I imagine he and his buddies have done this before. He brings the jeep to a stop right where I thought he would. He pulls up the handbrake and turns the engine off.

"How's this?" he asks.

I squint at him and frown. "Don't be a dick, jerkoff!" I exclaim, executing my standard "confuse the fuck outta him and then fuck the confusion outta him" protocol. And, boy is Jared confused. He looks like I just stole his basket of kittens and he's ready to boot me out and speed back to the base. I never seen a reaction like this before to my antics, but I think I just crushed his little fragile spirit, so I reel it in a bit. I smile and touch his thigh. "It's fine baby," I assure him.

Jared seems to be breathing again now, and I need to get things sorted to get back home, so there's no point in wasting daylight. I reach between his thighs and grab him. He's hard, but he pushes me away. I squint and frown at him again—this time for good reason, but I just dismiss it and continue my sexual advances.

I scoot my ass to the left and put my arms around him. I target his mouth and lead with my tongue, but as soon as I wet his lips he pulls back and pushes me off. Apparently, my sexual advances are somehow dare I say unwanted.

I move back fully into my seat. "What the fuck man?"

"I'm sorry, I-"

"Don't be sorry!" I exclaim. "Get your cock out. The fuck's wrong with you?"

"Can we just slow down here a little?" he asks.

I reach down and grab a Corona. I position it right on a metal bar near the dashboard and slam my free hand down on the neck to force the cap off. I spill a little, but I don't care. I put the bottle up to my lips and turn it almost vertical up in the air, gulping like a wild, thirsty drunk.

Jared tries to explain himself. "You are an amazing woman, I can see how fine you are, but it's just ... well, it's like I say, I'm committed to-"

I stop gulping for a moment. "You got a girlfriend?"

"Yes, well, no, not anymore we split."

I roll my eyes and continue drinking.

"See, I like you a lot, but-"

I put a finger up in the air and he stops talking. I finish gulping down my beer. Jared tries to talk again, but I wave my finger around and make a noise to suggest he shut the fuck up. I pull my sweatshirt over my head and toss it onto the back seat. I rub my big natural breasts with both hands and watch Jared drool a little, so I know he's not gay. I push my hands down into my sweatpants and start rubbing my clit and fingering my pussy. I take a wet finger and offer it to him. Unlike my tongue he sucks my finger, hungrily, licking all around it to taste every drop of my juices.

I roll my eyes and reach for another beer.

"You taste so-"

"Shhhhhh!" I put my index finger in the air again. Then, I bang open my next Corona. I finger my pussy while I drink and stare at Jared, who is about to find himself walking home if his cock doesn't find its way deep in my hot wet cunt.

I finish my drink, and I'm starting to feel a slight buzz. "You not drinking?" I ask.

"No ma'am, I'm still on duty," he replies.

"And, you're not gonna fuck me?" I ask in a frustrated tone.

He smiles this shit eating grin. "Yeah, about that, I-"

"So, you not gonna drink with me and you're not gonna fuck me, what the fuck you bring me out here for, asshole?"

"I'm sorry, I-"

"Fuck your sorry, boy! Don't say that shit to me. Wasting my goddamn time!"

Jared says something, but I'm too busy opening another beer and blessing his ass out.

"...The fuck kind of gay ass shit is this, you a serial killer or something?" I am completely belligerent now.

"No, I-"

"I-I-I, I DON'T GIVE A FUCK WHAT YOU SAY!" I yell, sitting there topless, getting bit by mosquitos, and knocking back beer after beer. I don't let him get a word in edgewise. "You're a little fucking bitch with a small dick, and I never should've wasted my goddamn motherfucking time on yo ass lil bitch!"

"HEY!" Jared yells, squeezing my left shoulder, his face scrunched up into the angriest little look ever. "You're gonna sit on my face and you're gonna squirt in my mouth and you're gonna shut the heck up about it!"

I wince a little. "You're hurting me."

We both look down at my body—all the bruises.

"I'm sorry," he says.

I start to tear up for reasons completely unknown to me. "It's okay, I whimper. If you want me to do that, I will it's fine, I just-"

"Hush now," he commands. He leans down and kisses my body, placing soft, gentle kisses on my breasts, tummy, and arms everywhere he sees a bruise.

Softly, I touch the top of his head and caress it slowly. His lips feel so good on me—sweet even—not like what I am used to with Tony or even Vanessa. Everyone is always in some raging hurry to fuck me, and this sexy little young man wants to take his time. In fact, he doesn't seem to want to fuck me at all. Strangely, this is turning me on even more.

Jared plants his final kiss just between my breasts where there's an awful blueish odd-shaped bruise right on my chest plate. He looks up into my eyes and says, "I'm sorry for hurting you, that's not what I'm about, but I asked you to do something, and I need you to do that for me now."

I lick my lips and nod slowly. Then, I push my ass up out of the seat and pull my pants down. I slide out of my slippers, stand up, turn around and take hold of the big bar across the top of the jeep. Then, I lift my right leg up and over to straddle him. I bend slightly over with a wide grip on the bar and Jared takes my ass in his hands and guides my pussy right up to his mouth.

Fuck me if this boy's tongue is not almost as long and wide as Vanessa's. No wonder he wants to eat pussy until he's married. With both hands gripping my ass tight, he literally smashes my clit up against his lips and he is doing this thing where he pushes his tongue against my clit and then runs it all the way down into my slit and up into my pussy hole. *Black Jesus, take the wheel!*

I cum right away, and this little fucker is laughing with his tongue up my pussy. I don't say a word, I just keep grinding on his face, harder and harder. As he slides further down and back in his seat, I squat lower and keep his big tongue inside me. It feels almost like a cock the way he is working it so deep, and all I can think about is the look on Tony's sensitive ass face when I tell him how many times Jared made me cum. He'll marry a Smurf before he marries my ass. Now, let me concentrate and count.

"FUCK, JARED, YOU'RE MAKING MOMMY CUM AGAIN!" I exclaim loud enough to scare every woodland creature in earshot. My voice echoes all around us. I feel his tongue on my asshole, and instinctively I turn around, grab the top of the windshield, and push my ass back in his face. I'm trying to suffocate him now with my fat cheeks, bouncing up and down on his face and smothering him with my ass and pussy. Whatever he is mumbling back there, I simply do not give a damn. All I want is him to tongue fuck me harder and harder from behind.

He gets bolder with his tongue-strokes, pushing into my pussy, teasing my clit, and rimming me from behind. Just when I think it can't get any nastier, he actually pushes his tongue inside my asshole. I damn near fucking flip up over the windshield onto the hood it feels so good. Jared grips his arms around my thighs and holds me into place, hungrily, wildly licking and sticking his big tongue in every pleasurable place he can identify. I cum again, and again, and again, blasting my love juices inside and all over his mouth.

Jared stops licking after what felt like an hour of me squirting. I turn around and sit on his lap, facing him. He smiles a toothy grin, my pussy juices glistening all around his mouth. I wrap my arms around his neck and move in for a kiss, but again, he stops me. He moves his head to the side and pulls me into a big tight hug.

"I want to get back with my girlfriend and I want to marry her, so even though we are on a break, I don't want to break our rules," he explains.

"But you tongue fuck my ass and pussy?" I reply softly. "I don't get it."

"Well, you know how some guys on the base cut hair, and some play pool or shoot dice to make extra money...?"

"Uh huh," I reply, still confused.

"Well, this is what I do," he confesses.

"Huh...?"

He clears his throat. "Yeah, I do this for-"

"Money!" I push myself back against the steering wheel.

"Uh-"

"You mean you're a fucking male whore? A goddamn gigolo?" I wait to make sure I understand exactly what he is saying.

"In a matter of speaking, yes," Jared responds.

He pauses for my response, but I just look at him.

"So, my girl knows I do this," he explains, "I mean, she's on base too and she lines women up so we can bring in more money and save up for a house, but I can't have sex with-"

I snap and slap him as hard as I can across the entire surface of his face. His eyes grow big. "Get me out of here, motherfucker! You just fucked this all up. We need to go now!" I climb off of him and start getting dressed.

Jared's tone completely changes. "I'll take you to the airport like I said I would."

"I don't care where you take me as long as you get me the fuck away from your whore ass."

Jared doesn't wait for me to get my top all the way down or even for me to buckle up. He just cranks up and spins us into a U-turn. I literally have to grab onto the dashboard to keep from being ejected from the jeep, which judging from the look on his face is perfectly okay with him.

Chapter 17

After realizing Jared is the worst kind of scum of the earth, I continue mumbling explicit insults just loud enough for him to hear over the roaring engine and the empty beer bottles clanking around on the floorboard. Jared is driving from our illicit rendezvous point back to the main road a lot faster than we came in, and I'm not mad one bit. We exit the dirt road, and I'm beyond pissed.

"I'm sorry," he says, eyes glued to the road.

"Whatever!"

"Really, I should've told you-"

"What! How much I owed you for the hour?" I snap. "Oh, my fucking God, you're a male hooker, that's so fucking gay!"

He frowns and says, "It's not like that. That's not nice, I have friends who are gay, and-"

"Doesn't surprise me, flyboy!" I cross my arms and look out the side of the jeep at the trees we are flying past, loading up more insults on my way to feeling better about myself. "Why don't you just tell me your station ID so I can send you a check, ho?"

"Hey, that's not fair!" he exclaims. "I'm sorry if I messed things up for you."

Jared gets a radio call, asking his location and he tells them he is in route, transporting a Federal Agent to Ronald Reagan National. We ride in silence for a few miles while I calm down and climb off my high horse. Hell, if I had a tongue like that, I'd be making all sorts of money too, and whatever he's charging I'd charge double.

"So, how much?" I ask.

"Come again?" he asks in a confused tone.

"How much money were you trying to rip off of my old ass, and why didn't you just tell me you were pay-to-play from the fucking beginning?"

"Because I didn't want you to pay," he replies, "I just wanted to play with you because I find you very attractive."

"I bet you do this to all the old bitches," I mumble.

"Huh?" He takes his eyes off the road for a quick moment.

"Forget it!" I exclaim. "Just get me to the airport so I can get home."

He nods. "Where you live?"

"None of your fucking business Mr. Prostitute. What the hell was I thinking with my old ass?"

"Please stop saying you're old!" he exclaims.

"Boy, I'm old enough to be your drunken rapist auntie or something."

He bursts out laughing as he merges us onto the interstate.

"Stop laughing!" I yell. "I'm serious. I knew this was too good to be true the moment I saw you trying to push all up on me. Aren't you afraid of getting court-martialed? Going to jail? Hell, I'm an FBI agent, what the fuck man, now I might lose my job for using prostitutes."

"You never shut up, do you?" asks Jared. "You didn't pay for sex, and I didn't ask."

"And, that doesn't make you any less of a goddamn whore now does it?" I shout. I have no plans of letting up on his ass and neither does Blondie. However, after a few more miles of loud wind blowing my hair back and Jared's angry driving, I guess I'm starting to soften up a bit.

"I didn't mean what I said."

He rolls his eyes. "Which part?"

I smile. "About you being a little bitch."

"Thanks, I guess," he replies. "What did I mess up for you?"

"I didn't say you messed anything up, I said you fucked it all up."

He shakes his head a few times. "Okay, what did I "F" up for you?"

"Ain't this some shit, a prostitute that don't curse, that's mighty rich."

Jared lets out a long sigh. "Just forget it. We'll be at the airport soon."

I curl my lips up and roll my eyes. Then, I stare at him for a while. *He's so cute and young and sexy. And, aside from the hooker bit he's nothing like that bastard Bill or that motherfucker Malik, or the host of other assholes who... yeah, but he tricked us into—oh, just stop it, Blondie. He's actually sweet.*

I bow my head and close my eyes to try and pray Blondie away as best I can. No matter the situation, she will find a way to ruin it and turn what could be a good opportunity into some raging, wild, ridiculous dramatic event. Besides, the male whore didn't charge me, so this could be a good situation when I come though Andrews. I just need him to put a condom on his tongue if he gonna be out sticking it in every slut's ass he comes into contact with. *Wait, did I just call myself a slut—bygones.*

"I'm getting married," I shout.

Jared looks over at me for a second. "I don't understand."

"He loves me, but he's a bit of a creep because he was my dad's friend."

Jared looks again. "Still not getting how I messed that up for you."

"I was going to tell him you fucked me."

Jared scratches his head. "So, you don't want to get married."

"No, I do," I reply, "I actually love him—I think."

"So, why would you tell him?"

I shut my eyes for a moment and breathe in deeply, contemplating on whether or not to tell all my business to a strange hooker.

"So, why would you tell him about us?" he repeats.

I instantly get catty again. "Hey, don't fucking rush me, and there ain't no us. Did you get fucked in your ass by your priest? Are you Catholic? Is that why you're a man whore?"

Jared gives me his angry look once more.

"Okay, okay, I'm not sorry, but I think I should say I am, so that's that, but it's just... honestly....?"

He looks at me and makes sure I notice he raises his left eyebrow.

"Okay, so honestly, I'm just an evil bitch, and I... like, I had this really hot girlfriend I was with for a while, and-"

Jared scoffs. "Girlfriend...?"

I frown. "Oh, fuck you, I'm not gay asshole! Just shut the fuck up, I'm trying to tell you something."

"For an FBI Agent, you're not very-"

"Do you want me to tell you or not, smartass?" I ask.

He gestures like he is zipping his lip.

I smack my lips. "So, we did a lot together, and-"

"Your girlfriend?" he asks.

"YES, SHUT THE FUCK UP!" I exclaim. "So, we did a lot together ... sexually, and I learned a lot about myself that started to make sense, and I like to hurt people—like I'm a sadist-"

"Yeah, I didn't notice," Jared retorts.

I gasp. "You're lucky to even have a whiff of this world-class high-grade pussy, boy, now shut the fuck up so I can tell you how you fucked all this up for me, gosh! So, anyway, as I was saying, this guy loves me, and I love him, and so when I thought we were going to die I made him promise to marry me and get me pregnant. Now, don't get me wrong I want that more than anything, but I don't want it, because I ... well, I just know it's going to ... I'm going to fuck it up, so I'd rather just hurt him now so he won't want me anymore than for it to go on for years and then I hurt him really bad ... because I love him. So, you were supposed to fuck me like a man versus licking me like a little bitch—no offense—I mean it was good, but I'm just saying if you weren't a male whore, I could've used the oral to my advantage, but now it just doesn't feel right. I feel like I owe you money and telling him I had a hooker versus I went out and found some hot young man who fucked my lights out wouldn't bruise his ego enough. You follow me?"

Jared is staring straight at the road. He doesn't look in my direction at all. "So, basically you don't think you are good enough to be in a healthy relationship, so you do a bunch of stuff to mess things up, so you never have the opportunity to be normal because deep down you don't want to be normal. Am I right?"

"KISS MY ASS!" I cross my arms and turn to the right, so I don't have to look at him. "The fuck are you Doctor Phil?" I roll my eyes.

"I've been kissing your ass for the last hour," he says, chuckling. "Look, I am not saying I'm a saint because I used to be doing a lot of stuff too, but I got a real nice lady, who believes in me, and don't get me wrong it's hard work, but she works with me, you know. Like, she knows I'm wrong, but she helps make me better. She overlooks a lot of things I do and even supports me in some of the bad. I guess what I'm trying to say is, she loves me for who I am. She takes the bad and the good and she doesn't judge me for the bad, she just takes me. And we all need that 'cause none of us are perfect."

I don't respond right away. "She was like that too. She actually loved all my bad. I think that's what I want with him, but I'm afraid he won't be anything like her. He will want to change me. I know I need to change, but I don't want to, and why the hell am I telling you all this shit, just forget it."

"Maybe because you need to?" he speculates. "And, maybe it's easier to tell someone you may never see again?"

I turn back to him. "Well ... what if I want to see you again...?" I ask in a very sweet tone. "I gotta pay?"

"Oh wow, you just want to abuse me, huh?" He laughs.

I punch his arm while he's driving. "Asshole."

"See you can't help yourself," he says. "Why you gotta be so mean...? You don't even know me."

I smile. "But I could get to know you. I'd like to get to know you. I can be nice."

He bursts out laughing. "Now you're lying to me."

"I don't lie unless I have to!"

He laughs even harder.

"Look, just take a weekend and come see me in New York. I got a beautiful place overlooking the city. We can go out and-"

"And, you want some—how did you say it—cock, right?"

"Uh, yeah, none of this *lick-her-license* bullshit, I need to feel you inside me." I reach over and put my hand on his thigh. I squeeze and rub him, inching my way to his inner thigh.

He grabs my wrist and throws my hand away. "No, I am not going to your place so you can accidentally get caught by your fiancé."

"He's not my fiancé!"

"YES, HE IS!" exclaims Jared.

I think for a second. "Shit, yeah, I guess you're right."

"Should be ashamed of yourself," he scolds.

I nearly hurt my side laughing out loud. "Well if that ain't the pot calling the kettle-"

"Hey, my girl knows what I do," he interrupts, "not like your fiancé."

"So, does she know you took me out to the woods to tongue-fuck my ass and you didn't charge me? A freebie? Does she know that?"

He sits quiet.

"THAT'S WHAT I THOUGHT!" I exclaim. "Look don't get all righteous on me. The day I get chastised by a goddamn prostitute, that'll be the fuckin' day."

He shakes his head. "You are sooooo mean."

I laugh the kind of laugh an evil Disney movie villain would. Jared just looks at me and continues shaking his head. I decide to stop beating him over the head and change the subject.

Another call comes over the radio, asking for our ETA. Jared responds, "About five minutes."

I ask, "You sure you won't get in trouble for being away all this time?"

"No ma'am," he says, casually. "We're just a few miles out."

"Well, thank you for the ride."

Jared replies, "You're welcome."

"...And for the freebie."

Jared repeats, "You're welcome," only a lot slower this time.

I'm pretty sure by now I've worn out my welcome because Jared is not saying much anymore. That or he is just good at oral and bad at small talk. I finally give up and just stare out over the water as Jared increases speed down George

Washington Memorial Parkway. I can see planes taking off and landing in the distance. The airport is literally right around the corner.

We finish the ride in silence. Jared drives onto the airport and pulls right up to the front of the terminal, where I see a man, who looks strikingly like Tony—my Tony.

"FUCK ME!" I say, louder than I'd planned in my head.

I startle Jared. "What?" he asks, looking all around.

"That's my fiancé," I reply, pointing.

Jared laughs and slows down. "You mean the big white guy standing there on the curb?"

It feels like my entire head bursts into flames. I turn and look at Jared like I want to kill him. I grit my teeth and talk through them. "You keep your goddamn mouth shut!" I mumble.

"You ain't even got to worry about me," Jared says in a serious tone. "He look like he just itching to kick a nigga's ass, no offense."

I frown. "I thought you didn't cuss."

"I thought you didn't date big ass angry looking white dudes!" he retorts.

I laugh loudly. "Pull up to him."

"HELL NO!"

"Jared, pull up, don't be a sissy, he's not like that...." I pause for a second. "He's my boss."

"He's your boss too? Oh, hell naw!"

He turns the wheel left as if he's about to make a U-turn, so I grab the wheel.

"STOP IT!" I whisper. "You're making us look suspicious."

"No fuck that, I know that dude," Jared says, softly, "that's the Director of the FBI-"

"Deputy Director," I correct.

"No! Director. I saw him on the news. YOU ARE FUCKING THE DIRECTOR OF THE FBI! YOU GOT TO GET OUT THIS JEEP RIGHT NOW, LADY!"

"Pull up to him, I'm not gonna bust your shit, I swear!"

Jared shakes his head. "I knew I shouldn't've waited for you, man this is bad!"

I continue giggling as Jared slowly creeps up to Tony. I wave at my man and get ready to hop out while the jeep is still moving. I look over my shoulder at Jared, who is all but driving with his head down. Finally, he stops a few feet away from Tony. Tony steps down off the curb, and I jump out of the jeep and into his arms. I kiss him, and he kisses me and squeezes me like I haven't been squeezed in a long time. I instantly start feeling bad again.

"What are you doing here?" I ask, kissing him slowly and passionately. "God, I missed you baby."

He kisses me back several times. "I spoke to President Wood, and the guys at Andrews told me you were coming, so I just wanted to be here for you."

I nearly throw up in the back of my throat. He's already starting with this nice farm boy bullshit. "Ahem, Tony, I'd like you to meet Jared, who was kind enough to give me a ride." I turn and smile at Jared. As dark as he is, he's turning white right before our eyes.

Tony steps forward and reaches across the passenger seat of the jeep for a handshake. "Thank you, Jared. You've been a great help today."

Jared nods. He manages to look Tony in the eyes towards the end of the handshake, and replies, "Just doing my duty, sir."

"Thank you," Tony repeats, releasing Jared's hand and stepping back up onto the curb with me.

Jared looks up at me one last time, nods a little, and then burns rubber to get away from us. I don't blame him either. Tony looks like one bad ass motherfucker today in his suit and tie and his little shades. His shoes are on point too. *Since when did he start dressing up like this? And, who are the two goons standing in the background with earpieces? Tony's got security now? Okay, this is seriously turning me on.*

Tony looks me up and down. "I like your slippers," he says, sarcastically.

I smile so big. "Ass." I punch him a few times in the arm, and ask, "Director? Seriously?"

He smiles back and nods with a hint of pride that's impossible to miss. He seems very satisfied with himself.

"Apparently saving a damsel in distress actually works," he jokes.

"Oh my God, you're such a fucking ass!" I laugh and kiss him again. "Can we go now?"

Tony rolls his eyes. "And, you're still a demanding little-"

I jam my finger up in his face. "Don't say it, or you will not be getting any pussy tonight!"

Tony looks back to his guys and nods. They instantly start moving.

"This way, Mrs. Crane," Tony says.

I twist my lips up so hard. "Yeah we gotta talk about that."

"We have a lot to talk about," Tony warns.

I give him a strange look. "What?"

"Later," he replies.

"Hey, don't do that to me, I been through way too much to be-"

"Alex, what did I say before?"

I sigh and roll my eyes. "Fine, I trust you. Lead the way."

I follow Tony and his newly acquired goons through the terminal and out the other side of the airport. I have no clue who these guys are. I guess I have been out of the office for way too long. I can't wait to just sit my butt down at my desk again and breathe in the bad air and germs that come with a government office. The building is old, and there's this air conditioning vent right over the far side of my desk that continuously drips oil or dust bunnies—you name it—right on all my stuff. It's disgusting, but I miss it.

We walk to the other side if the airport and out through a hangar. Outside, I see an FBI helicopter perched on a yellow line on the ground. Tony has really moved up. I mean, they are letting him use a helicopter to go pick his "wife-like" associate up? Yes, that's what I'm calling it at this point—"wife-like" associate. To be honest, if I'm not pregnant, the deal is off because he didn't keep his part of the bargain. Personally, I just hope he says he doesn't want to go through with it. I blew my wad with that asshole Jared figuratively and literally. I may do many things, but I don't lie ... well, I don't lie about cheating. If I cheat and have an actual fling, that's worth something. I can fuck up a relationship really good with that but getting ate out by a hooker just doesn't really feel the same to me—it's like kissing a strange girl at a club. That doesn't incite enough jealousy in a confident man like Tony, and I think that's the only way I will get rid of him based on how he keeps looking at me. I need him to catch me right in the act with some big, burly, harry ass black man with a huge cock, resting his balls on my chin.

The big guy leading us walks around to the other side of the helicopter, opens the door, and climbs in next to the pilot while the other agent holds the back door open for me. I climb up and scoot over to the other side. I lock my seatbelt in place. Tony climbs in and sits beside me. The other man shuts the door and waves. Tony gives him a nod and the pilot starts the chopper.

"Here, put these on," Tony says, handing me a pair of headphones.

I put mine on, and he puts his on too.

"He's not coming with us?" I ask, pointing at the man walking backwards away from the plane with his head down.

Tony shakes his head. "He'll meet us back in New York." He smiles really big and reaches over. He touches my hand and then grips it tightly.

I stare into his eyes for a moment. "You okay?" I ask.

"I should be asking you that," he replies. "I'm glad you're back safe. I … … it's good to have you back."

"It's good to be back, sir" I reply.

He smiles again. "You lost weight, or those sweats are too big."

I frown. I'm about to offer a snappy, witty yet bitchy comeback, but a voice over the radio interrupts me. I listen for a second, but I don't really care what they're talking about. I can tell it's all work stuff. Tony immediately gives the agent his attention, which is fine by me. I just tune them out and look out my window down at the busy runway as we take off.

The hour and a half it takes for us to get to New York is chock full of Tony running his damn mouth. In all our years together, I never realized just how much he can talk, but he is getting on my nerves. Nothing, and I mean nothing short of a giant octopus attacking the White House deserves more than 30 minutes in my opinion. Just say what the fuck you gotta say and get off, but no, not Tony. He's yammering like a little schoolgirl. Now that I think about it, I think I'm doing that thing I said I wouldn't do—trampling on any chances I have at happiness. I always try and go for quiet time to sort things out in my head, but all this noise up here is distracting—maybe in a good way. I can see what Blondie is doing, being so annoyed with everything Tony does, but I'm not going to let her win this time.

I look at Tony, reach over, touch his hand, and smile. He turns and looks at me. He smiles and squeezes my hand. He gives me that nod he gives people when he's all satisfied with himself, and instead of me conjuring up some negativity in my mind, I close my eyes, shut that crafty bitch, Blondie, out of my head and mouth the words *I love you. Now you can shove that up your ass, Blondie.* I feel satisfied as if I have one-upped her—at least a little while. Time will tell.

I've been away from New York for far too long. Twenty-six Federal Plaza never looked so sweet. I don't think I've ever seen it from this high up—at least I never actually paid it any attention. The Federal Police vehicles parked down out-front look like little marshmallows from up here. A helicopter lease is definitely on my wish list now. Hopefully these assholes were smart enough to unfreeze my assets—that is if Pearson actually was able to freeze them at all. He could have been lying about that too. I can't wait to see him jammed up in a tiny box.

We head right for the helipad atop the Jacob K. Javits building. As the pilot hovers over the rooftop, I feel a surge of excitement rush through my body. *Almost home,* I think.

Chapter 18

The chopper finally comes to rest on the roof of the FBI building and the pilot switches the engine off. *New York, home sweet home, I missed you so.* Tony ends his business call and motions for me to hop out, so I do. I follow him and the mysterious agent into the building. Tony vouches for me, since I don't have my credentials, and after the guard reluctantly lets me in, we head down the stairs. We pop out on the top floor and snake our way around to Tony's new office, which is the biggest I've ever seen in a government building. He has a brief sidebar conversation with the agent walking with us, who then immediately takes off. I can't see where he goes, nor do I really care. I'm fixated on Tony and doing my best to be a good girl for once in my life.

I wait patiently for him to talk to his assistant, and finally, he opens the door to his office and waves me in.

I walk inside Tony's office and look around. He hustles over to his desk and sits down, sliding his smart card into his laptop and unlocking it.

"Have a seat, Alex", Tony says, clicking away on his keyboard.

I mosey on over to his desk and sit down in the guest chair on the right. I sit back deep in the chair and put my hands together, interlacing my fingers.

Tony checks his email and his voice messages. Then, he checks his phones, and finally, he turns to me. He smiles really big. "Are you alright?" he asks.

I maintain eye contact and nod.

Tony keeps smiling. "You eat?"

I shake my head. "I'm not hungry."

"You get a chance to get cleaned up?" he asks.

I nod again.

He nods too. "Good ... good. Listen, I brought some of your things from the house."

My eyebrows shoot up. "What house?"

"Your apartment," he replies. Tony points over to the other side of the room.

I look over my shoulder and see a small bag on top of his conference table. "Thank you, baby."

"You're welcome," he replies, slowly. "You wanna get changed?"

I nod again.

"If you want, you can go in the bathroom," he says, pointing to the other side of his massive office.

I smile. "No, I'm okay." I stand up and walk over to the conference table. I unzip the bag and stretch it open. Inside he has me a pair of my black cargo pants, a polo shirt, socks, boots the whole nine. I'm glad too because these cheap house slippers are pretty much done for. I dump the bag out on the table. Then, I sit down to undress. I pull my sweatshirt over my head and look over at Tony, who's still seated at his desk, but is intently staring at my boobs.

"You said we had a lot to talk about," I say, kicking my government issued slippers off. "What did you mean—wait, is that my stuff?" I spring up out of the chair. "That my stuff from my office?"

Tony stands up. "Uh, yeah...."

I give him a strange look. "Well, why is it in here? And, where's my badge? My credentials?"

"Alex-"

"What's going on, Tony?"

He lets out the biggest sigh ever. "Alex, we-"

"Don't Alex me, Tony, what the hell is going on?"

"Just calm down, Alex, I need to-"

"FUCK CALM!" I exclaim, topless and tits out, standing wide-legged in the middle of his office with my hands on my hips. "WHERE'S MY SHIT, DIRECTOR?"

"How about a little respect?" he replies, sharply.

I start rolling my neck. "HOW 'BOUT YOU GET MY GODDAMN CREDENTIALS, AND-"

"ALEX, YOU'RE DONE WITH THE BUREAU!" he yells, his face now beet red.

My mouth drops open. "I... I... I-"

"Listen to me, let me explain. You-"

I throw My right slipper at him. Tony ducks and it flies over his head. I want to stomp over and pulverize his goddamn ass.

"YOU FIRED ME...?" I speculate. "YOU GODDAMN, BACKSTABBING, CRACKA-ASS-MOTHERFUCKER!"

I spin and continue getting dressed as fast as I can. Tony is trying to talk some ole bullshit to me, but I ain't listening.

"THE FUCK IS MY BRA?" I yell. "YOU CAN'T PACK ME A FUCKING BRA, BUT YOU CAN FIRE MY GODDAMN BLACK ASS, YOU HATEFUL ASS SON OF A BITCH!"

I continue cursing for the better part of the next few minutes. I'm fully dressed now, and I've called Tony every horrible name in the book.

Tony just stands there behind his desk with both hands palms down on top of it. His head is hung down low. He looks up at me and says, "Alex, can we please talk about this at home?"

"WHAT FUCKING HOME YOU KEEP TALKING ABOUT, TONY? FBI DIRECTOR!"

"Your apartment," he replies, clearly frustrated with me. "You told me to move into the apartment, so I did and got it ready for us to-"

"US...? SHUT UP! JUST SHUT YOUR FUCKING MOUTH! DON'T YOU SAY A GODDAMN NOTHER WORD TO ME!" I walk up to him and angrily point my finger right at his face. "You stay the fuck away from me, or I will put you in a goddamn hole."

Tony's mouth drops open and his chin damn near hits the floor.

I mean mug him, and then walk slowly all the way to the door while he shakes his head in disgust. I open the door wide. I stare him down a little more, and make sure he's looking right at me. I flip him a bird high in the air and yell, *FUCK YOU* really slow for dramatic effect. Then, I slam the door and walk across the floor. I'm headed towards the elevators, and I feel like I'm going to throw up, but I suck it in and press on. I probably shouldn't be walking around without at least a visitor's badge, but no one seems to give a shit, so neither do I. I don't recognize anyone, and my team is obviously somewhere else in the building because I just walked past where we used to sit, and no one is there. This is a nightmare. A lot may have changed, but the elevators are still in the same place. I push the down button and wait impatiently for the doors to open.

Just as expected, Tony comes stomping around the corner. "Alex, hang on a second."

I shoot him a bird, and he starts walking faster. I all but beat the down elevator button, hoping it will hurry things up because Tony is getting closer by the second.

"Alex, let me talk to you for a moment," he says from midway down the hall, still hustling to get to me.

Tony's legs are swifter than I remember because he is almost on me, but then I hear an electronic voice from behind say, "floor 41 going down." I turn and see the circle above the elevator on the other side light up red. The doors crack open. I turn to Tony, smile, give him a double middle finger up before darting into the elevator.

"COME ON, ALEX!" he yells.

I hide over near the elevator buttons. I hear Tony's footsteps still coming, so I start jamming on the button to close the doors. Tony looks mad as hell. My heart races and I can't help but smile. *He is angry and coming after me. I keep this up, embarrassing him in his precious Bureau, and he will be done with me for real. Fuck this marriage shit!* I skip backwards and press my back against the rear of the elevator, holding on to the rails with both hands. One more step and he can stop the doors from closing, but it's too late. The doors shut and the elevator goes down.

I instantly get bold again. Cracking my neck and stretching my arms. "Motherfucker fired me!" I pace around as the elevator continues to descend. "Can't believe this fucking shit!"

I get downstairs and bolt outside to hail a cab. A yellow taxi pulls right up to the curb next to me. I fling the back door open and crawl in. I slam the door shut and tell the cabbie to take me to the financial district just in time to see Tony running out of the building like a love-struck puppy. I take the liberty of shooting him another bird as we pull off. He stands there with both hands up shaking his head.

"Goodbye and good riddance," I say under my breath.

"Trying to get away from your boyfriend?" asks the cab driver.

"FUCK OFF!"

"Jeez lady," he replies. "Was just joking."

I stare up into his review mirror. "Do I look like I'm joking?"

"Lady, you fuckin' look mad as hell."

"OH SHIT!" I exclaim.

"What? What'd I say?"

"You gotta stop the cab," I say.

"Why?"

"I don't have my purse or anything. I-"

"Nothing...?"

I shake my head. "I'm sorry, just let me out."

"I bet you wish you'd been nicer to me now, huh?" He laughs loudly. "Look, I'm about done on my shift, so where is it you're trying to get to?"

"55 Wall Street."

"You live over there?" he asks.

I nod. "I used to," I say softly.

"Look, it's none of my business, but if you live over on Wall Street you can do better than a cop."

I squint and cock my head to the side a little. "What' makes you think he's a cop?"

"That asshole's got cop written all over him," he replies. "Look at his shoes ... who wears those shoes? A fuckin' cop, that's who."

"Yeah, well maybe I like cops. Are you gonna stop or not? I have no cash on me."

"Maybe you like cab drivers?" He laughs again.

"OKAY, STOP THE CAR, I'LL WALK!"

He continues laughing and driving. "Relax lady, I got you. I got a few charity bones in my body. This one's on me."

"I'm not a fuckin charity case!"

"You wanna get home or not?" he asks.

I smile. "Fine...! Thank you," I say softly.

"Don't worry about it," he replies. "What's your name?"

"Alex."

"Alex, I'm Tony," he replies, making a sharp left turn.

"Oh, Jesus are you fucking kidding me?"

Tony looks back over his shoulder for a moment. "Whuh, you don't like cabbies? You don't like the name Tony either?"

"That's my boyfriend."

He bursts out laughing louder than ever before. "I guess it's just your lucky fucking day huh, Alex?"

I settle back into the grimy backseat and reply, "I guess so, Tony. I haven't been home in years."

"Why so long?" he asks.

I chuckle a little. "I was in jail."

Tony laughs uncontrollably and asks, "Ya boyfriend do that to you?"

I roll my eyes. "Hardly! Some asshole, another asshole, and a bunch of other assholes lied on me and did a bunch of general asshole shit. Took a lot for me to get righteous again."

"And your cop boyfriend...? Was he there for you?" he asks.

"You're a real nosey fucker, aren't you? Is this fucking Taxicab Confessions or something?"

Tony laughs so hard that he spits all over the windshield. "You're some kind of crazy, lady," he says, still laughing and coughing. "I need a girl like you in my life. My old lady is like-"

"HEY BE NICE!" I exclaim.

He laughs again. "Well it's like everything I say is a broken kite and that shit just ain't gone fly, ya know what I'm sayin'?" He continues laughing.

"Yeah but are you a nice guy or are you a fuckin' asshole, Tony, 'cause it sounds to me like you can be a real fuckin' asshole."

He stops laughing and takes a long pause. Then he starts laughing again. "Yeah, well it takes one to know one. Yeah, I'm a fucking asshole dammit this is New York. She's from the south ya know, Florida. Talks ... real ... slow ... like ... this, and I'm like spit it out I ain't got all day." Tony turns around and looks hard right, then he jumps a lane over.

"So, you love this woman?" I ask.

"Yeah, I fucking love when she has dinner on when I get home, yah know what I'm sayin!" He laughs his loud annoying laugh once again.

"Yeah, you're a fuckin' asshole man. She's gonna throw some hot grits in your face one day!"

He waves his right hand up in front of the rearview mirror. "Yeah and fuck me with this grit shit. Who the fuck eats grits? She wants grits. I don't eat that shit!"

I laugh now. "Okay man that's where I draw the line, I'm from Atlanta and that's how we get down! Nothing wrong with a bowl of cheese grits with some freshly cracked black pepper!"

"Oh, that's how come you're taking up for her," he says. "You're not a real New Yorker!"

"Fuck you, I'm straight outta Brooklyn!" I exclaim.

"BROOKLYN MY ASS!" he yells, "Fuckin' Wall Street rich country girl, you need another boyfriend or somethin'?"

I burst out laughing and snorting. "You're a dirty ole bastard, aren't you? You made me snort!"

Tony pulls the car over to the curb. "Well, we're here," he says, turning right and putting his arm up on the back of the seat.

I smile at him. "Thank you. Give me a second to run up and get some money."

"Alex, fuck that," he replies. "You ain't no Brooklyn, but you're good people to me. I ain't worried. Meter wasn't even running. I'm going home, baby!"

I smile again and touch a kiss to the security glass between us. "Thank you, Tony, the taxicab confession host."

"Just ask for me next time you call in a cab, okay? I'm usually working all day in this area."

"You got it, man." I hop out, close the door, and wave, but he pulls off so fast, he doesn't even notice. *New Yorkers.* I look up at my building and just stare for a moment. It's been so long since I been home. Feels good. Smells good. Smells like New York. I take two steps and then I hear tires screeching behind me. I turn around, and I see Tony—my Tony—stepping out the back of an all-black SUV with tinted windows.

"NO, NO, NO!" I exclaim, backing up.

Tony shuts the back door and pulls his coat together. He looks at me, and I bolt inside. With all I've been through, I just can't. I run as fast as my legs can carry me. A man I don't know opens the door and tries to greet me, but I fly right past him and up to the front desk.

"Where's Ralph?" I ask frantically.

"I'm sorry, ma'am, but he's no longer with us," he replies. "He … he had a heart attack, and-"

"Nooooo!" I shake my head. "No, no, no!" I look and see Tony at the door talking to the doorman. I turn back to the man at the desk and check his name tag. "Okay, Noah? Noah, I'm-"

"Miss Southerland."

I pause and raise an eyebrow. "Yes, whatever, listen are my car keys down here?"

"Yes, Mr. Crane had all your cars valeted. I can bring one around for you if you-"

"Just give me the keys!"

Noah points to the left. "Go right down there and ask for Gary. He'll get you sorted. Hey, Mr. Crane, welcome back."

I freeze in my tracks.

"Noah," comes Tony's voice from behind. "Good to see you … Alex, you just took off without letting me explain. Can I please just talk to you for a moment?" he asks softly.

I can feel him, breathing down my neck, so I don't even turn around. I sprint away from the desk and head for Gary.

Around the corner, I'm shouting, "GARY…? GARY…? ANYBODY KNOW GARY?"

Finally, a young man speaks up. "Ms. Southerland, I'm Gary. How may I-"

"KEYS! NOW!" I yell. I can't stand in one place. I am off the deep end, running like a little girl from Daddy. *What the hell is wrong with me?* I wonder, but I just wanna get the fuck away from Tony's stalking ass. I hear footsteps behind me as Gary's flipping through my keys inside this box on the wall. I see the DBS keys and yell, "Aston Martin, now!"

Gary takes the key off the hook and holds it up. "I can pull it-"

"Just give me the fucking key!" I yell, snatching it from his hand. Then, I make a run for the parking garage.

"Alex this is ridiculous!" exclaims Tony from behind. "Would you ... just stop for a second, please!"

I shoot him another bird and run straight to my car. I have this vision in my head of me spitting in Tony's face as I peel out of the parking garage. I aim my remote at the car and press *unlock*, but nothing happens. I press it again, and again, and again, and still nothing happens, so I jam the key into the lock on the driver side and fling open the door. I hop in, slam the door right in Tony's face, and lock it. He knocks on the window, but I give less than a shit. I shoot him yet another bird, mash the clutch to the floor and press the start button. Unfortunately, nothing happens, and I mean nothing. *These assholes didn't keep my battery charged! It's dead as hell, just like how I feel about Tony.* He keeps knocking on my window, but he can knock until his knuckles wear off because I ain't opening this door. *Fuck that backstabbing little bitch!*

Chapter 19

Tony might be just as stubborn as I am. More than an hour has passed, and this idiot is still at my car door. The air is getting thin in here, and I'm sweating like a pig, but I'm still trying to wait his ass out. I keep shaking my head and trying to figure out if this is Blondie again messing up a good thing, or if I really am mad as hell. *Guess what? I really am mad as hell. Way I see it, Tony took away everything from me. That job was all I had left, and he didn't fight for me, I know it. I don't care what comes out of his lying ass mouth. I know he didn't stand up for me one fucking bit. Jesus, it's getting hot in here. I can't stay in here much longer.* I tug at the neck of my top and try to slow my breathing, but it doesn't seem to be helping. This car is sealed at every corner, and without power, it would seem there's no getting oxygen in here.

Tony stands outside my door with his arms crossed. I wait a few more minutes, and finally I give in. I slowly crack open my door and then kick it open with my left leg, hoping it smashes right into Tony and leaves him dead on the ground, but he's far too crafty for that to happen. He steps back and the door swings in front of him. He reaches up with his left hand and braces the door to keep it from bouncing at the hinge and shutting again.

With my head tilted down and sweat dripping off every corner of my body, I swing around and plant both feet on the ground. Tony tries to talk, but I stick my finger up in the air and he promptly shuts up. I put my elbows on my knees and palm my face with both hands. Then, I pull my sweaty hair back and look in Tony's eyes. "I don't want to talk to you. If you say one word, I swear to God, Tony, on my daddy

I will do everything I can to take your gun away from you and kill you with it."

Tony gasps as if he is taking me seriously, but I imagine he is just patronizing me. He better not press his luck because I am dead fucking serious.

I grab the car door and drag myself up. Tony acts like he wants to help me out of the car, but he is smart enough to keep his hands to himself. I get to my feet and shake my hair out of my eyes. Then, I point my finger in his face and say, "Take me to the Four Seasons, and don't say a goddamn, motherfucking word to me or I swear to God I will end your trifflin' ass. Nod if you understand?"

Tony nods.

I take a few steps to my left and he shuts my car door. Then, he turns halfway to his right and gestures for me to go.

"I DON'T WALK IN FRONT OF BACKSTABBERS!" I exclaim. "Lead the way, asshole!"

Tony shakes his head in silence. Then, he walks away and heads back to the lobby. I follow him, but I keep my distance. I don't want to hear his voice. I don't even want to smell his cologne. I want to hit his ass with a brick. Lucky for him, there are none loose in this parking deck or he would be leaking cranial fluid.

The men in the lobby try to speak to us but Tony and I blow them off and keep stepping. I follow Tony right out the front door and down to his SUV still parked on the curb running. An agent hops out of the front driver side door, circles around, and opens the back-passenger door for us. Tony walks up to the back and turns to me. I stop dead in my tracks and shake my head.

"No, you get in first," I order, pointing inside the vehicle.

Tony rolls his eyes, but then he climbs in and scoots over. I walk up to the agent holding the door.

"And who the fuck you supposed to be?" I ask rudely.

"Ma'am, I-"

"OH, PUT A SOCK IN IT!" I exclaim holding my palm up to his face. "I don't wanna hear your shit either." I plop down on the back seat and the agent shuts the door. I scoot over to my side as far as I can against the car door. I don't want to be anywhere near either of those motherfuckers.

The driver gets in and puts the truck in gear. "Where to, sir?" he asks.

"Four Seasons," Tony replies.

"Yes, sir." The agent looks left, and then pulls off from the curb.

The further down the road we get, the angrier I become. "So, what, it's you, Wood, and Keller now. Bunch of peas in a pod? I know too much, so you fire me and you wanna take me out now, huh?"

Tony leans over a little and says, "Alex, I am trying to-"

"DON'T YOU DARE FUCKING TOUCH ME, TONY! You better watch your fucking back around me. A shit ton of assholes have tried to kill me, and I'm still fucking here, so if you bastards are coming you better bring a motherfucking army—A WHOLE GODDAMN PLATOON! You drop me off and I better not ever see you at my place or in my rearview or I'm gonna put two in your chest." I turn left and look him square in his eyes. "Now, tell me I'm bullshittin'!"

Tony opens his mouth to say something, but then he doesn't. He just shakes his head. "I can't talk to you when you are like this, Alex."

"Like what?" I ask.

"Like this," he replies.

"Oh, like I can't see through your bullshit, you showing up, stalking me and shit everywhere I fucking go. You firing my blackass? Huh?"

"Alex, I didn't-"

"DON'T YOU FUCKIN' DARE!" I scream so loud I startle our driver.

"Everything okay back there?" he asks.

I shoot him a bird. "Oh, shut the fuck up and drive!"

"ALEX!" Tony shakes his head and closes his eyes for a second as if I am just wearing every ounce of patience out of him. "We're fine," Tony tells the agent.

"No, we're not fucking fine," I mumble. "Hey up front, how close are we?"

The man clears his throat. "We're about 15 or 20 minutes away."

"If I had known this, I would've not even gone home!" I say, my attitude getting worse by the moment. "You better get your shit out of my place, or it's gonna get put out in the fucking street."

"Okay, Alex, that's'-"

"SAY ONE MO' GODDAMN WORD TO ME! I FUCKING DARE YOU, TONY! I FUCKING DARE YOU! KEEP MY GODDAMN NAME OUT YO' MOTHERFUCKING MOUTH FROM THIS MOMENT FORWARD UNTIL ONE OF US IS DEAD IN THE GROUND, YOU GOT ME?"

He doesn't respond. His phone buzzes. He checks it and starts texting.

"Fucking right. Check your shit, and don't say shit else to me."

Disappointingly, Tony complies. He doesn't say another word. In fact, the three of us ride in silence the rest of the way. I almost feel like crying because he didn't fight me how Bill used to. Tony got right back to work as if I didn't mean a thing to him. I guess that's how he could fire me so easily. All these years I thought he was the one really looking out for me, and as soon as he fucks me, he throws me away like garbage. Tony is no different than all the rest. They get what they want, and then they shake me to the left.

In my heart of hearts, I know they are going to try and kill me. The things I know, I could take all of those bastards down. But they better be coming with the hand of God. I'm not going down without a fight. I don't know what has happened with Vanessa's stuff, but from what she told me her suite is paid up for years to come and that place was stocked with the three things I need most right now—liquor, weed, and guns—lots of guns. Even if I can't access her suite, I don't give a shit. I will fuck a bell hop and get a room and some cash to get back out and find Tony's ass, and—*wait— what am I saying? And, we're at the hotel. Did I really just spend 20 minutes plotting on Tony's life in the depths of my mind? It feels wrong for some reason, but my little voice says I should go to war, and my little voice is rarely wrong.*

The agent pulls up to the front and stops the vehicle. I unlock my back door and jump up out of the car, slamming the door as hard as I can. I walk for the entrance and hear Tony's voice behind me.

"Alex ... Alex ... ALEX!" he yells.

I violently turn around. "WHAT!"

Tony is standing with the back door of the truck open and he has one of my clutches in his hand. "HERE!" he shouts, waving it towards me.

I stomp back over, cursing and yelling, "YOU COULD'VE GIVEN ME THIS SHIT BACK AT THE APARTMENT YOU GODDAMN CRAFTY BASTARD!" I snatch it from his hand and open it. Inside I find my ID, credit cards, a check book, cash, everything I need to stay the fuck away from his ass.

"FUCK YOU! DIE SLOW!" I swing my leg back and roundhouse kick the door right into his face. The blow damn near knocks him out, and blood gushes out of his nose.

"GOD DAMN YOU, ALEX!" he exclaims, tilting his head back and pinching the bridge of his nose.

The agent up front yells "Sir!" He swings open his door and puts his hand on his gun.

"STAND DOWN!" Tony yells before the agent can dismount the vehicle.

"OH MY GOD, TONY!" I yell.

"STAND DOWN!" Tony repeats, waving at the agent.

The agent reluctantly complies and sits back down on the driver seat. Then, he turns almost all the way around and monitors us through the window.

"It's okay," Tony assures him, calmly.

I kneel down, drop my clutch on the ground, and then put both hands on Tony's face, using my thumbs to check his nose. I'm crying now. "I'm sorry, I didn't mean to do that, oh my God, I'm so sorry, baby!"

Tony's nice bright white shirt and fancy grey tie looks more like a maxi pad at this point, and I am trying to use the end of my top to stop the blood from flowing.

"Ouch!" he exclaims. "Alex, wait, hang on." He reaches into his inner jacket pocket and pulls out a hanky.

"I'm so sorry!" I repeat.

Tony balls up the hanky and presses it up to his nostrils. He nods. "I'm okay, it's not broken."

I'm still sobbing. "Well, just ... fuck you ... and everything and like whatever." I bend over slowly and pick up my clutch up off the ground. I try and straighten my clothes, but my shirt is sticky at the bottom from Tony's blood. I frown and hang my head down low. I take a few steps back and apologize one more time. Then, I run into the lobby. I don't look back—I just run from the man I love once again, for the last time.

Chapter 20

I'm sitting here, pondering what love really is. Over the years, I've developed quite a few ideas on the subject, and I wanted to love someone, anyone, so badly. In fact, I've said the words *I love you* more times than I care to admit, but did I mean it? I don't think so. Even if I did, I'm certain I didn't want to mean it. Only a few people have really seen through my bullshit. Truth is I know how to simulate love and make other people feel loved, but I'm rotten down to the core. There's nothing good about me. I know this because I assume the worst in others right off the bat. Yet, here again, I'm sitting here, completely naked, on my dead ex-girlfriend's bed, and even though I'm thinking about what love is, I feel like I'm far more concerned about why Vanessa isn't here making me feel good. She used to make me feel like a queen, but I wonder if I made her feel good too. I dunno. I hope so. Actually, I wonder if I make anyone feel good? I just don't know.

It's funny—not only did the people down at the front desk know me when I arrived, they had some high-level dude sit me down. I don't know if he is an attorney or not, but he had all this paperwork to give me. Evidently, Vanessa left me everything—me, as in Alex! Sole access to her suite until the prepayment runs out, her money, cars, clothes, shoes, jewelry—I mean everything. And, do I need this stuff? No, and she knew I didn't. Back when we were together, I had access to all my money. I wasn't a criminal, so she knew a bitch was rich, but she left it all for me anyway. Is that love? Maybe so. It's hard to tell.

Speaking of criminals, I guess I can strike that off my list of attributes. President Wood actually pardoned me just like he said he would. I have immunity from federal prosecution from any and all acts prior to me stepping foot on U.S. soil again. I talked to my family too. They're just fine down in Atlanta. They're waiting for me to come visit them. I guess they love me too. No matter what, everyone seems to know how to love—everyone but me. I want to blame it all on Blondie, but that's not being intellectually honest. There's a big part of me that wants to be a failure at love. I can't figure it out, but whatever it is it's keeping me from being happy.

It's been more than a few months since I last saw Tony. He calls every day without fail, but that's not why I agreed to meet him today. Something's going on with me, and I'm not sure if I should share it or even how. Either way, this is one secret I can't keep to myself.

I know Tony loves me because he treats me like Vanessa and my little brother and ... and Daddy, but I'm afraid I don't know how to do that. I feel like Daddy taught me how to protect myself a little too well. It's like I don't know how to open up to anyone, and the only one who cracked my shell open wide enough to get in was Vanessa, but she's gone now.

Everywhere I look around this hotel suite reminds me of Vanessa, which sounds stupid, because it's all her stuff, but it doesn't make it any less worth mentioning. It all smells and feels like her. I don't want to wear her clothes anymore because I don't want to have them and not have her. I can't be alone anymore either though. I think somewhere between strong black woman and getting my ass beat 40 ways from Sunday, my heart has grown softer, and I need to feel the way I did with her again.

It was stupid of me not to listen to Tony. I should've given him a chance to explain why he fired me. It was silly to think he would hurt me. I know that now. He's on his way over today, and I want to look nice for him, but I can't. I haven't left this room since I checked in, and I can't even stomach wearing one of Vanessa's silk robes that I used to lounge around in every chance I got. I hope it's not too late for me. People around me probably think I'm bipolar, but I'm not. It's just when I get an idea in my head—especially if it potentially involves someone fucking me over—I roll with it no matter what. I can no longer do that if I want to be happy again. The phone rings, and I answer.

"Hello?"

"Ms. Southerland," comes a voice.

"Yes, Judy?"

"You have a visitor in the lobby."

I pause for a moment. I know who it is, but I ask anyway. "Who is it?"

"A Mr. Crane," Judy replies.

I take a deep breath. "Send him up, the door is open."

"Yes, ma'am."

I hang up and start fidgeting. I feel like I need to get dressed, but I can't move. Every second it seems like I hear the door open, and I want to jump up, run to it, and wrap my arms around him, but that's not a good idea. Last time I saw Tony I threatened to kill him and damn near broke his nose. When I called him last night, he didn't sound happy to hear from me, so maybe he's moved on. I feel like a cheap slut, sitting here butt ass naked, but I don't want him to see me in my ex's clothes. It just doesn't make sense to me no matter how I look at it.

Finally, I hear the door open. Then, I hear footsteps.

"Alex...?" comes a voice.

"I'm in here," I say, my voice cracking. "I'm in here, Tony."

Slowly, he creeps into my room. He looks right at me, and acts like nothing in the world is wrong. He walks over and sits on the edge of the bed and turns to me. He smiles a very handsome smile, sitting there in his dark suit with his smart card badge hung around his neck.

"You're handsome," I say.

"You're beautiful as always," he replies. "...and very naked."

I smile a toothy grin. "I'm not trying to seduce you, I just-"

He holds up his hand and I shut up for once. "Alex, you always do the talking. Let me do the talking for once, okay?"

I nod slowly. I'm sitting Indian style and suddenly all the slut in me disappears. My cheeks feel flushed and I realize I am actually embarrassed. I should've put something on. I slowly try to pull the covers up, but Tony puts his hand down to stop me. I smile in sheer embarrassment because I don't know what else to do.

"Too late for that now," he says softly. "Just relax, Alex, okay?"

I nod again. I can't stop smiling. I'm such an idiot.

"Good. Listen, Alex, I didn't fire you."

I part my lips, but Tony is quick on the draw today.

"Wait!" he exclaims.

I sigh and give him the respect I rarely do.

"President Wood and I have been working closely together on a number of efforts, including yours. Your return presented so many complications I don't want to even get into, but the President decided you could do more good in service to him the way Vice President Keller set you up. You are Navy ... you're an officer. You're not eligible for reinstatement at the FBI without a discharge. He won't allow the Secretary of the Navy to release you back to me despite my best arguments, and I have been arguing with him for a while now. You wanted your FBI credentials, but I could not legally give them back to you. Here...." Tony pulls a folded envelope out of his inner jacket pocket and lays it on the bed. "This is your security clearance letter and all your DOD credentials."

I take one look at the envelope and exclaim, "One second!" I tumble, crawling over the bed, and then I fell off onto the floor headfirst.

"Oh shoot, Alex...?"

"I'M FINE!" I shout, high tailing it to the bathroom. I run inside and slam the door shut and drop to my knees, trying to pull my hair back before it all comes flying out. I get my hair up just in the nick of time, and then I spend what feels like 10 whole minutes puking up the breakfast I was sure would stay down this time.

Tony knocks on the bathroom door, but I tell him I'm fine and ask him to give me a few minutes. I take my time and steady myself. Then I brush my teeth and rinse with mouthwash. I'm sweating from all the heaving, but I try to pull myself together. I slowly walk back over to the bed and sit back in the same spot. I clear my throat. "Ahem, you were saying?"

Tony shakes his head. "Hangover? Alex, you have got to stop all the heavy drinking. It's just not good for you."

I roll my eyes at Tony, but I don't say anything. I pick my envelope up off the bed, open it, and thumb through the contents.

"Anyway, like I was saying, Alex, I didn't fire you. I just couldn't keep you even if I want to, I can't."

"What's this?" I ask, holding up a piece of paper.

Tony leans in for a look. "I believe those are orders."

"It says One Federal Parkway...."

Tony shrugs. "Okay...?"

"No such thing as One Federal Parkway in New York-wait, it says Quantico, holy shit you gotta be kiddin' me!"

"What?" Tony seems just as surprised as me.

I sigh heavily. "I do not want to go back to Quantico. Wait a minute I'm not FBI anymore, so...."

Tony grabs the paper from me. He shakes his head. "This isn't an FBI building. That address doesn't exist ... not that I'm aware of. Misprint maybe?"

I frown. "Doesn't surprise me. We do work for the government, right?"

He smiles and nods. "Look Alex, I didn't fire you, and I didn't take your career away or anything like that. I've known you long enough, and I've heard you talk about all your relationships to know you don't trust men with your heart, but...." He pulls a box out of his pocket.

I cover my mouth with both hands. "No! No! No! No! No! No!"

Tony slides off the bed and gets down on one knee.

"No, stop it, get up!" I'm so giddy, I can't sit still. "Don't do this, Tony!"

He slowly opens the box to reveal a beautiful diamond engagement ring. The stone is square and there are smaller diamonds all around the setting.

"No! Don't do this! Please! Oh my God I'm so embarrassed, you can't do this and I'm like this!" I burry myself under the covers.

Tony plays tug of war with me, but finally pulls the covers back. "Alex Southerland...."

I scream.

Tony laughs, but continues, saying, "I have scoured the earth to find you, and before I did, I thought I'd lost you. I am not perfect, but I know perfection when I see it, and you are damn near my perfect everything. I need you to be my wife too. Alex, will you marry me...?" He takes the ring out of the box and offers it to me.

My little voice was wrong after all. I can't hold it in any longer. I leap off the edge of the bed and tackle him, kissing him everywhere I see an un-kissed spot—his lips, his cheeks, his neck, his forehead, his eyes, his chin, his nose. I kiss him literally all over and start to get so hot. My pussy is aching for the man I've hated for months yet loved for years.

"Yes!" I kiss. "Yes, I love you!" I kiss him again.

He grabs me by both shoulders and pushes me up a bit. "Wait," he says. He looks around the room a bit. I don't understand all of this with her, but I know what she means to you now, and ... I'm not forcing you to marry me ... I just ... if you want. I can never take her place or even your dad's or David, but I want to take a place with you, and I want us to have a life together."

"And what about your ex?"

He shakes his head. "She's history."

"Well, my ex is dead, so you're not going to come home and catch us in bed together."

"That ... that's a terrible thing to say, Alex," he says solemnly.

"And...? It's true. You know the men, who cheated on me, and I don't want to ever feel that way-"

"Alex...?" he interrupts.

"Yes?"

"You're doing it again."

I squint at him. "What?"

"Trying to convince me of all people you're some kind of helpless victim versus the one who terrorizes everyone else."

I cock my head to the side and give him a very mean look. I try to punch him, but he's got my arms locked up pretty good.

I struggle and whisper, "I'm gonna fuck you up!"

"Can you marry me first?" he asks, sarcastically.

I sigh. "You're such an asshole!" I laugh out loud. "Yes! Yes! Here give me this thing before you change your fucking mind and run out of here!" I snatch the ring from him and try it on. It fits perfectly. I lean back and admire my first ever engagement ring as it sparkles under the bright lights above us. It looks amazing.

Tony props himself up on his elbows and smiles.

"You did good baby, real good," I say. "I need to tell you something...."

"What?" he asks, but then his phone rings. Tony pulls a phone out of his pocket and looks at it for a second. "Oh, this is yours," he says, handing me the phone.

I take the phone and answer, "Hello?"

"Captain Southerland?"

"Who? Captain? Hold on a second." I pull the phone away from my ear and cover the receiver with the palm of my hand. "Tony...."

"Yes, Alex?"

I lean in close and whisper, "I'm pregnant."

Tony dumps me off of him and tumbles backwards up to his feet, stuttering and tripping all over himself as he tries to back up out of the room. I put the phone back to my ear and say, "Sorry, hold on a minute." I mute the phone, and then drop it on the bed. I take off after Tony. This time, he's the one running.

"Wait! The hell are you doing?"

"I gotta ... I ... I gotta go I don't...." Tony turns and rushes to the door.

I just stand in the middle of the entry way with my mouth wide open. "Are you shittin' me?"

"I'm sorry, I ... I gotta go, I'm sorry, Alex, I'll call you I-" Tony gives me one more strange look, and then he bolts out the door.

I stand in disbelief, but then I remember the call I put on hold. I rush back into the bedroom. Luckily the caller is still waiting. I pick up the phone and look at the caller ID. It's the White House. I quickly unmute the call and put the phone up to my ear.

"Hello?" I answer. "Sorry about that. How can I help you?"

"Captain Southerland, how are you?" comes a voice.

"Well, I think I just got divorced before I even got married," I reply.

"Tony's a good man," comes another voice, "I'm sure you two will work everything out."

"I'm sorry, who is this? President Wood? Mr. President? Oh God, I'm sorry, sir I didn't-"

"I'm on the line too, Alex, it's Jim."

"Vice President Keller ... gentlemen, it's an honor to speak with you again."

"You can cut the honor shit," Wood snaps, "we've got work to do."

I rummage through the papers on my bed and pick up my new military ID. Sure enough, my rank says "Captain". *I just got a serious promotion!*

"Alex...?"

"Yes, sir, Mr. Vice President?"

"Get your boyfriend sorted, and then get yourself on a plane. You have your orders, yes?"

I clear my throat. "Sir, yes sir, I do, but the address for my duty station is wrong. There's a typo ... it says One Federal Parkway in Quantico, but there's no-"

"Alex, it's no typo," Keller replies. "Find your way to that address Monday at 0800. Bring your credentials. There's something I need to show you."

I hesitate to respond, but finally I say, "Roger that, sir. I'll be there."

"Godspeed," says President Wood in the most presidential tone I've ever heard.

"See you soon, Alex," Keller says.

The call disconnects, and another one comes in immediately after. I don't recognize the number, but I pick up anyway.

"Southerland," I answer.

"Alex, it's me, I'm so sorry, I just freaked, I-"

"Tony, you're about to be a husband and a father, are you up to the task? I need to know now."

"Alex, I love you. Yes. I'm so happy! Yes! I'm gonna be a dad! It's just ... you just shocked me is all. I'm coming back up now."

"No!" I reply as I smile and breathe a sigh of relief. "Don't come back up here. This is the past, Tony, all of it. You, the baby, y'all are my future. I love you. I really do. Let that new door man know I'll be home for dinner."

"I'll cook something nice for us," says Tony.

"You fuckin' better. You don't want me to cook right now. I'm so tired it'd surely be something out of a can."

Tony laughs and says, "I think I can do a little better than canned food. I'm sorry about-"

"Husband!" I interrupt. "I'm coming home. I'll see you there soon, okay baby?"

"I can't wait," he replies.

I hang up and take one last look around the hotel room. I never got a chance to say goodbye to Vanessa, and I never will, but no matter how I start to feel, I'm not coming back to this place again. I pick up a framed picture of Vanessa from the table near the sofa. It's amazing how glamorous she looked in real life—even better than she did in all her photos. I press my lips against the cold glass of the picture frame and hold them there as I close my eyes and breathe in slowly. I give her one more kiss for the very last time. "Goodbye my love," I say, holding back my tears. I carefully set the picture back down on the table. "Tony is a good man, and I need to be better now for all of us ... I need to be here for him, and for the baby. I wish you were still here. Wish you could see the baby being born. I hope it's a girl ... anyway, I guess I'll see you in my dreams, Vanessa. This babygirl's got a new fiancé to lasso and a wedding to plan."

I exit the hotel and hail a cab. Now I'm on my way to a new experience. I rub my tummy and ponder what it will be like to walk through the door of our home and see my own family for the first time. I'm actually nervous—not so much about living with Tony, but about being a mom—especially if it's a girl. I fear I may treat her the way my mother treated me. I fear she may grow up and resent me like I resented my mother till the day she died. I don't want that in my life. I don't want my past to dictate my future. I've always said that I want to live my life free from the people. I realize at this point I just want to be free from myself. I want to feel brand new. I thought earning my freedom would make me feel the way I know I should, but it doesn't. So, maybe—just maybe—I can find peace in my new life with my very own family. I send Tony a text that reads *in cab OMW* with an entire line of hearts immediately after. Then, I settle back on my seat, shut my eyes, and get myself mentally ready for the next episode.

www.ingramcontent.com/pod-product-compliance
Lightning Source LLC
Chambersburg PA
CBHW060915250626
47159CB00008B/3024